Faith and Fortitude

The life and times of
John Rogers
Martyr

Crispin Rogers

Grosvenor House
Publishing Limited

This book is published by
Grosvenor House Publishing Ltd
Link House
140 The Broadway, Tolworth, Surrey, KT6 7HT.
www.grosvenorhousepublishing.co.uk

This book is a work of fiction. Although there is some basis in
historical fact, many events, characters and conversations are purely
fictional and the book is not intended as a factual, historical record.

All internal images are within the Public Domain
or are reproduced under licence

A CIP record for this book
is available from the British Library

Paperback ISBN 978-1-83975-995-6
Hardback ISBN 978-1-83975-996-3

Dedication

For my dad.

"Ich bin der Gott deiner Väter"

Foreword –
The Story Behind the Story

It was in early April 2021 that I received an unexpected and delightful call.

"Crispin? It's Cecil Riley, from the Old Bailey"

It took me just a moment to make the connection – then I recalled the guide I'd met at the Old Bailey some months prior who had shown my daughter and me around the premises where the infamous Newgate prison had stood in London.

"Hello Cecil – how very good to hear from you! Is all well with you?"

"All good thanks, Crispin – I've got some rather interesting news for you … I think you're going to like it!"

I had no idea where this was going – so more out of politeness responded "Oh yes, well that sounds promising. Have you found some more detail about Newgate prison to help with my research?"

"I can do better than that", he responded. "You might want to sit down for this."

Now he really had my attention. "Ah OK – so what's the news then?"

I could hear him drawing a breath. "Do you remember where we had that coffee in the yard by the old prison wall?"

"Yes, Cecil – of course – it was very good of you to take so much time and interest in my research". I paused and waited for him to tell me more.

"Well I'm glad I did, Crispin. Because … that old lean-to was taken down last week, we're replacing it with a new visitor experience centre."

"Sounds good" I said, feeling somewhat deflated that this was the news.

"And behind the shed, inside the wall – in a crack in the wall with some loose bricks around it … we found something …"

He paused.

I waited.

He continued.

"Do you want to know what we found, Crispin?"

"Well yes, Cecil – you've got me hooked – what did you find?"

"A manuscript!" – he fairly exhaled the word.

"A manuscript? Really?" I was intrigued and properly interested now, but still uncertain where this was going. The day's date also flashed through my mind – having just watched a far fetched piece on BBC Breakfast featuring a talking dolphin.

"By John Rogers!"

I froze.

"Crispin? Are you there? Did you hear me? It's a manuscript by John Rogers, your ancestor, the martyr you were telling me about! I thought you'd be interested. It looks authentic. It's a sheath of papers in a roll – clearly very old – and with a beautiful handwritten script, although quite hard to read. And it's dated. The earliest date is February 1554. Does that sound right?"

I finally let out a breath and came to. "February 1554? Yes, yes, that would be right. He was sent to Newgate in January of that year – and was there until the following year, right up until he was burned. Are you serious? Is this an April fool?"

"No, no, honestly Crispin – I'm deadly serious. I thought you'd said 1554 was when he was imprisoned – and he died in 1555, right? So I've had a word with my boss and he's agreed that as long as you can prove you're going to use this for historical research within the next 12 months, he's happy to lend it to you. Does that sound OK?"

"OK?" I said. "OK? Cecil – that's absolutely amazing! I can't thank you enough – but … I can't get my head around this, it's amazing! Honestly Cecil, I can't thank you enough. Do you know the timings on this – when can I come and collect it?"

And so we finalised the details and, sure enough, true to his word, within the week Cecil Riley introduced me to the

Provost of the Old Bailey, Sir John Mills who had prepared a short contract for me to be able to borrow the manuscript.

But I'd better re-track; let me first explain why this excited me so much.

My dad always said we were related to John Rogers, the first Protestant martyr under Queen Mary who was burned at the stake on 4th February 1555.

Which would be an honour.

Dad's cousin, Sidney John Rogers, had undertaken a mammoth piece of genealogy in 1950 and had managed to trace the familial line back through thirteen generations (so fourteen generations back from me – and sixteen from my grandchildren). There's a little confusion around the four generations of John Rogers of Penryn through the eighteenth century – which my dad successfully unravelled (one infant John Rogers death and a later surviving John Rogers born to the same family seemed to resolve it).

There was circumstantial evidence enough too – the Rogers name of course (but it's fairly common), the prevalence of similar familial first names - my father's name was also John, with Thomas and Samuel also running through the generations in our family line in the twentieth, nineteenth and eighteenth century as it does in the Martyr's line in the sixteenth and seventeenth centuries. I can even see a likeness in the portraits of the Martyr and my own father – not least that strong Roman nose!

But maybe the most compelling case – certainly for deep affiliation if not for definitive relational evidence – is the strong

Protestant, Christian faith that runs through the generations of our family. The tenets of faith on which the Martyr stood firm – justification by faith, that it is what God has done for us, not, in any way, what we try and do for him that restores our relationship with the living God; the nature of the sacrament of holy communion, that it symbolises the ultimate sacrifice made by God's son and draws us close to the presence of Jesus, but is not transforming into the literal body and blood of Christ; and the supreme authority of Scriptures ('God breathed') and the power of that Living Word to enrich and sustain us in our everyday lives, in our everyday language – these are the foundations of my faith, of my father's faith, his father before him and back and back through the generations.

Each new generation being nurtured in these truths, but ultimately, wonderfully finding out for themselves as individuals the deep contentment and enlightenment that comes from finding that personal relationship with Jesus Christ.

My dad had a sharp intelligence (both a linguist and Cambridge graduate – like the Martyr) and a keen intellectual curiosity that led him to explore not only our family genealogy, but also the life and times of his sixteenth century namesake.

So it was that I grew up witnessing not only the 1861, definitive biography of John Rogers the Martyr by Joseph Lemuel Chester sitting proudly aged and ageing amidst his eclectic library of books in his study – but also the sporadic exchange of letters with distant relatives or namesakes or simply interested parties across the country on the same hallowed subject.

No line of enquiry was too obtuse once it had peaked his curiosity and he found numerous like-minded souls who replied to his fluid, handwritten letters in similar, if often less legible vein.

I have those letters and the box file of articles from newspapers and magazines that referenced anything related to the extraordinary story of the extraordinary man, John Rogers the Martyr.

I have also my dad's nineteenth century copy of Foxe's Book of Martyrs – more accurately Book of Acts and Monuments. The ghoulish and fearsome descriptions and etchings show saintly soul after saintly soul meeting the grim end of burning at the stake with a fierce defiance and acclaiming their certain hope in a blessed life in the hereafter thanks to their saviour on whom they have stood firm and true.

I was probably about ten years old when I first tentatively peaked through those pages and was confronted with the wonderful horrors within. This rich and potent mixture of faith, history, drama, evil, goodness and no mercy was bound to etch itself into my memory and psyche.

Maybe I was thereafter destined and bound to study history at university – literally a stone's throw (come to think of it) from the Oxford Martyrs' Memorial outside Balliol College marking the exact spot that shortly after Rogers was burned there was the equally public burning of Bishops Latimer and Ridley (Rogers' good friend and erstwhile boss) and commemorating Archbishop Cranmer's martyrdom nearby soon after.

Admittedly my career then followed more closely that of my father – into commerce and marketing specifically

– but I had always had a nagging idea that one day, one day I would return to the fascination of historical study and specifically I would personally visit the story of John Rogers the Martyr. I was keen to understand not just what happened, but also *why?* What was it about the Martyr's beliefs that were so at odds with the temporarily restored Roman Catholic creed that the latter sought to obliterate him by fire and the former felt compelled to walk through a fiery end rather than acknowledge any other view of his faith?

So this was as much a spiritual journey and exploration for me as it was a historical project. And my turning 55 – likely the age of the Martyr on his execution – and a change to working status threw up the opportunity, at last, to pursue this particular dream and see where it led.

I surged headlong into my research – and once the dreaded pandemic allowed, finally moved from online research at home to visiting in person the key locations in the John Rogers story. Including, of course, the location of Newgate prison where the Martyr spent his final days –just over a year in fact – which is now the location of another ancient stalwart of the English justice system, the Old Bailey.

And so, fatefully, as part of my research and eager to escape the confines of lockdown now that the stay at home restriction was lifted, I visited the Old Bailey with my youngest daughter Lucy (29) and was fortunate enough to get a guided tour by the aforementioned Mr Cecil Riley. It was only Lucy and me on the tour that day – so we had plenty of opportunity for discussion and naturally I shared with him the particular reason for my interest.

His eyes lit up.

It transpired that he had married into the Rogers line – his wife Sarah nee Rogers – some 30 years prior. But this was the first he'd heard of the Martyr, let alone that the ground on which he walked every day of his working life had been where John Rogers was imprisoned.

Most of the buildings were of much later construction, but Cecil was eager to show me the 'ancient wall' that abuts Amen Corner – which is the last surviving wall of the prison itself.

It certainly looked old. And one could only imagine the horrors it had witnessed.

In the courtyard itself there was a lean-to building that housed various maintenance paraphernalia – paint pots, ladders, brushes and the like. With a sink and a kettle – which Cecil kindly put to use for a brew as I regaled him of the extraordinary tale of John Rogers and he responded with inspirational infill of detail about life in the prison back in the sixteenth and seventeenth century.

So that made for a fulfilling and informative afternoon – we exchanged contact details and I promised to let him know when my revised biography of the Martyr had been published.

And then, apart from writing up my notes on the insights he'd given me on the daily lives of inmates of Newgate Prison, I thought nothing more of it.

Until he called me with the extraordinary news of this new manuscript, which I found myself in possession of and fiercely holding onto having left the Old Bailey to return home.

I dared not open it up and look at it on the train home – much as I was dying to – but rather went straight into the dining room when I got home (I even left the door open of the car in my haste!) and gingerly lifted out the roll from the holdall in which I'd put it.

I spread it over the table and placed makeshift paperweights on each corner.

And there in front of me was the manuscript.

The writing clear, mainly in black ink but with certain words in what I imagine would have been a vivid red, but was now a kind of sepia colour.

The first page was dated – 'Foreword. February 1554'. And then it began …

"I find myself detained …"

I read and read – had to slow myself down as I started to skim read – reminding myself that no one had seen these words for 467 years! And that in fact, in all probability, no one had EVER read them excepting the author himself. John Rogers had committed to writing down the extraordinary events of his extraordinary life perhaps more in hope than expectation that anyone would get to read them.

Toward the end of his entries, he mentions how he had been hiding the manuscript in the wall of the exercise yard – and his prayers that not only will he be able to do so in a clandestine manner so that the (admittedly apparently slack) guards would not see, but also that he would be able to get word to his wife about where to find them when his mortal life was over, which he knew would be all too soon.

And now I present this extraordinary tale of an extraordinary life to you that had such immense consequences on countless souls. I've used the lightest of editorial touches, really only to help convey meaning into modern day English and occasionally in the rare instances when the writing became harder to read, very likely due to tiredness and the tribulations of another day in the unforgiving harshness of Newgate prison.

I challenge you to read this first hand account of history – with an open heart and an open mind. Remembering that he who wrote it was from another era, from a culture that has flashes of familiarity but which is in many ways alien to us today. Read it and see the man who committed these words to paper. The same man who had committed the words of the first authorised English translation of the Bible to paper too – and in so doing lit a fire that rages to this day. Who himself faced the fire – and faced it with the most extraordinary bravery and steadfastness, rock solid (there can be no doubt) in the certainty of his hope and faith in his Lord Jesus Christ and in the certain expectation to be united with Him and his God – as well as, in the fulness of time, with his beloved family in friends – in heaven for eternity.

I think of him there now and pray a prayer of thanks for his witness.

And the feeling I get?

That he's loving seeing his story told and retold – not for any personal glory or gain, he's very far, so very far from having such a care – but rather that a new generation will see his witness pointing once again to his own Lord Jesus Christ, whom he now sees face to face.

And who do I imagine sitting next to him, enjoying the unfolding story and drama and delighting in the gaps in his own knowledge being filled?

Well, I'd love to think, it's my dad.

***

A Life Lived for the Glory of Jesus Christ

PREFACE

February 1554

I find myself detained in most unpleasant conditions, although surprisingly blessed with the gift of time.

Time to reflect on the extraordinary pathways that God has led me on and the journey I have been on in better understanding true Christian ways.

A journey toward the Light you might say. A journey not yet complete – although I sense it nearing the ultimate destination. I have a certain hope for Heaven: But an increasing certainty that the way to it will be ... an adventure in itself, shall we say.

My surroundings right now are grim. My prison cell is dimly lit with only the five shafts of light pouring in from the small, barred window just

1

above head height. A wooden bench serves to sit, rest and sleep – fortunately I am blessed to be able to sleep in just about any circumstance. Undefined grime and slime covers the floor – I'll waste no time or nerves on seeking to understand it nor describe it any more.

And yet ...

I truly give thanks to the Lord for my circumstances. As Paul gave thanks for his sufferings in the name of our shared Lord Jesus Christ, so too do I. All the more so, in fact, as – just like Paul (I only now realise) – I am permitted at least to have sufficient quills, ink and paper to do what I have so far failed to do, by dint of life's distractions both professional and familial: That is to write down my own version of events in my life that have led me to this privileged position of being persecuted for standing on the truth of the Gospel and thereby to stand for Christ.

I cannot say whether I will be granted the time to complete my record.

I can say that this record will stand firm against any scrutiny, whatever my enemies may say. May it be a true and accurate account – from my perspective at least – that may enlighten my family, friends, congregation and maybe even others over the mystery of time (who knows?).

Further that it will cover that eternal human search for intellectual and spiritual truths (in truth intertwined and inextricable) – that can only be reconciled and revealed via revelation from Him who made us and made us curious.

It will cover more mundanely my travels across foreign lands that were to become not foreign to me. Come with me across those lands and I'll show you places and people like no other ; and yet places and people just the same. (And I would welcome a mental sojourn from this place, in all honesty!).

I will share my thinking in taking the paths I chose when presented with a crossroads, according to the Lord's will. God only knows where I would otherwise be right now if not for those pivotal decisions. But I am glad He also knows I am here right now.

And most especially, I will share tales of **Love**.

The love I found for my dearest wife Adriana, that grew and multiplied as our wonderful family grew and became such a blessing and solace to me.

And the brotherly love I found for those special soldiers in Christ along the way – dear Ridley, the prodigiously gifted Tyndale, the incomparable Melanchthon to name but a few. You will meet them all – and marvel, like me, at the richness of character of these men and women made in God's image and made for just such a time as this.

Love for the Holy Scriptures, of course – upon which I had the privilege to labour to release in familiar tongue to any Englishman who would have the wisdom to look upon it and receive it. What a blessing to me! And, I pray in certain hope, a blessing to every Englishman – and woman - who reads it.

And through that, surpassingly, the love I have found in Christ Jesus. Gentle. Kind. Patient. Forgiving – and forgiving again. And now supreme and victorious, reigning in Glory and worthy of all wonder and praise. The beginning and the end and in whom all things now hold together.

Whatever it might look like or feel like for us along the way.

Love will win.

Love always wins.

Thanks to Him.

***

Chapter 1 – Deritend, Early Life

"FIRE !"

The shout jolted me from my slumber, alarm surging through my veins.

"FIRE ! FIRE ! Everyone out !" I recognised my father's voice and leapt to his command.
My younger brothers Will and Edward jumped from their bunks and instinctively came running over to me, wide eyed and seeking instruction.

"Come on you two, you heard father, we have to get out quickly – just like we practised", I said, calmly but urgently.

"Is this another drill, John?" asked Will, seeking my reassurance.

"I don't know, Will" I replied honestly, although I had a strong sense from the urgency of my father's voice that it was not.

Sure enough as we ran down the stairs from our sleeping quarters we saw my mother clutching my sister Ellenor's hand and cradling baby Joan as she scurried toward the door. "Quickly boys, out of the door and run toward the pond!" Behind her I could see smoke billowing down the stairs that led toward my parents' and my sisters' bedrooms. My father was already at the door and was waving us out – "Out now, everyone, this is for real! Save yourselves! Assemble by the pond!"

The next moment it is Ellenor crying out, "Annie !" and in the same instant snatching her hand away from our mother's grasp, turning on her heel and running back toward the stairs and bedroom from whence came the smoke. "Ellenor ! Ellenor come back here immediately, it's too dangerous!" my mother cried out.

She took no heed, headstrong as always she scampered up the stairs, her smock seeming to blend with the billowing smoke as her small frame disappeared up the stairs and out of view.

I instinctively shoved my brothers toward my mother and the door and called to her "I'll go mother, you take the others to safety! Father must raise the alarm and alert the fire patrol." And with that I ran toward and up the stairs, shutting out the protestations from my parents as I sought to rescue my sister.

The moment I stepped through into my parents' room I was physically taken aback by the hellish scene confronting me. What I had known as the heart of peace and gentility, drapes across the four poster bed, floral wall coverings of the finest materials and elegant furniture was unrecognisable.

Fire.

Everywhere fire.

An inferno licked it's way up the drapes and over the bed, it sprung from the walls and the roar from it devouring the wooden furniture assaulted my hearing.

And yet I was not scared.

Coming immediately to mind, as if placed there from the Lord, was Shadrach, Meshach and Abednego. Would the Lord save me and my sister from this firey furnace?

Surely He could.

Surely He would.

In that moment I saw my sister run in from the adjoining room, clutching her precious Annie doll close to her chest. She began to cough and slow as she saw how the flames were engulfing the room so much more fiercely that when she had just come through.

Her eyes were wild with fear now as she stood motionless and stared at me across the flames.

As if in slow motion and with a sense of peace I can only now describe as supernatural and from the Lord, I smiled at her as I raised my arms to calm her from a distance and to instruct her to stay put. In one motion I grasped a drape that had not yet caught the flames and raised it to my face as I then strode toward my sister, waving the flames away with my free arm. I then wrapped the drape around her as I swept her up into my arms and then darted for the door.

At that moment the flames raced across the floor in front of me, but undeterred I ran straight through them as if they were nothing but shafts of light. I felt the heat singeing my bare feet and catching my night clothes but nothing would stop me reaching the door and racing down the stairs with Ellenor in my arms – still clutching her priceless Annie – across the smoky parlour and out to the sanctuary of the outdoors.

I saw both relief and renewed shock flash across my mother's face – and then heard Will cry out in alarm "John, your clothes! You're on fire!".

"Take Ellenor!" I instructed, as I passed over Ellenor, still wrapped in the drape and still clinging on to her doll. And with the next stride – and a cry of "Lord, save me!" I leapt confidently into the cool embrace of the pond water, allowing my full body, face, head and hair to be fully submerged into the green-brown water.

8

As I surfaced back from under the water I saw my concerned family crowding around the water's edge. Ellenor, standing now – but still clutching her Annie doll to her chest – was the first to speak. "John – are you alright? Are you hurt?". I strode through the lillies and past the rushes, dripping wet and seeking to identify feeling across my body. But apart from the cool sensation of the water dripping from me and the squelchy embrace of the muddy pond floor, I could feel nothing.

No pain.

No burning.

And still no fear.

"I''m fine Ellenor, just rather wet. It seems the Lord is not finished with any of us yet! Although if you bring that doll near me again I shall personally throw it into the pond myself!". And with that we laughed together in relief, a little delirium and love.

Behind my gathered family I could see my father ordering the human chain to convey the pales of water to fight the house fire. Being already in the water I volunteered to draw the water as the first link in the chain. We worked three hours, but in the end the fire was conquered and the house, thank God, was saved.

Perhaps it was through this incident that I transitioned from a boy to a man – at perhaps 12 years old.

***

It had started with the tiny flickering flame of a candle, apparently. A robe cast too carelessly across the table at bedtime. A seam frayed from too frequent use and too infrequent repair. And a breath of wind drifting from the window that brought the two into contact for a defining moment, sufficient for the flame to catch.

Funny how such a tiny flame could trigger such a monumental event.

But it was a temporary inconvenience, thank the Lord. Not only did our neighbours rally to form the fire patrol that morning to put out the fire and prevent the whole house burning, but also fellow members of my father's guild clubbed together to provide all of the assistance we needed to restore the house to being a home.

It was a comfortable house and a happy home. Our family were of the middle sort and we lived in the middle of England.

Deritend in the Parish of Aston in the County of Warwickshire was a town like a hundred and more across the land. A happy enough place in the heart of England – perhaps both geographically and by sentiment.

My father, also John, was a loriner, making the metal parts for horse harnesses. He'd built a good business from years of hard and highly skilled work and now had several smithies in the villages surrounding Deritend with a team of other loriners and a stream of apprentices.

As such he afforded his family a good home and a good education. Our home comprised several bedrooms accessed from two staircases off the main parlour – as well as a separate kitchen area for food preparation. We even had a privy fitted upstairs, instigating a long running argument between my brothers and me when it came to clearing out the slop pile. As the eldest brother I'm afraid to say that was a task I became more used to supervising than labouring over !

My mother, Margery née Wyatt, I have loved dearly, not only as the matriarch of our healthy brood of a family, but also as my earliest spiritual mentor. We would don our finest clothing to attend mass on a Sunday at Deritend Chapel – my earliest memories are of us perched on stools on a rough, reed matting; and I recall our corporate pride in modernising to smart wooden pews, with the second and third rows allocated to the Rogers family.

The provision of the pews, as indeed of the chapel itself and all associated furniture, candles and so forth, was provided by the Deritend Guild – of which my father was a proud and leading member. The Guild provided also for two priests – one managing matters spiritual including the leading of mass and the other our school teacher.

Thus it was that one Richard Mathers imbued me with all the knowledge I needed to embark into the world with a solid foundation of understanding. He taught all of my siblings too and we shall forever be in his debt. I wonder whether he still lives?

But it was from my mother that I learned the fear of God. By which I mean not to take fright, but rather to come to a place of awe and reverence in His presence and in recognition of His great goodness. Looking back now I wonder that she had such an insight given the false teaching and antichristian practices she was forced to endure by the Romish Church of the time. And yet despite all of that – the absurd obsession with long deceased saints, the incessant and obsolete demands for prayers for those passed and in supposed purgatory and the obscene obsession with the Virgin Mary – she had a spiritual soul that I have rarely encountered despite the abundant richness of my acquaintances since.

Now I come to think of it, it was from my mother too that I first learned to be a Protestant.

My beloved grandfather, Thomas – my father's father – had sadly passed away. A larger than life character, my father naturally wanted to venerate him appropriately. My father raised the subject with the Guild and a payment was agreed for the provision of lights for a perpetual thirty day period initially and then monthly for a period of ten years. A levy was proposed on Guild members in order to cover the cost – and this in a year when the harvest had been poor, sickness covered the land and household budgets were already stretched.

My mother was concerned that rather than venerating Grandfather Thomas' memory, this levy would bring ill feeling and resentment onto the family.

"But why must there be a levy, John?" my mother asked as we shared a family meal together in the parlour. "For the lights, my dear", my father replied. "And light needs candles, candles need wax and wax must be bought. And furthermore we need our priest to pray to the saints for his soul. I would have my father freed from purgatory at the soonest moment. It is the least I can do for him."

I thought for a moment – and then piped up "How do the lights help Grandfather in purgatory, father?"

"How indeed!", replied my mother. "Easier to answer how the levy helps line the pockets of our priest."

"Margery!", my father shouted in a whisper (if you can imagine such a thing). "Ours is not the place to question the ways of the Guild and the ways of our mother church. Our elders and betters have shown us the way for decades and who are we now to do anything but follow their lead?"

My mother – headstrong as well as smart (likely where our Ellenor got those traits) – retorted "Well if we're not to question it I scarce can see anyone else around here that will." But she knew when to respect her husband also and she let the matter drop.

But I never did get an answer as to how lighting candles for the departed and paying extra for prayers by the priest for their souls in supposed purgatory could help them (a subject that future study would demonstrate to me was a fantasy conjured by the church of the Antichrist, by which I mean the Romish Church, for their own edification and enrichment).

The thought and conversation lodged with me, but it was to be many years before I found for myself the truth to answer these questions and others I had around the inconsistencies and injustices I witnessed in the false bride of Christ, being the Romish Church. I knew little at the time of the Reformist views that were already rising like a spring in the land and which in later life I would be blessed to encounter, bringing true life to me and eternal life to my soul.

***

The Guild itself, however, was an honourable undertaking. As well as providing for the education of the young, it also provided an outlet for sport and social recreation.

One particular such event I recall now – the brightness of the day and the gaiety of the mood in such stark contrast to the dimness of my surroundings now and the melancholy that threatens to surround me if I were not equipped with the armour of God as Scripture instructs.

It was soon after the fire at home – when I was around twelve years old – when word went out that King Henry had instructed, through the full weight of Parliament, that all male children should henceforth practise the noble skill of archery. So it was that our Guild – ever keen to demonstrate their loyalty to the crown and love of our country – determined to organise a festival to feature an archery competition for all lads to the age of sixteen. It was to be under the auspices of St Sebastian, the patron saint of archers – midway through the year to his saint's day.

The prize to the winner – a suckling pig to share in feast with the boy's own family.

It occurs to me now that the reader of this may not be familiar with my countenance, so let me explain.

I was never tall, but I was ever strong.

Even at twelve, perhaps from many hours helping my father in the smithy, but perhaps mostly because of a stocky and stout build I had strength beyond my years and beyond the expectation of my friends and foes alike. My calf muscles have always had a prominent curvature about them (although ever smooth and hairless) and my arms would stretch the cloth of my summer shirt, so muscular have they always been.

In my circle of school friends I would go by the name of Ox. And although I mostly eschewed confrontation out of respect for living a Godly and peaceful life, occasionally I had reason to scrap and rarely came out the worse.

I mention this, because my strength enabled me to prevail at this St Sebastian festival. The competition had started light heartedly and with light challenges. Targets shaped like deer, wild boar or rabbits were arrayed before us – so close that even the youngest of the boys could make a strike. Proud parents and grandparents cheered as the targets went down, one after the other.

Gradually the targets were drawn further back and so it was that the younger contingent found them to be out of range. The older boys ploughed on though and with a strike within three arrows kept their place in the competition.

The group of juvenile contestants diminished as the task grew more challenging and arms tired. Until there were only two – myself and a certain Tom Hughes, a sixteen year old lad, a yeoman's son. Three rounds we remained neck and neck – I hit the deer twice and a rabbit once, all on my second shot; he the boar, twice on his first shot and then the deer on his third and last chance.

It seemed the whole village was watching on, some cheering me and some Tom, depending on their family ties and friendships – but all was in good spirits. The targets were moved back once more – a further ten paces back, likely to the limit of both our young frames. He first – the arrow falling short and to the left of the boar; then my shot, veering to the right of the deer's head. He again – overcompensating and sailing just over the boar. I pulled my next arrow from the earth where I'd planted it – and took aim at the boar again. Overcompensation from me too – with the blade of my arrow high and to the left over the deer. Him again – still aiming for the boar and this time surely, if his strength held, he would have his eye.

Time to act. As he started to draw the bow and take aim, I too snatched my arrow and instead of aiming at the deer once again, I shifted the bow toward Tom's target. Drawing back the bow to my usual strain I drew a short breath and tensed my muscular arm with all the strength I could muster, drawing the bow back a fraction further.

He released his arrow, but as he did so, so did I.

The extra draw I had given the bow sent the arrow accelerating toward the boar at a great speed – such a speed that to the amazement of all watching, it surpassed Tom's arrow mid air and struck the boar first on the shoulder. Down went the metal silhouette of the boar, just as Tom's arrow arrived. With the boar no long standing, his arrow sailed on until it landed, spent, into the bare earth beyond.

I had won.

A loud cheer went up from all watching – Tom's supporters as well as mine – and to his credit he let out a loud laugh and patted me firmly on the back, congratulating me for my skill as well as my resourcefulness.

Next to my side my father, face beaming with pride and with a manly pat on my back: "I didn't know you could do that!", he exclaimed. And I replied, "To be honest dad, neither did I!". Our laughter was joined by all around as we went to claim my prize - a wonderful suckling pig that my friends and family devoured and enjoyed well into the night.

That was a happy day.

In happier times.

**

Chapter 2 – Cambridge and Oxford, University Years

It was not long after that happy event that I secured my heart's desire of a place at Cambridge University. I had been a diligent student under Richard Matthews at Deritend, easily the star student of my generation. Learning came easily to me, if truth be told. I was able to recall readily what I had read and the structures and frameworks of language were as logical to me as the mathematics I studied.

Thus it was I made the long journey to the fens and Cambridge University, with my small collection of possessions and many books packed in a trunk. Through contacts of Richard Matthews it was Pembroke Hall that was to be my home and place of tutelage for the following years. With a proud history of nearly 200 years, Pembroke Hall was everything I had hoped it would be.

The regime was a strict one, but that suited me well enough. The study was initially a significant departure from what I had been used to and it was something of a shock to find I was no longer (at first at least) the most able student in class. The syllabus also was broader than I had been used to, with a focus on logic, classical literature and philosophy – but I soon learned to love it, to love the variety and intellectual stimulation and stretch. I could feel my capabilities and academic foundations building, which in turn gave me further and further confidence in both my abilities and my place in this world.

There is no doubt that, meanwhile, God was stirring and at work to draw the people of England back to Him once again.

And at the epicentre – Cambridge.

So it was that I was witness to the birth of Reform in England during that time.

Although I was slow to appreciate it. Perhaps by nature I am cautious, given to respecting authority and therefore not quick to adopt new ideas nor to accept that scathing criticism of the status quo can be valid.

But I consider things earnestly.

And I reflect on them deeply.

Until, with the help of the Holy Spirit, I make up my mind,

Thus it was that I observed and absorbed the extraordinary events of the time and pondered them in my heart the long while.

The initial spark came from Erasmus' translation of the New Testament into accessible Greek. It dawned on me over time – a dawning that was to have long term ramifications on my life – that the translation was so much more than an academic exercise, as might be any other literary translation. As Erasmus himself reflected, the translation opened the sealed door that the Romish Church had guarded for centuries and allowed for long, long standing errors to be brought into the strictures of bright daylight and finally corrected. So too it enabled the Holy Spirit once more to breathe life into the words of the Gospel and to challenge afresh a new generation – and generations to follow also – with the wonders of God's plan.

Fanning those flames, Martin Luther (with whom I was to become well acquainted during my time in Wittenburg) boldly called out the worst exigences of the Papist church. His character then was modest and humble and he demonstrated considerable restraint in the manner in which he drew attention to the blasphemous and rotten practices into which the greed of the Romish Church had become accustomed. Now it is clear that Luther was

remarking only upon the peripheral out-
workings of the church that had become the
domain of the Antichrist, whilst at its core
was the poisonous lie of justification by works.

Contrary to the Gospel, the Papist church
had built new layers of law upon the Law and
constructed its own blasphemous economy to
enrich and engorge itself upon a gullible and
defenceless people. Long will it live in
condemnation for the same.

However, these sparks had not the effect in
England as they had on a Continent more ready
and dry to receive this word. The form of the fire
in England looked only to be that of Wolsey's,
that High Priest of the Papist church who
constructed his own pyre of Luther's works that
he had deemed heretical (heresy to challenge the
source of his boundless spoils and riches, more
like). The burning of the paper was futile, of
course, as even Wolsey found out that whilst
he could destroy a monastery it was far harder
to destroy an idea. And when that idea is the
True Word of God – impossible to destroy
for eternity!

Such were the topics discussed amongst my
generation at Pembroke Hall and across certain
other colleges of Cambridge. Nowhere more so
than at "Little Germany', our nickname for The
White Horse Tavern where those open to these

new Reformed ideas would meet and earnestly seek out truth from heresy to find (and ultimately rescue) the true catholic church.

It was on such an evening that I first encountered William Tyndale. Already he had renown for being a highly gifted linguist, with eight languages in his tongue – and as such he was someone whom I held in high esteem and regard. It was shock then to find myself in opposing argument with him. We had been discussing Wolsey's Lutheran book pyre ...

"This won't end before more than books are burned, mark my words", said Tyndale.

"There is already truth in that, William", it was Nicholas Ridley, a mentor of mine already, foreshadowing a long and blessed friendship, although forever he was to remain my senior. "I hear of the people rebelling in London and it's eastern and western flanks – with statues ripped from their age old spots in churches from across that area and piled with rood screens to make a pyre the likes of which England has never seen. What say you, justice or heresy?"

I could not hold my tongue, "Criminals at least, heretics at worst!", I replied. "Surely good Christian men are called to obey the law and live quietly and peacefully? Not to go about causing disruption and destruction?"

"Mark my words", came Tyndale, "many a good Christian man will themselves fuel the fires before this work of the Lord is done. There is no law against those that fight injustice nor those that speak out for the Truth of the Lord".

I retorted, "But how can these folk know the truth of the Lord when they are but merchants, farmers and labourers? Are they not the sheep rather than the shepherds? Should they not bow to the knowledge and wisdom of their superiors for the sake of an orderly society and for their very souls?"

Tyndale again – and I recall these words so well, him at ease with himself, sitting by the hearth with a dozen learned and earnest men, good men, waiting upon his every word – "When Scripture itself is released to all men – and women – there will be such revelation that revolution must surely follow. A revolution of hearts. Who once were sheep will discover the joy of finding their own way and their shepherds will be revealed as thieves. His Kingdom cometh and it cometh by His Word. But that road is lit by fire – the fire of the Godly. And it will be a Holy Fire – one that will light up the world and burn for an eternity".

At that moment, the fire around which we sat in comfort in that tavern gave a loud CRACK as the logs gave themselves up to the fire and settled anew. A moment of levity that broke the tensions amongst us.

Many such conversations were had around that fire – with young men who were to be so much used by the Lord in reviving his Word in this land – the likes of Thomas Cranmer, Hugh Latimer, Robert Barnes, Thomas Bilney and many more.

My conservative and obedient nature could not readily take to this talk of revolution and this extreme language disturbed me. So I decided to dwell on these matters further without needing to have a ready answer on my lips. The Lord was still working on my heart.

Whilst these were private conversations and the atmosphere of Cambridge University, especially under the spirit of Erasmus, allowed for and encouraged this frankness of speech, it was only at the Christmas of 1525 that this talk finally reached the pulpit.

Another occasion that has stood the test of time and stands clear in my memory.

It was Robert Barnes who spoke that night at the traditional midnight mass. But his message was far from traditional. One of the more outspoken against the crimes and excesses of the practices of the Papist church at the time, he spoke first about the false pride and pomp of priests of the land who dressed themselves as peacocks to strut their parishes. And worse of their greedy trickery in deceiving the people that they could accelerate and secure their way to a heavenly future despite their sinful nature and actions by the appropriate payment to the church and therefore, in essence, to them, to fund their devilish and selfish lifestyle.

These things had been heard before from the pulpit, so stark were these injustices and contraventions of God's ways – but it seemed then that the Holy Spirit came upon him as he embarked upon a new direction. Ostensibly he began to challenge the legitimacy of one Christian suing another via the courts, laying out the true scriptural direction for resolving disputes between good Christians. But the Spirit then inspired him further to declare the fundamental truth that salvation in the Lord comes not from what we do, from our acts and actions, but rather is in its pure entirety a gift from the Grace of God Himself.

So the marker was laid down as a challenge to the Papist church that their antichristian reign was declared bankrupt and coming to an end.

I describe and see this now as a clear marker from the Lord, as clear to me as Joshua's pile of stones to mark the way to the Promised Land would have been to his people. At the time I was more intellectually curious than excited (blind that I was!), and for the most part strove to keep in the background from the tensions that followed.

Barnes was held to account by Wolsey, archdeacon and prime beneficiary of the evils of the Papist church as he was (as I now also see clearly), despite his future contentions on behalf of his king. Threatened with the fire, Barnes did not hold firm at that time – but no doubt God was able to use his weakness to show His own strength as Barnes became a useful envoy to facilitate relations between England and Reformed Germany.

(His escape from the fire was to prove temporary, as it transpired – perhaps the Lord had determined His will that it should be so, to enable a wrong to be righted – and much later, still in the reign of Henry at a time when the Reformist tide was out, he stood firm as he was consumed by the flame).

To recall the threat of war as an ever present backdrop to this time. Henry had been poorly served (again) by his advisers in an ill fated attempt to raise funds (unfairly) for his proposed invasion of France. And The Emperor Charles succeeded in sacking Rome, essentially taking captive the Pope and removing any prospect of Clement acceding to King Henry's urgent demands for an annulment to his marriage to Catherine – the Emperor's aunt.

Perhaps the hand of the Lord was in that too, disentangling the realm from centuries of Papist stranglehold and setting in motion the process of Reform and a series of 'victories for Christ' (as I call them) as He reclaimed his church over the following decades.

The tide might be out once again for Reform right now in England due to the current devilish circumstances, but doubt not that it will rise again – and rise higher at that!

***

From Cambridge then to Oxford, having established some degree of distinction in my studies at Pembroke Hall I was then invited to attend the new Cardinal's College which Wolsey had established and where were sought the finest minds and men of potential in the land.

The premises were nonetheless austere, comprising as they did the buildings previously constituting St Frideswide's Monastery. St Frideswide's had been sequestered by Wolsey as were so many, countless other such disreputable houses at that time as Henry sought, in part at least, to cleanse the worst abominations of the slidden church. I convinced myself at the time that the intent from Wolsey was sound and holy and that there was a pleasing harmony in building something learned, holy and good from the very platform of evil monastic excess.

Over time, of course, I have seen Wolsey for what he was – the arch-priest of his own branch of the Romish Church and as such presiding over sustaining the church of the Antichrist. But whilst at Cardinal's college, there was too much of intellectual interest and stimulation for me to concern myself too much about the great affairs of state and we saw little of our benefactor.

Other Reformists came with me to Oxford and debate regarding the ongoing evolution of Reform on the continent spread across the university – although I found myself withdrawing somewhat from it. My family, of course, had great pride in my elevation and the honour that brought to them. Few indeed from Deritend had matriculated at Cambridge and indeed fairly few was anyone from my county able to claim matriculation at both Cambridge and Oxford too.

I recall a visit from my mother and father, coming to meet me at my rooms at Cardinal College and joining me in Hall for supper. It was good to see them again after so long – and I enjoyed hearing news of Deritend, friends and family back home.

Although their stories reminded me how small the world when viewed from Deritend.

We retired back to my rooms after supper, where my father was able to speak to me freely.

"John, you know how very proud your mother and I are of you, for all that you have already achieved?"

I was touched, I did know this of course, but my father was not often given to praise nor to outward expressions of affection and so to hear this from his lips struck me deeply.

"Thank you father. Anything I have achieved is only thanks to the upbringing granted me by you and mother – and by the Grace of God" I replied, ensuring I looked each of my father and mother in the eyes to convey the depth of my true gratitude and appreciation. Because it was true.

"But we do worry about you", it was my mother who interjected. "These are shifting times and we hear of dreadful events all over the land. And always over the church. John, we're worried about you getting caught up in this storm. It is said that the universities are the breeding ground for all kinds of new ideas which may be heresies and that England may follow the path of Germany into anarchy. You will be careful, won't you?"

I understood her concern. There was an air of brutality abounding that pervaded all places, with examples of ordinary people taking extraordinary actions in response to the turbulence of the times. Churches continued to be raided by aggrieved men taking out their anger on the greed of the rotten clergy. And naturally, the response of the authorities was decisive and brutal – with the use of the noose all too frequent across towns and villages, especially in the south of the kingdom.

"God will protect me", I reassured my mother.

"Are you sure of that?" my father asked. "Can you be sure that in this world full of evil you will not be on the wrong side of even a righteous battle? We could not bear for you to be in trouble, my son; for all of your talents and skill and cleverness to go to waste over some arcane debate amongst mortals."

"I promise I will have a care", I told my parents.

I promise I will have a care.

And I meant it – very much. At that time my love for my parents could not be bettered. Indeed, ashamed as I am to admit this – sinner that I was – in reality at that time my love for my parents was perhaps greater than my love of God.

I wished to do nothing to cause them worry or upset. And so I resolved to walk a safe path and to ask the Lord for safe passage along it.

How could I have come from that earnest
promise to my parents to this present
circumstance – jailed amongst thieves and
murderers and awaiting an uncertain (or perhaps
all to certain) fate for standing firm on my faith
in my saviour Jesus Christ? I have become a new
man, that is how. My eyes have been opened
through the Holy Spirit such that now,
honouring the memory of my mother and
father as I still surely do, may God rest their
souls, I acknowledge only the Lord over all
of my life.

***

But I am ashamed to say that another, more
colourful, more ghastly event also shaped my
decision to follow the broad path into the church,
tainted as it was by all types of rotten practices
(and indeed rotten eggs conducting them!).

I had taken a rare trip from Oxford to London
with several of my colleagues – my tutor believed
we would benefit from visual confirmation of the
places of which we studied and of the main and
historic places of worship in our capital city.

So it was that we found ourselves swept up in a
loud and rowdy crowd gathered at St Paul's.
There was an animation to this group of people
that reminded me of a living animal, as it swirled
and pulsated and began to drift off, to move off

toward Newgate. I asked a woman, waving what appeared to be a kitchen roller, what was the reason for this commotion.

"It's the cook's execution day!" she said, with a somewhat deranged glee.

"The cook's execution? Why, what had he done? And why such interest in the execution of a cook?" I asked – having to raise my voice above the rising voice of the crowd-beast.

"It's the boiling!" she shouted, with a disgusting degree of glee. "It's Rochester's cook – he sought to poison his master and good King Henry has decreed he must be boiled alive! Over at Smithfield – we're heading over now to see it for ourselves!"

My stomach turned at the news and yet I found myself swept along by the beast with the noise level rising as it grew in size as we neared Smithfield. Finally we came out into the open and to what looked like a stage set for a theatrical play.

There on a platform, lifted for all to see, the faggots were set and already alight. Even from where I was standing I could feel the heat from the roaring flames. But there was no stake upon which to attach the miserable prisoner. Instead, there was wooden frame, ss if for a hanging, but larger and with a further platform above

head height. And beneath it – chillingly
(oddly) - a large, very large rounded pot.

Already the water in the pot was beginning to
agitate and boil and spit as if in anger. Some
say it was salted to increase the temperature
further, all I know is that it's violent bubbling
added to the roar of the flames made for a
terrifying spectacle. The flames would spit
themselves and rise when the water boiled
over and onto the faggots – as if in some
eternal war between the elements.

There must have been over a thousand people
come to watch this grisly spectacle – I wonder
still why they were there? Was it to see justice?
Was it for education? There were certainly
numerous children amongst the crowd. I suspect
in fact that it was mostly for entertainment –
such is the depravity of sinful man, I'm
afraid.

There was then a cry that began to ring out
from the crowd-beast, first from the southern
side of the field and then rippling across the
beast, as all could at first glimpse the wretched
man, the cook, being dragged to his dreadful
doom.

They say he'd claimed his innocence, that the
'poison' was meant only as a mild laxative, as a
prank played on his colleagues in Rochester's
household. His 'joke' led to the death of a

poor woman, whom the household had been supporting out of Christian charity, but whose misfortune was capped by this poisoning unto death. Afeared of being poisoned in his own house – and therefore forever fearing every meal even in the heart of his own home – Henry sought to curb anyone further from trying such a heinous crime and so it was decreed that a new, most dreadful execution be the fruit of any such endeavour.

A prank, now led to this.

Not laughing now, the wretched man had been stripped to only a loincloth – I imagine to increase the visible drama (were that possible?) and to increase the suffering of this poor man. His hands were tethered behind him. His eyes were wide, not able to take in the horror of his circumstance and unable to comprehend how so many of his Christian brothers and sisters could have become co-conspirators in his nightmare. They dragged him up the steps of the framework construction and onto the platform.

He was resisting now, fighting and shouting out as if a wild animal and who could blame him? Beneath him the snarling cauldron, inviting a demise most awful.

The sheriff raised his hands to seek the quiet of the beast – and to my surprise it did subside.

He read out the charge, his voice ringing clear
across the becalmed Smithfield – all leaning in to
hear and to bear witness to the full drama of this
unholy theatre.

No response was required from the cook – but
he called out, again and again "Mercy! Mercy!
For Christ's sake mercy!"

But mercy was there none.

Two burly and masked gaolers grasped the
unfortunate cook by the upper arms and lifted
him easily off the platform and over the angry
pot. The poor man's legs, white and plump like
the thousand chicken thighs he must have
placed in the pot over the course of his toil,
curled up beneath him in an effort to pull
away from the heat.

But there was no escape.

One of the gaolers chose to have some sport
and with a wink to his brawny companion he
called out in a loud voice that carried about
the building roar of the beast, "Ten, nine ..." The
beast knew it's cue and as one counted down,
"Eight, seven, six, five ..."

**The cook's cries were drowned out now under
the sound of a thousand voices, "... four three,
two ... ONE!"**

And with that a sound that will be with me to
my grave. The gaolers released their resisting
charge and at first there was the dull sound of a
splash; but there followed the most eerie and
haunting scream I have heard in all my days.
I would never have known a person could make
such a noise – his roar came from his very soul
as the agony of the boiling water scalded first
his skin, his limbs, his face.

The crowd-beast's own roar gave way to a quiet
fascination as it witnessed what no human eye
should ever see.

But that mood soon turned as well.

The cook was fighting for his life, with no
opportunity to be saved he yet fought and
fought – so strong is a man's desire to live
rather than die for no reason. He managed to
free one arm and with that arm to reach up and
grasp the scalding edge of the pot to part pull
himself up and peer over the side as if in
accusation of the one thousand persecutors.

The beast recoiled.

His head already half boiled, red skin falling from
his face and his eyes protruding diabolically and
staring perhaps unseeing at his last earthly view.
As his drooping mouth gaped his strength finally
gave way and he slipped into the embrace of the
boiling cauldron.

Those closest to the spectacle groaned and women, children and men alike were seen to faint and empty the contents of their stomachs where they stood.

"Lord save us!", cried some, of a stronger constitution. "Christ give him comfort!" cried others.

And me?

I felt a deep sense of shame at having witnessed something so ungodly and spoke an unspoken prayer to the Lord to forgive all of us sinners and to give this poor man the peace in the next life that he was denied in this.

And why do I dwell on these things now? Sat as I am only a short stroll from that same Smithfield, which may yet offer me the same last earthly view.

But it isn't that.

It is to seek to explain to you that, at that time, together with that conversation with my parents, my fear of the authority of the King and his rule was in that moment sealed.

And that in turn sealed my intent for the next stage of my life. I need not seek out controversy or walk the hazardous path of pioneer in these ideas of Reform in which I had dallied at university. I felt my parents were right. I had no desire to cross the awesome power of the King's decrees – I'd trust in the Lord to fight the spiritual battles and then I could go along with that.

Am I ashamed as I write this now?

In all truth, no – for I did not yet know the full power of the Armour of God nor did I fully comprehend the all consuming greatness off His goodness and mercy for me.

So I resolved to go into the church and to take a living, to nurture my congregation quietly and in a Godly manner, seeking a quiet and orderly life. Was that not what Paul had written to the Thessalonians?

'... make it your ambition to lead a quiet life: You should mind your own business and work with your hands, just as we told you, so that your daily life may win the respect of outsiders and so that you will not be dependent on anybody.'

That sounded very attractive to me at this time, with the worried tones of my parents combining with the frenzied and painful cries

of the cook ringing and echoing in my ears.
And so I determined upon the easy path.

But the Lord was not done with me yet and
His plans for me were to prove to be very
different.

***

Chapter 3 – London,
Life as a Priest

It was as Cardinal College was about to be dissolved and King Henry was reinstating it under his own name that I went into the ministry and was offered the living (through some contacts from my Cambridge days) at Holy Trinity the Less in London.

London life was more dense and frenetic than that of either Cambridge or Oxford and it took quite a while to acquaint myself with the closeness of living to be had there. My congregation took to me well enough, it was a small living but it did put me in a place to witness the developments of state at first hand.

It was not long before King Henry finally abjured his first wife, Catherine and suspicion was rife that his new wife Anne Boleyn would sponsor and encourage him toward further Reform of the church.

I stuck by my pledge to my parents and myself to be the quiet observer.

Thus it was, even before the marriage of King Henry and Anne, that I was on the streets with some of my congregation outside our church on Knyghtrider Street to see the great King Henry himself process with his newly betrothed. An Act of Submission from Parliament had formalised affairs and the future Queen Anne could finally take her place with some legitimacy at the side of her future husband.

Then as now, the great politics of state and the affairs of the church were intermingled and the suspicion that I witnessed the people of London greet Anne with that day was surely as motivated by suspicion over her influence in Reforming the church as it was over any residual loyalty (of which much resided) in the old Queen Catherine and her Romish, imperial connections.

Even on the normally joyous occasion of Henry's marriage to Anne, the crowds were strangely subdued.

I think the mass of people are reluctant to see change. I think for the most part hearts are hard and familiarity is friend to most, sometimes more than truth itself. Certainly it seemed so as slowly, so slowly did the momentum for Reform in the church build – in London itself, let alone across the more conservative, superstitious and backward parts of the land.

Was it Anne's doing or for the convenience of the King that the edict came down to all priests that the Pope should henceforth be known only as the 'Bishop of Rome'? Was it in recognition of the wrongdoing of that Romish Church over the decades and centuries or was it to facilitate further earthly powers to a King hungry for them? Perhaps we will never know – and perhaps it is not for us ordinary folk to know the mind of a monarch.

But surely the Lord knew and the Lord could work in all things for the good, as always.

Stalwarts such as Hugh Latimer, one of my tutors at Cambridge and stout Reformer, continued to preach bravely the cause of Reform and to accuse the continued grievances of the Romish Church. Word of his preaching in Bristol reached us in London and I felt the pangs of guilt that I kept my services anodyne, being sure to follow the latest instruction from my diocese.

But my spirit was restless. The Lord was at work on my heart.

The violence toward the emblems of Romish Popery that my parents had warned me about was escalating and they were occurring closer to my home now. King Henry was ramping up his authority and did so with much blood – with hundreds facing the executioner, mostly for

failing to acknowledge his primacy over the
church and for mistakenly clinging on to the
teaching and indoctrination they had received
about their antichristian Pope.

Many fled the land, seeking refuge and people
who carried the same sympathies as they.
Papists fled to France and Spain, Reformers too
enthusiastic for Henry to the Protestant states.

And I harboured a fearful heart.

I sensed sympathy with the Reformers for
I began to see the superstition and hollowness of
the Romish Catholic ways just as I was forced to
practice much of them daily with my expectant
congregation. I recalled the debates in "Little
Germany" and understood better the rottenness
which the likes of Tyndale, Cranmer, Bilney and
Barnes had accused the Papist Church.

But I could not bring myself to speak out just
then, for fear of finding myself ahead of the pace
of change that King Henry had set for us. I had
seen just how dangerous it could be to get too
far ahead. And I had the promise to my parents
to keep.

"These be no causes to die for" became the
popular refrain for those of us on the edges of
these traumatic events. And in that argument
I found good merit.

So I found a way to escape myself and (so
I thought!) thereby escape undue scrutiny or
the consequences of having to make any stand
one way or another in that volatile climate.
(How the Lord must have sighed then, knowing
the plans he had for me which are being revealed
only now! Again, I eschew shame regarding
this for being not yet 'reborn', I 'knew not what
I did').

One of the most burgeoning guilds at this time
was that of the Merchant Adventurers, riding
the rise in demand across Europe for finished
English cloth – long since the finest in the
world. A thriving trade had led to a strong
affiliation with Antwerp, gateway to the
European market – and my old friend from
Cambridge days, William Tyndale had trodden
the path before me to join the chaplaincy there.

It was through a mutual contact of ours that
I was then offered a way out of the tempestuous
climate in England (I speak figuratively of the
emerging Reform in our land, conflicted as it was
with eddies back and forth that could catch the
most careful sailor). I was invited to join the
chaplaincy of the Merchant Adventurers in
Antwerp – and it felt to me then an opportunity
to safely ride out the storm raging in England.
At the same time, I felt I might affiliate myself
with those who had an earnest desire to know
truth and live a Godly life – in a place where

I could explore these Reformist ideas cautiously and in safe harbour where I could take my time to make up my own mind.

Whilst living a quiet life.

How little I understood the way of the Lord!

But relinquish my living I did, leaving the souls of Holy Trinity the Less to the care of the next curate and leaving these shores for I knew not how long.

I would return a man reborn. Married. With eight children ! Compiler of the first authorised Bible in our native tongue. And with a burning love of the Lord of which I could not have dreamed when I left clutching my few belongings and seeing the white cliffs of Dover diminish beneath a typical English fog as I sailed across the Channel.

The Lord works in mysterious ways indeed!

***

Chapter 4 – Antwerp, The Holy Work

My accommodation in Antwerp was initially with one Thomas Poyntz, a wealthy merchant well known amongst the Merchant Adventurer community who was already host to one of the other chaplains – none other than William Tyndale.

Poyntz was not only known by everyone in Antwerp, but I would venture to suggest was liked by everyone too. Sitting atop his business which had made considerable monies from the growth in finished English cloth exports into the Continent, his appetite for trade was matched by his appetite for life. Although a Godly man (to which his future conduct would attest in full), he was also fond of company, fond of food and fond of bright and high quality attire.

I recall gently challenging him on his expenditure on exotic and expensive clothing on one occasion, but he was unrepentant.

"But John," he chided, "it is my business to encourage the wearing of quality clothing for there be none finer than that made from our own English cloth. Would I not be a hypocrite if I were not to act equal as to what I say?"

He paused a moment, before letting out a loud "Ha!" and slapping me firmly on the back.

"John," he teased me, "you're a fine and learned fellow, but you need not be so earnest ALL the time!" He had that social assurance which perhaps comes only from centuries of breeding – he was from a landed gentry family hailing from Essex and (as he was proud to share with us many a time over supper), his grandfather and uncle had both held the elevated position of Lord Mayor of London.

As the second son, Thomas had gone into trade – and his sharp mind together with his affable character and social confidence ensured his success.

Beneath the finery and social Graces, however, was also a kindly and Godly soul. Thus it was that his generosity extended to providing living quarters for William Tyndale and, on my arrival, myself also.

I recall my arrival at his private home, where he welcomed me as if I were a family member. It was good also to see William again, it had been many years since our discussions and debates over the hearth of 'Little Germany' in our briefly overlapping Cambridge days.

Tyndale already had some notoriety by this stage, having completed his translation of the New Testament Scriptures into English in the year I had graduated from Pembroke Hall, 1526. He had retreated to the relative safety of Antwerp, having spent time in Wittenberg with the Reformers there – including Martin Luther himself.

William Tyndale was to have a profound effect on my life.

Perhaps more accurately, the Lord was to use William Tyndale to transform my life – to enable me to be born again, into everlasting communion with our Lord through Jesus Christ. I will seek to capture some of the discussions we had in those intense times in Antwerp to give you a flavour of the man and a glimpse of how our Lord God works in mysterious ways.

Soon after my arrival at Poyntz's house, we were in discussion over supper about the progress of Reform and barriers to the same back in England.

"For me, John, it was the Erasmus translation that lit the flame of passion that led me to my translations. I observed how, perhaps inadvertently, his edition laying out the Greek alongside the Latin had ignited the power of Scripture amongst us once again. After perhaps centuries of dormancy, whilst the Romish Church cloaked the truth from us all, we at the universities could finally see the Lord's Word laid out for us to see and understand clearly."

"I certainly recall the strength of our debates in Little Germany!", I commented. "But then, does that not suffice? Is it not enough for men of learning to refresh their understanding of the Scriptures in order to be able to give right teaching and counsel to the common man?"

"But that's just it," replied Tyndale, animated now, "it hit me like a thunderbolt from the sky that if WE were enlivened and inspired by seeing the Lord's Word in a familiar tongue, why then would not EVERY man – or woman – be so inspired if they were to be able to read it in a tongue familiar to them. In English. The Lord so stirred my heart that day – I had been tutor to the Walsh boys and seeking to impart knowledge to them, when I began to see that ALL people could learn and be inspired directly from the Word of the Lord ! And one day, the plough boy with pure heart will know more of the Scriptures than the Pope himself !"

"And so you completed your New Testament translation?" I asked, a rhetorical question.

"But what good can it be if even the Bishop of London forbids its use? And if, as I have heard report, such is his determination that he buys up every copy in print over here, only to see all copies burned amongst the faggots in St Paul's Cross?"

I noticed Tyndale look to Poyntz and a wry smile be exchanged between them. "Ha!", exclaimed Poyntz, "Tell him, William!"

"Tell me what?" I asked.

"Well, John, you are right that Cuthbert Tunstall sent an envoy to buy up all the copies from our printers. Quite a clever and cunning plan! Except perhaps he should have checked a little more closely on the associates of his envoy!"

Poyntz laughed aloud again.

"For it transpired," continued Tyndale, "that he was rather well known to a certain W. Tyndale, currently residing in Antwerp! We agreed to provide the copies his master desired – although the price was high ... so high in fact that we were able to create THREE further copies for every one we sent for burning and to increase by far the number of souls we could reach in England with these English Scriptures!"

I was amazed – at their audacity as well as their bravery in contravening the authority of the Bishop of London (I had yet to shake off my misdirected deference to unjust authority – but the day was soon to come!).

"Well that would explain why so many of my acquaintance in London claimed to have had sight of your translation – although few confessed to me to own one."

"Are you surprised?" asked Poyntz, "Could they have known you wouldn't have reported straight back to your masters and placed them under examination, rsulting in their burning?"

I looked away, ashamed at how they must view me in that moment – my equivocation stark against their bravery and bold action for our Lord.

"But how could you continue to import these copies, under the very noses of your enemies?" I asked – not wanting to respond to Poyntz's remarks.

Poyntz looked at Tyndale, who nodded, as if granting permission to speak.

He looked me directly in the eye as he explained, "By God's Grace the Port of London is under the control of brothers in Christ from Germany. Being sympathetic to our cause, they turn a blind eye to certain imports of commodities from Antwerp – including sacks of flour that might be mysteriously weighty or oddly angular!"

"You mean you were smuggling English New Testaments in sacks of flour, less than a thousand yards from the residency of the Bishop of London?" I asked, flabbergasted.

"Correct!" replied Tyndale.

"'Well, bless my soul!" I retorted. And then, quick as a flash, quipped, "Man shall not live by bread alone, but by every word that proceeds from the mouth of God'" – which brought about much unrestrained laughter and another slap on the back from Poyntz.

"I told you he was a good fellow!", said Tyndale to Poyntz.

***

There was method to their entrusting me with the secrets of their project, as I was to find to my initial consternation and then delight.

Tyndale began to share with me his approach and methodology in translating the Scriptures and it was not long before I found myself contributing my own thoughts to help bring further order and organisation to this extraordinary work.

I consider myself gifted in languages, readily picking up the rhythms and structures of each of those that I have studied – Greek and Latin of course, but also Hebrew and Aramaic. But what gifting I have and had there paled against the natural abilities of Tyndale, which allowed him to combine speed with an elegance of turn of phrase in English which served so well to bring out the true meaning of the texts for God's glory.

I began to categorise Tyndale's output and as I reviewed past manuscripts I began also to annotate with comments the text, drawing out the marvellous relevance of certain verses to enlighten us in our dark times, so long shrouded in Papist obfuscation. The effect of this was twofold:-

Firstly, Tyndale delighted in my additions to his most excellent translation and grew in trust of me to co-ordinate the full collation of the translated Scriptures and to make a complete commentary across the all the Scriptures he translated.

And secondly, most marvellously and most mysteriously, this process of my annotating the English text with my own commentary allowed me to reflect more deeply than ever I had on the POWER of those words. Despite my proficiency in language and my familiarity with the text in Greek, Latin, Hebrew or Aramaic, somehow there was a culmination, a denouement in reviewing the Scriptures in English that finally broke the shackles and chains under which I had been

bound by the devious endeavours of the Church
of the Antichrist that is the Romish Church.

'All Scripture is God-breathed and is useful for
teaching, rebuking, correcting and training in
righteousness, so that the servant of God may
be thoroughly equipped for every good work',
wrote the Apostle Paul to Timothy.

God-breathed.

And so it was that God breathed through His
Word that I studied, analysed and sought to
explain and reveal in native tongue – in MY
native tongue to my fellow native tongue
speakers. And words and phrases that I had
passed over in dry academic study for the
purposes of completing dissertations at
university suddenly leapt out at me with a
force that quickened my heart – literally
quickened my heart and drew shortness of
breath in me.

How could I have missed the unsurpassing Good
News of God's unfolding plan revealed to us
through His Word? Of a Christ who has done it
all to reconcile us with our Creator, dying
and being raised again to the right hand of
God in Glory so that we are forever reconciled
with Him.

No more condemnation then. No longer sinners,
but saints all – who believe.

What purpose, then, indulgences to buy further favour from the Lord? He cannot love us any more nor can he love us any less than he already does! He loves us as a son, he loves us as he loves Jesus.

He loves us as he loves Jesus.

He loves ME as he loves Jesus.

It was like being filled up from my toes to the top of my head, filled – tingling with a warmth up my spine as it went - with what I can only describe as overwhelming spirit of Love. That God should love me so and cleanse me so and desire me so – even to sending his own son to die for ME!

What value then my own feeble achievements to date? How foolish my pride in anything I had accomplished in comparison to this all consuming Truth?

I grasped at last that the Lord would indeed work in all things for the good for those that love Him – and now I truly did love Him ! Nothing could separate me now from the love He has for me. Nothing can separate us. My fears of earthly authorities and my desires to serve those false masters fell clean away as I found myself on my knees at the feet of my True Lord.

Directly at the feet of Jesus.

NOW I knew Jesus! Now I am truly born of God and neither the evil one nor the church of the Antichrist can touch me.

And now I knew also my destiny, why He had brought me here under this roof and at this time – to help Tyndale in this Holy Work to complete the translation of all of the Scriptures and present in orderly and accessible fashion to every English speaker so that they too may grasp how wide, how long, how great is the love God has for them!

Truly I understood how I had been chosen and appointed by God to bear fruit – just as the Apostle John had described. That I am a fellow worker with God as Paul explained to the Corinthians. And that despite my fears and anxieties – regarding personal safety or how men might view me – as Paul exclaimed to the Ephesians, I can do all things through Christ who strengthens me!

I was a man reborn.

I belonged – and will always belong – to Christ.

***

Tyndale was one of the first I told about my true encounter with the Living Christ and his delight for me was heart felt and real. Of course he also had been reborn in the Lord and now

I understood his zeal and energy and passion to complete his work. I redoubled my efforts to support him – and there was a short and marvellous period when we were fully engrossed together in the Holy Work and made great strides forward in the endeavour.

It was Poyntz who one evening raised the subject of safeguarding our work.

"You know you could lose it all in the flames in a matter of moments?" he remarked, almost casually.

"We trust in the Lord that this is His work and that it is His will that it be completed. There can be no better protector" replied Tyndale calmly.

"No better protector indeed," he replied. "But I spent some time reviewing your translation and commentary on Peter last evening. And his words about our enemy the devil prowling around us like a roaring lion resonated rather too strongly for my liking. Peter exhorted us to be vigilant. To be frank, I don't believe we are being vigilant enough."

"But only a few know of our full endeavours – and I have scarce left the safety of your premises these four months", Tyndale replied.

I felt a stirring in my heart. "Thomas is right, William" I interjected. "Proverbs tells us that the wise are cautious and avoid danger ..."

Tyndale laughed scornfully at this and exclaimed, "Avoid danger?! I think we're rather past avoiding danger John. If you're still wanting to avoid danger I suggest you flee our company and go back to your Papist friends in London!". He could be irascible, William Tyndale, but I knew the few hours sleep he'd had and the amount of hours he'd dedicated to the Holy Work these last months – and so I did not rise to his uncharacteristic unkindness.

"Let me finish, William" I said gently but firmly. "I was meaning only that we should use all wisdom to ensure the success of our venture as best we can. And with some simple steps I believe we can take away much of the risk we're currently under."

"I'm sorry, John" Tyndale was quick to apologise. "Tell us you plan."

And so I explained how I proposed to leave their company for overnight accommodation: One of the other leading Merchant Adventurers – Richard Hawkins - had offered me lodging in a wing of their home not two streets away. I would have more space and comfort there – and most importantly, I could use the extended space I had there to store the translated manuscripts until we could have them reproduced and printed.

I explained further, "I am not yet well known here and as part of this endeavour, whereas those that know you are aware that it is here at Poyntz's that you reside and work. So if they come looking to confiscate the work, it's here they'll come looking. And Richard is a good man who will speak of this to no one, of that I'm sure."

And so it was agreed and within two days I had removed myself along with all of my belongings and – secretly – all of the translated manuscripts to my new accommodation.

The Lord had his hand in that.

Within the week things were to take a rapid turn for the worse. A certain Henry Phillips had made his way into Tyndale's acquaintance, despite Poyntz's misgivings and mistrust. But Tyndale was of a trusting nature and I think hungry for new contact having been holed up within the residence for many weeks.

Phillips had increasingly been spending time in the evenings with Tyndale and I think provided some refreshing distraction for him as he brought a fresh perspective to our gatherings. For some days he had been encouraging Tyndale to leave the oppressive confines of Poyntz's home to enjoy an evening walk and perhaps a meal down in the harbour.

I'm sure that if Poyntz had been at home he would successfully have dissuaded Tyndale from such a risky diversion from our safe and secure habits. But he was away on business at one of what he described as his 'Zoom meetings' – at the Easter Fayre at Bergen op Zoom – and so there was no one who had Tyndale's ear to dissuade him from Phillips' invitation.

He had invited me to join him also, but my natural caution and the fact that I had much work to catch up on meant that I was over at my new accommodation with Hawkins on the evening Phillips persuaded Tyndale out of the house.

He regretted it immediately he stepped out of the door.

There outside the door were two burly men who promptly arrested him the moment he stepped away from the safety of the Englishman Poyntz's house that was under the protection of the Merchant Adventurers itself.

"On the authority of the Procurer-General, you are placed under arrest on the charge of heresy!" announced the larger of the men.

"On what evidence?" challenged Tyndale, shooting a look at Phillips, whose inability to look him in the eye confirmed his betrayal.

"There will be evidence enough inside, of that we have no doubt!" responded the law enforcer.

With that he grabbed Tyndale by both arms and tied his hands behind his back. With a shove he pushed him down the road and toward his incarceration. As Tyndale glanced back, he saw the other law enforcer reach into his pocket and pass across a purse to Phillips. And he thought he heard him say, "This is yours, Judas. I hope you're proud of yourself!" It seemed he had sympathy with Tyndale and perhaps the cause – but not sufficient to renege on his duties.

We heard it report that Tyndale was escorted to the castle outside Vilvorde near Brussels and were not surprised when Poyntz's residence was searched from top to bottom by the authorities. They confiscated quills and pens and some generic texts – but thanks be to God, they found none of the translated manuscripts which were safely in my possession.

I eschewed visiting Poyntz from that moment on – not out of fear (I was afeared no more since my encounter with the Living Christ), but out of wise caution and according to the plans we had agreed only the week prior.

Poyntz made every effort to seek the release of Tyndale, vouching for his good character and promising to stand guardian over him until he could return to England. He was at one point confident of succeeding in this, letting me know via one of his servants that he had written to his brother in England who was well placed at the

English court to exert the influence needed to bring about Tyndale's release.

But to his great cost, he was mistaken.

The 'Judas' Phillips had not finished his diabolical work and informed the authorities that Poyntz was himself an arch Reformer and a danger to the community – resulting in his arrest and examination. Several months passed and the fate of Poyntz as well as Tyndale looked bleak. Poyntz was stoic when imprisoned, but when he was being moved to a more secure prison he saw his opportunity to escape, otherwise he knew he would face execution.

I wonder if the same guard that accused Phillips of being a Judas had a hand in aiding his escape?

I do not blame my friend Poyntz for fleeing his inevitable execution. He had more than fulfilled the task the Lord laid before him and I was glad to hear that his familiarity with the lay of the land allowed him to escape the oncoming search of the horsemen. Some time later I received report that he had made safe journey back to England – although he was banished from ever setting foot in the Netherlands again and as a result his flourishing business was undone and collapsed. A heavy price to pay for supporting our Holy Work.

I was sorry for my friend – whose wife refused to join him also and who now lives out his time still in a comfort far less than that to which he had become accustomed in Antwerp.

No fine clothes for him any more. I pray the Lord will provide for him and restore his fortunes one day soon.

***

With Tyndale imprisoned and Poyntz fled back to England, the Holy Work fell squarely on my shoulders. Inspired by my encounter with the Lord and emboldened by the Holy Spirit, I redoubled my efforts to bring Tyndale's vision of an English Bible alive and available to every Englishman.

Although I had all of the translated manuscripts from Tyndale (most complete, some in part) and a number also that we had been revising from Miles Coverdale, my first task was to bring order to the array of papers, writings and commentaries. My friend Tyndale was the most marvellous linguist – but (I am sure he would not mind me sharing) did not possess the same sense of order and management that was second nature to me. I think that was why he was keen we work together – we complimented one another.

Now it was down to me alone.

Fortunately the bulk of the translation work was completed – my own linguistic experience had at least prepared me for this task now and I was able to complete those Scriptures that had not already been completed by Tyndale or Coverdale. Tyndale's translations I found most excellent and on review needed only modest revision and the addition of my commentaries in the margin to shed light on how the Scriptures related to our current circumstances.

I was grateful to have Coverdale's manuscripts, although I found it necessary to pay greater scrutiny to his translations and to make certain significant amendments that I felt could not be left to stand.

It was arduous work.

It was lengthy work.

But it was also marvellous work!

A Holy Work!

Bringing the Word of the Lord to our native tongue, the Lord continued to make Himself known to me more and more intimately as my own intimacy with His Word increased. What marvellous revelation revealed from God to His people! How exhilarating to consider how the Holy Spirit would work in the hearts of the very many people who would now be able to read and hear these Scriptures for themselves!

It was with great anticipation therefore that I turned my attention to seeking a means to get the manuscripts printed and published – to release this Word to the English speaking peoples.

The Lord was already preparing the way so that when I began to inquire through my contacts in the Merchant Adventurers, I quickly received word back that two publishers had been asking after the opportunity to publish an English Bible. I needed to be cautious, with Tyndale still imprisoned and enemies abroad - so I had asked one of my closer associates at the Guild to spend an evening with the two gentlemen to ascertain their intent before allowing them to meet me directly. He reported back to me that he felt their intentions were earnest as well as honourable – although he also cautioned me that these gentlemen saw the venture as a commercial one, not just a holy one.

Thus it was that I met, in great secrecy, Messrs Richard Grafton and Edward Whitchurch. I was impressed by their credentials and also by their connections back in England. In particular, Richard Grafton had notions to use his familiarity with key members of the English court to have the translation authorised at the highest levels – and I mean the very highest levels! -and promoted across the land. This stirred my spirit and outweighed any

concerns I harboured about the commercial
nature of their engagement. Frankly I could see
no other way than involving commercial interest
in sustaining the work. Although not my own
motivation, I was prepared to work with any
party that shared – for whatever reason – the
same mission as me, to see the Scriptures made
available in the English language to the whole
of the English people, from high to ordinary
to lowly.

One area of heated debate was regarding the
Apocrypha, which came near to thwarting our
partnership.

"It must be the COMPLETE Bible," asserted
Grafton, "nothing else will suffice if we are to
achieve formal authorisation and court
sponsorship of the translation."

"On that we can agree," I answered,
misunderstanding his meaning, "we must of
course include both the Old and New
Testaments. I have taken it upon myself to
complete the work Tyndale had commenced,
which together with the Coverdale chapters
will give us the full Scriptures."

"And the Apocrypha? Is that not also the Word
of God?" asked Whitchurch.

"The Apocrypha doubtless contain men's
wisdom for the instruction of man. But it has

no place in the Scriptures, which are the God-breathed Word from the Lord to mankind. One cannot equate them."

"And yet we have, the church has for many centuries ..." Grafton again.

I interrupted, "The Papist Church, yes, which has misled the people over the longest of times into the most superstitious and antichristian practices ..."

Grafton now interrupting, "So the Apocrypha are of the Antichrist? Is that your view? Edward, we are perhaps mistaken to shackle ourselves with a heretic. This could blacken our names and lead to ruin."

"You must listen to my argument, Mr Grafton, not build your own arguments on the foundations of mine! I stated that the Papist Church has mislead the people in numerous ways. As such it has led people not toward the Lord but away from Him. It is therefore the church of the Antichrist. Amongst those ills, but by no means foremost amongst them, has been the equivalence of place given to the Apocrypha with the Living Word of God that is the Old and New Testaments."

"Then it is to be discarded as rubbish on the heap? Or would you have it burned at St Paul's Cross?" asked Grafton angrily.

"Allow me to finish, Mr Grafton. I say that these books of man are useful instruction as they contain the wisdom of man interpreting the true Scriptures. But Scriptures themselves – inspired and the living breath of the Holy Spirit, they are not!"

An awkward silence ensued.

The fire cracked as the logs settled in the hearth.

It was Whitchurch who spoke next. I had warmed to Whitchurch, he seemed to have a conciliatory spirit and a gentle nature that I recognised as Godly.

"John, you are a learned and well read man. More so than Richard and myself who are humble men of business. But please listen to us and understand that we do know and understand our business. We have a very real opportunity – and a small window of time – to do something remarkable, advancing the Word of God in our land. But we cannot take too extreme a stance or we will not succeed. Honestly John, we will not succeed unless we include what the majority of Englishmen would expect to be in a full English Bible – all eighty books - perhaps wrongly as you suggest, but they will expect it nonetheless."

Another moment of silence. I looked from one to the other. I saw the agitation on Grafton's face and hoped it was not the passing of a money making opportunity that made him so aggrieved. But on Whitchurch's face I saw what I discerned to be true concern.

I spoke calmly, "Well, we only have Coverdale's translations of those – which do not even include the prayer of Manessah. His standards are not those of Tyndale. Would you have me burn the midnight oil toiling over correcting and annotating texts that I have such little faith in?"

The question was directed at Whitchurch.

"Perhaps not." he replied. "If you could just include Coverdale's Apocrypha, as they stand, with the least amendments possible we could simply allow them to stand between the Old and New Testaments. No commentary or annotation required. It would be clear then that your own role in this is as Compiler, without your having to put your name or reputation to this part of the translation."

I knew then that they were right.

I hold strong views on the beliefs I have come to hold – through reasoned evaluation of true Scripture and weighing up arguments fully and objectively. But I also know when to stand firm and when to set an argument aside for the working of all things for the good.

"I have listened to you and I understand your case. And I agree to it." I looked them both in the eye as I said this and held my hand out, first to Grafton to demonstrate my reconciliation with him and then to Whitchurch, with a nod to acknowledge his role as peacemaker which had kept the venture alive.

"Just one more thing." I saw their faces drop as I said this, clearly alarmed that there would be another obstacle I was about to place in the way of proceeding. "About putting my name to this."

"Yes," replied Grafton, "naturally you shall be credited for this major work you have achieved."

"No," I replied "you misunderstand me. I do NOT wish my name to be associated with this. Not because of the Apocrypha, but for these reasons – which I have thought about and prayed over these many weeks since I took over this work from Tyndale."

"Go on" said Whitchurch.

"I seek no fame from this venture, I seek only God's approval for any small role I may have played in releasing the power of His Word on the people of England. Furthermore, this work – apart from being truly from the Lord – has also been the work of many people. Tyndale and

Coverdale of course, but also numerous others in the provision of support, encouragement and practicalities. I would not seek to claim the universal credit for this work that putting my name to this would imply."

"We understand," replied Whitchurch. "but it must have a name by which to be known, surely?"

"Yes, indeed" I replied, "and if I may I'd like to use any position of influence I do hold from the tasks I have undertaken to propose we give this work a pseudonym comprising the two names from the Gospel that have influenced me most spiritually."

"And what would those be?" asked Grafton.

"Thomas Matthew" I replied.

"To Matthew I owe my appreciation of the life and life changing teachings of Christ, explained so fully and marvellously in that Gospel. And in Thomas I see a disciple like myself who took time to come to know who Christ truly is and needed additional proof to commit himself fully."

"The Thomas Matthew Bible. So be it. May the Lord bless the Thomas Matthew Bible and use it for His glory in our kingdom!" announced Whitchurch.

"Amen to that." I replied. And we laughed together and set about making the Thomas Matthew Bible a reality.

***

Just as my spiritual life had been transformed by my encounter with Christ and my professional life had been transformed by being thrust into sole responsibility for the Holy Work of getting the English Scriptures published, so too it was at this time that my personal life was to be transformed also.

It was as Grafton, Whitchurch and I were seeking a printer for the Thomas Matthew Bible in Antwerp that I made the acquaintance of Jacob van Meteren, who had previously facilitated the printing of Coverdale's version. Although not a rich man in the worldly sense, he was rich in the spirit of the Lord. Rarely have I met a more virtuous man and as our business relationship developed over the printing of our Scriptures, so too developed our friendship.

Thus it was that he was in due course to invite me to his family home for supper – which I almost passed up, so engrossed was I in the Holy Work on that day.

I will forever be grateful that my assistants insisted that they could manage in my absence, for on that evening I was to meet my future wife.

Adriana.

Adriana was the eldest of three daughters at that time and so was the first in line to greet me as an honoured guest. The moment I looked upon her, I saw her differently from any other woman I had ever gazed upon.

Her eyes were an emerald green, with a sparkle that betrayed a vivid spirit beneath her demure exterior. She curtsied and seemed to blush on greeting me – which I found disconcerting for it was I who felt aflush in a manner I had never experienced before. Over supper the discussions were lively and entertaining, with my hosts continually courteous and considerate of my views. We discussed the progress of Reform in England and I was impressed at Adriana's willingness to contribute as well as the extent of her knowledge and insight into matters of Reform despite her having little understanding of the state of affairs in England.

"So the execution of Queen Anne could bring an end to the progress of Reform in England?" Adriana asked.

"Indeed", I replied, "there is no doubt that the parties connected to Anne were true sympathisers of Reform and she has surely enlightened King Henry in these matters. I fear her betrayal may harden his heart once again, but I pray it will not be so."

"And these 'Ten Articles", do you consider them to be true to the Scriptures about which you know so much?"

"In part," I answer. "There are doubtless some victories for Christ in these positions, most notably in the primacy of place given to the Scriptures – which is so helpful to our own endeavour, Jacob – and in the recognition of the role of faith as pre-eminent over works. But many superstitious legacies have been retained – the absurd devotion given to the saints, for example and the encouragement of dressing priests in rich vestments like peacocks; and the ambivalence over purgatory, insisting still on prayers for the dead."

"Do the dead not deserve our prayers?" asked Adriana.

"Adriana! Mind your tongue in front of our honoured guest!" her mother interjected.

"That's fine," I chuckled, encouraged and entranced by her spirit. "Christ has already done all that is needed for the dead, my dear. Their fate is up to the Lord now, whatever we may say or wish and whatever prattling we make here on earth."

"Prattling?" Adriana raised her eyebrows. "Please have a care, Mr Rogers. We Pratts have a pension for 'prattling' and cannot but

help to 'prattle' every time we open our mouths."
I understood she was alluding to the anglicised
version of her name – being Pratt and having the
meaning 'meadows'.

I laughed. "Your prattling I can stand and
would welcome, for certain!" I reassured her.
"But I would request to hear it whilst alive
rather than waiting until after my death!"

And our conversation turned to lighter matters,
although I valued the earnest discourse with
virtuous and honest people, as I always have.

It transpired my words were to prove prophetic.

I had several restless nights where my spirit was
disturbed. The image of Adriana's face and the
lightness of her voice stayed with me as a
constant presence day and night.

She filled my thoughts.

More than that, it felt as though she had
touched my soul.

I felt disquieted and shameful that I should be
so transfixed on this young woman, that I knew
was different in nature from any other feelings
I had ever felt.

It was deep in the night one evening that I was
unable to sleep and came down from my rooms

to sit awhile downstairs with a glass of milk in the candlelight. I saw the light from another candle flickering as someone else was coming down the staircase.

It was Richard Hawkins.

"You're up late! Or are you risen early?" he asked.

"I'm sorry if I woke you: I apologised. "I'm afraid I cannot find rest."

"You've been restless these last few days, John, I've noticed." He said. "What ails you?"

I thought for a moment, uncertain whether to share my true feelings so openly with someone else. Even speaking them out loud would make my predicament more real and mean I could ignore them no longer.

But Richard had been a good friend to me and I trusted his counsel. And God's Word tells us in Proverbs "Listen to advice and accept discipline, and at the end you will be counted among the wise": and "Get all the advice and instruction you can, so you will be wise the rest of your life."

And so I confessed to him my preoccupation with Adriana in the dimness of that deep night.

And a wonderful thing happened.

"But John," Richard gently chided me, "are you not always exhorting me to follow the Word of God as laid out in the Scriptures?"

"I am" I acknowledged.

"Then what does the Bible tell you about marriage?" he asked. "Does it prohibit any man from having a wife?"

"It does not." I answered. "But the church prohibits me to marry as a priest."

"In England yes," he replied, "but we are not in England now. And Adriana is not English. I do not have the knowledge of the Scriptures that you have, but even I know that the Lord said of Adam that 'It is not good for man to be alone and he made a suitable helper for him'. Do you not deserve your own suitable helper?"

Richard could see me wavering and wrestling with these truths. Was this a temptation from the Evil One that could lead to the damnation of my soul? Or could this be the final missing piece to make my soul feel whole?

"Have you worked on the translation of Jeremiah yet, John" he asked.

I was wrong footed by this apparent change of tack. "Well yes," I replied, "it is the first of the translations not yet printed and so was one of the first of Tyndale's books I have toiled over. What has that to do with my predicament?"

"And you got as far as the Israelites' exile in Babylon?" he asked. I began to see where this was heading. "So you tell me – what was the Lord's exhortation to the people of Israel for those people, who found themselves in a strange land."

I picked up the thread and recited from memory, "'Build houses and settle down; plant gardens and eat what they produce. Marry and have sons and daughters; find wives for your sons and give your daughters in marriage, so that they too may have sons and daughters.'"

"So?" he asked.

"So," I replied, "I shall seek Adriana's hand in marriage!"

"Just so!" he answered, "I am so very glad for you, John, you deserve to be happy and enjoy the wonderful gift from the Lord that is family life. Shall I pray for you now?"

"Please," I replied. And my friend Richard Hawkins prayed for me and for Adriana and for the life and family we might enjoy together, God willing.

And I felt my spirit stir and the Holy Spirit upon me again – and I knew that Adriana would be my wife, that she would be my constant helper and companion and that we would have many wonderful children together.

And so it has been.

***

Whilst my personal circumstances were blossoming, I was ever conscious of my friend Tyndale's precarious situation still imprisoned. By agreement there had been no contact between us and I was grateful (and still am) for his discretion in keeping my name out of any examinations he underwent.

Once Poyntz's endeavours to solicit the royal court had failed and he himself had had to flee for his very life, there was a certain inevitability about Tyndale facing the ultimate penalty for his stance.

And yet I knew he would consider it gain.

Thus it was that he was finally led to his execution and I determined that it would be safe and fitting for me to show my respects by attending his execution. I was careful to maintain a low profile as I travelled to Brussels and to keep anonymous amongst the thronging crowd.

The crowd began to stir and I had the same queasy feeling in the pit of my stomach as

I had had that day Rochester's cook had met such a grisly demise.

The crowd-beast lived aboard as well as in England.

This time I maintained a distance from the emotion by praying for my friend's steadfastness throughout. I had conflicting feelings. Here was a wonderful man of God being executed only for doing the work of the Lord. I was sorry to be losing a friend.

And yet.

I was also so very proud of my friend, the gifted William Tyndale whose translations would ensure his Holy Work would outlive his own body and whose trust in our Lord Jesus Christ would doubtless lead his soul to an eternity in the presence of the Lord in Heaven. A certain hope I knew we shared.

It was no surprise to me then – although the lack of surprise did nothing to diminish my pride and love of him at that moment – that my dear friend William Tyndale was stoic and steadfast for our Lord unto the end.

Execution practices in the Spanish Netherlands were somewhat different to those in England. The faggots and stake were familiar, but there was also a structure that was intended to allow for simultaneous strangulation of the victim.

As if man could thereby kill the victim not once but twice – once by burning and once by strangulation, as if that might double the punishment.

I prayed for a peaceful and speedy end for my friend.

But what came next was both marvellous and unexpected.

As in England, the victim was permitted some final words – so the crowd-beast quieted to hear what this true Englishman had to say with his last breath.

He called out in a bold and fearless voice, "Lord, open the eyes of the King of England!"

At that very moment I knew that our Holy Work, our venture to place the truth of the Holy Scriptures in English into the hands of every living Englishman would prevail and prosper. This was surely a prophecy and I felt also that it was an encouragement from my friend and co-worker.

At that the executioners took up position to light the fires and simultaneously strangle the Lord's martyr Tyndale.

But my prayers were answered.

Through some confusion and doubtless the
hand of the Lord, the executioners tasked with
strangling William Tyndale were over-eager in
their task and quickly took the strain such that
my friend passed quickly over to the Lord and
slumped down in forever sleep before the fires
of the faggots could take hold.

The fires then took hold and consumed him,
but they could bring him no harm now as
he was already secure in the comforting arms
of our Lord.

**

We had word from England that an attempt
by the Catholics of the north, led by Robert Aske,
to rise up against Henry's Reforms had been
thwarted. It appeared that the progress that
Reform had made in the land was now more
secure, although Grafton and Whitchurch
remained anxious that the optimum timing for
succeeding in gaining not just the acceptance of
our English Scripture translation, but also its
authorisation at the highest levels in England
was imminent. Further, that the continued
volatility of matters of religion in England were
such that if we did not strike while the iron was
still hot, there may not be such a God-sent
opportunity again.

We therefore worked tirelessly to complete the
task, including my own taking on the task of

helping the reader with some navigation and summaries of the key tenets of true belief which were to be placed at the beginning of the book. This was a task that I thoroughly enjoyed, summarising as it does the extraordinary truth of God's love for man over the centuries and its ultimate expression in sending his son, Jesus Christ, to die for us all to reconcile us with Him forever!

What a wonderful God we serve!

How faithful, unchanging and true!

And we together grew in confidence and faith that the good works he had started through Tyndale (God rest his soul) and Coverdale would indeed be completed by His good Grace.

Grafton was true to his word in giving this venture his full support and sank what must have been close to his full fortune in it (perhaps £500!). This enabled us to print 1,500 copies of the Thomas Matthew Bible which we then set about distributing overseas to England.

Grafton was also true to his word in seeking to use the contacts he had to gain acceptance of the translation at the highest levels of the English Church and indeed of the King's Court. He had asked me to write a direct eulogy to Henry as a preface to the book which I had prayed over and then toiled over to ensure that I achieved the

appropriate level of reverence and respect due to
the anointed King of England.

I believe I achieved that aim.

Grafton had the wisdom to send a copy of our
Bible to none other than Thomas Cranmer,
Archbishop of Canterbury and second only to
Henry himself as head of the church in England.
It was with great joy that I heard report back
that so taken was Cranmer with the quality of
our work that he in turn sent it on to the great
Thomas Cromwell, Viceregent for Ecclesiastical
Affairs for all England.

Vitally, Cromwell had the ear of King Henry
himself and the Lord so stirred his heart that
he personally vouched for the quality of our
translation. Furthermore, that he argued for
the appropriateness of furthering Reform in
England by having an AUTHORISED version
of the Bible in English for every Englishman to
have access to the true Word of God in their
native tongue.

We had covered this Holy Work in prayer since
its commencement and we did not stop now.
The Lord heard us and was gracious unto us
as not only did Henry immediately accede to
authorising our Thomas Matthew Bible, but
he went further. Every parish in the land was
instructed to obtain a copy and to make it
available to be read by the parishioner

themselves or for them to have a reader read them the Word of God in a language they could understand, even if they could not read!

Now any Englishman or Englishwoman could read and hear what a marvellous God we have in Heaven and how wonderfully he has saved us for all eternity, if only we will repent and BELIEVE in His Son, Jesus Christ. Nobleman, yeoman, ploughman or merchant – no one now would be barred by lack of linguistic ability or profession from engaging directly with the Word of God.

Our dream – started by the Martyr William Tyndale and with me and my colleagues taking on the torch – had become a reality.

What a marvellous thing!

And how blessed am I to have been chosen to play a part in it!

Grafton had designs on achieving a monopoly of the supply of our Bible as the only version to be allowed in the land, but rightly proud as I was of our translation I was not so arrogant as to assume that our efforts could not in future be improved upon.

Nor would I claim to be the only humble vessel through whom God might work to spread His Word in the future.

I have told you I have always been strong, but no man's shoulders are broad enough to take on that responsibility.

Grafton – typically and driven I believe by greed, I'm afraid – pressed ahead with his plans to achieve this; but I am glad to say his efforts were thwarted.

***

But in other respects Grafton had proved correct. The Lord worked a miracle in enabling the Thomas Matthew Bible to be not only published, but Authorised by the King himself in that year of 1537. How remarkable that Tyndale himself was a fugitive from his native land only a few short years before this came to pass – with his works being set afire at St Paul's Cross by Wolsey under the very same monarch, King Henry.

But the Lord 'can do immeasurably more than we can know or imagine' and so why, really, should we be surprised?

I have learned to 'trust in the Lord in all things and to lean not on my own understanding'. But I have learned also that 'the Lord's thoughts are not our thoughts and His ways are not our ways'.

And so it has transpired that the path of Reform in England has not been a straight one, even after the release of His Scriptures in English across the land.

Within two years many of the 'Victories for Christ' (by which I mean Reforms of the rotten Papist Church) had been reversed, culminating in the Six Articles, or as we referred to it in Antwerp amongst our fellow Reformers, 'The Bloody Act'.

Notwithstanding the truths called out – even by myself in the commentary – in the Thomas Matthew Bible, such is the black heart of man and the scheming of 'the devil who prowls around us seeking to devour us' that Reform seemed to be halted before it had taken root in the land.

So it was that the absurdity of the presence of our Lord Jesus' actual body in the mass was sadly once again affirmed, congregants were allowed communion in one kind only and clergy such as myself were forbidden again to marry.

Even Cranmer himself – the Archbishop of Canterbury! - had to send his wife and children back over to safe keeping in Nuremburg, Germany.

Clouds had gathered over the land – the Antichrist was not so easily to be deposed.

Finally, in the year of our Lord 1540, Cromwell himself – so long first amongst all ministers in

King Henry's court, chief sponsor of Reform in England and so instrumental in helping us achieve the authorisation and distribution of our Thomas Matthew Bible – was executed by order of King Henry himself for treason.

How fleeting is fame and fortune on earth! That someone risen so high, such as Thomas Cromwell, albeit from such lowly beginnings, could end his days so abruptly and be brought so low by temporal powers. I hope and pray that he held firm to True Faith until the last.

The cause of Reform in England appeared lost indeed.

But I trusted in the Lord's Grace to finish the work He had begun, just as His word promises. Only He knew when that would come to pass.

***

It was Christmas 1536 that I married my dear Adriana, on an icy clear day that matched the brightness of my spirit. It was a small ceremony, with my dear friend and confidante Richard Hawkins acting as Witness together with Stephen Vaughan, head of the English House at Antwerp for the Merchant Adventurers and a loyal supporter of my work and of the work of Reform in general.

Adriana herself shone like the sun that day, her emerald green eyes sparkling with delight and enhanced by the green velvet gown she wore, with exaggerated width at the cuffs and a fulsome skirt which accentuated her every movement.

I had no residual compunction in taking a wife, so convinced was I – and am I still – that it was the Lord's purpose for me and a good and rightly thing for any man. But we needed to be cautious and we therefore kept the wedding party small, with only our most trusted friends and Adriana's family.

My father had passed away by this time and there was no question of my mother being able to visit, nor my siblings. I was sorry I could not share this happy day with my parents in particular, but I felt sure my mother would be glad of the news. It was from her and my father that I had learned the humble pleasures of a happy family life – and it was that that I now looked forward to with anticipation and excitement.

What a twelve months had passed! My Thomas Matthew English Bible had been authorised and distributed across England, I had entered into marriage with my dear love Adriana – and then in October the following year theLord gave His blessing to our marriage with the arrival of our healthy first son, Daniel.

I had quickly settled into the warm comfort of married life with Adriana. We would laugh together – in a way I had not laughed since being with my dear siblings back in Deritend – we would eat together, we would pray together, I would conduct my pastoral and ministerial duties for the Merchant Adventurers during the day and by night we would enjoy the soft delights of one another's company in our bed.

And our little son Daniel was such a revelation to me. I had handled babies for christenings of course, but nothing prepared me for the outpouring of love and care that came over me when I first held that little miracle of new life from God. How wonderful that God's Glory could be found in the tiny perfection of my son's little fingers and toes and sparkling eyes, emerald like his mother's. Truly we are fearfully and wonderfully made by God and life is so very precious as a result.

Having a wife and son tilted my view of the world. Life for me was no longer just about my own desires and will – nor even my own search to do the will of God – but now encompassed caring for and sustaining my dear wife and now my precious young son. This itself was a sacred responsibility I had taken on as head of our new household.

Who would look after their physical needs and who would be there to love them and care for their wellbeing if anything were to happen to me?

This made me far more aware of the risks I had undertaken and continued to take – which began to play on my mind, more and more in fact.

My lodgings at Hawkins' home continued to provide comfortable accommodation for me and now for my family, but when my second son John arrived in January 1539 we knew we had outgrown my friend Hawkins' hospitality and that it was time to take our own lodgings. With the support and sponsorship of Richard Vaughan, we were able to do this and finally set up our own household near the centre of the city with easy access to the Merchant Adventurers' factory.

But by the beginning of the following year my wife was growing anxious for our safety.

She was with child again and we were taking a stroll in the early evening around the harbour when she stopped and turned to me, the alertness in her bright eyes conveying to me that a serious conversation was imminent.

"Husband, you know how much I love you?" she asked. Unsure whether this was a rhetorical question or whether I was expected to provide a reply, I chose the latter for the sake of safety.

"Of course my darling Adriana!" I replied. "And you know I will always love you with all my heart. But something is troubling you?"

She glanced around and then led me by the hand to a bench overlooking the harbour and sat herself down carefully toward one end, making it clear that I was expected to sit down alongside her. She went on, "You have achieved so much here in Antwerp and I thank God daily for bringing you here to me. I love this city and would love to see my sons and our new child build a life here ...", she stroked her swelling stomach and glanced lovingly down at our latest miracle, "... but most of all I want them to grow up happy and strong and safe."

"Of course ...", I replied – but she continued determinedly, "And with a father to guide them." She turned and looked at me intently again. "John, I'm concerned that the tide is turning against us. I'm scared. Scared for your safety and scared for us should anything happen to you."

"But we have the protection of the Adventurers?" I offered, although as I say it I hear the hollowness of my defence and am not surprised at the reaction it provokes.

"Protection?" she exclaims. "Like they protected poor William? Like they protected Poyntz? And that when Reform was blooming in England! Now we have The Bloody Act and Reform is in retreat in your homeland – perhaps forever beaten down ..."

"Do not say it!" I interrupted, although with kindness, for I knew her heart.

"I pray not, John, as you well know," she replied, "but we have to accept that currently the climate is oppressive for Reform in England so we cannot expect protection from the Adventurers and their sponsors in Court much longer. And your role in the Thomas Matthew Bible is no longer a secret. I fear you are in danger, John."

"I trust in the Lord ..." I began to protest, but my wife cut across my words.

"John, I know, I know. You know I know. And you know I love your love for the Lord. You inspire me in that and you always will. But you have already done great service to the Lord and put yourself at great risk with the Holy Work. But things are different now. The Lord has provided you a wife and two sons and this wonderful new child of ours," she placed the palm of her hand on her stomach again. "I could not bear to lose you, John. I could not bear it. I need you by my side. I need you for me and I need you to be a father to our children. To see them grown, to nurture them, to teach them Godly ways and just to love them. I cannot do it alone, John!"

There were tears in her eyes now and I saw that her fears were real. I reached out and held her. "I am hearing you, dear wife. I have every intention of doing all of those things – and more besides to show my love for you and our family. I will pray about this and see whether the Lord has new plans for us now. Let us continue discussing this together and pray together. And the Lord will show us the way."

And so we did.

We explored our options, we discussed the pros and cons and we prayed together to seek God's direction in this. And out of those discussions, we increasingly became drawn to the merits of moving to Wittenberg to join the Reformists there in relative safety. It excited me to think I could develop my own theology with some of the finest minds in Europe and to grow in closeness to the Lord in this special place where the Holy Spirit seemed to be most especially at work in the hearts of men.

And finally we determined that I would seek a place at Wittenberg and we set things in motion to achieve this. Our third son Ambrose arrived in the May and we determined to move as soon as Adriana was recovered from the birth and fit to do so.

Our decision to move from Antwerp was then twice affirmed. First by the execution of the great Thomas Cromwell, true friend to Reform in England. And second then by the execution of the Reformist Robert Barnes, whom I had greatly respected at Cambridge and who had led the Reformist cause bravely. Illustrating the volatility of matters of religion at this time in England, on the same day as Barnes' execution two other good Reformists were martyred whilst so too were three unrepentant Papists.

The spiritual battle for the heart and soul of England was raging.

***

Chapter 5 – Wittenberg and Meldorf, Halcyon Days

I have been fortunate – I would say blessed in fact – to have met some truly remarkable people in my life to date.

William Tyndale was an inspiration to me, brilliant in mind and outstanding in character. He was also instrumental in my coming to know Christ fully and to appreciate the marvellous depths of the Holy Scriptures. And his steadfastness in remaining faithful to the Lord, even amidst the faggots of the fire, has left an everlasting and abiding impression on me. Would that I could emulate that bravery and constancy if ever I should be so tested.

Another such giant of our generation is one Philip Melanchthon.

I say 'giant', I don't mean that literally - he was diminutive in stature, shorter even than me, and somewhat frail also. Indeed one's first impression of the man physically was that he was rather weak and slightly freakish in appearance

(I say this with all due respect and love – he himself admits it). His eyes were buried deep into his head – although shone with a fearsome brightness – his forehead protruded unnaturally and his nose as sharp as it was misshapen.

But what God omitted to provide for physically, he more than made up with other qualities in this extraordinary man. Melanchthon had been instrumental in smoothing the way for me to come to Wittenberg and I soon came to appreciate my good fortune in having close and regular access to this man's extraordinary mind.

Martin Luther, no doubt, was used powerfully by the Lord to trigger this Awakening of His people that we call Reform. His was the spark that ignited the work and he has continued to fight bravely and speak out against the injustices and lies of the Papist Church. Perhaps the Lord chose Luther for this task due to his force of character and fiery nature. But I have learned that people in general need more than the grand gesture from a powerful speaker to truly take stock of their lives, to repent and follow the true path.

They need reason

They need a rational and well organised argument.

They need to be able to understand how all parts fit together.

And it was for this reason, I believe, that the Lord provided Luther with Philip Melanchthon. Just as He provided Moses with Aaron, though not brothers in blood, Melanchthon became like a brother to Luther as he took his insights and revelations and brought them into a full argument and system to justify their truth.

I admire that.

If a statement of faith cannot be defended with reason, on the basis of the revelation of Scripture, then it cannot be defended at all.

My friend – for he became my very good friend during my time in Wittenberg and even later when I took on the congregation at Meldorf – had a wonderful ability to bring order and structure to Lutheran thought, to develop it indeed into a truly defensible doctrine, itself demonstrably based upon the Holy Scriptures themselves.

I recall the first time Adriana and I were invited to supper at Melanchthon's wonderful home – just a few weeks after we had arrived following our long journey from Antwerp. We had met already at the University, but it was typical of the man that he wanted to extend the hand of friendship by offering us hospitality in his own home. It was also an opportunity for Adriana to meet his wife, Katharina, as well as some of the other good folk of Wittenberg.

The house itself was remarkable in its elegance, three stories high and topped with six pillars on which were supported five domes.

"They represent my 'crown'", he joked, "one for my wife and one each for my four children!". Although he spoke in gest, this spoke of truth as was evident from the moment I saw him with his wife and children: his love for them was clearly very deep and very real – and I recognised there also a kindred spirit to my own.

"You are most kind to invite us to your lovely home", I ventured.

"Nonsense," replied Melanchthon, "the kindness is yours in coming to our humble home and in allowing us to meet your lovely wife!"

"My husband speaks the truth," said his wife Katharina, "good company is one of the great pleasures of Philip's life. Spending all day with his nose buried in books I think he needs to socialise of an evening to put into practice all of the instructions he has been taking on board!"

"That is true indeed!", he replied, ever ready to speak with humility. "There is nothing sweeter nor lovelier than mutual intercourse with friends." I was touched by his affection, although I soon learned that this was a favourite phrase of his – albeit none the less earnest for its frequency of use.

As the evening went on, Adriana and I relaxed into the presence of this wonderful couple and their like-minded friends and we had never felt so much at home in company. The conversation flowed freely from joviality and triviality to matters of earnest faith. I was proud to have my wife beside me, able so fully to engage in the stimulating conversation.

"Philip, how do you manage to stay so humble and grounded when all the Christian world is waiting on your every written word?" she asked.

Katharina was quick to interject, "Oh, the children and I see to that, don't you worry Adriana!" and we laughed, knowing there to be more than a grain of truth in this.

"That is true, my dear wife! But I have other reasons too to know my true place in this world and under God" he replied. "As St Paul wrote to the people of Galatia, I ask myself 'Am I now seeking the approval of man, or of God? If I were still trying to please man, I would not be a servant of Christ.' I have no need of the praise of man, being already a fellow worker with God – as we all are around this table. There can be no higher calling than that, whether man speaks well of me or poorly of me, it matters not a jot. The best of our efforts on earth count for nought when weighed against our sins and yet the worst of our offences are wiped clean by God's most perfect and wonderful Grace. Truly, whether people think well or ill of me matters not in the scheme of things under God and therefore not to me."

I loved his candour and honesty and the ease with which he expressed the depths of the Gospel even in this relaxed and informal environment.

I admired this man already and knew I could learn much from him.

Later in the evening, I shared privately with him my admiration for his easy exposition of the Gospel even whilst offering hospitality in his own home.

He laughed.

"But of course, John, and why not? My home is itself a little church of God and if we cannot be true to ourselves in our own homes, where can we be?"

We continued to discuss earnest matters as I shared my own experience of encountering the Lord and being filled with the Holy Spirit, with which he empathised.

"What I find more of a challenge," I ventured, a little concerned at speaking the thoughts of my true heart so openly, "is sustaining the exhilaration and ardour of that first encounter through the trials and tribulations of everyday life. How do you do it, Philip?"

He looked at me with those bright and alert eyes that seemed to glisten with the opportunity to share a truth that he had learned and treasured and loved to pass on to those he loved.

"One word, John. Prayer. Pray to the living God at every opportunity and about every thing. Prayer connects us through the power of the Holy Spirit to the heart of God and to Christ himself. I don't need to remind you of all people, that He speaks to us through his Word, so I treasure my daily meditation on some verses each day. I don't mean in order to write an exposition or lecture to instruct others. I mean as a personal and intimate exercise to align my heart with the Lord's. You know He speaks through his Word and that - incredibly, wonderfully, unbelievably! - he yearns - YEARNS, John! - to speak to us. And just as He speaks to us personally through prayer and our daily meditation of His Word, so too he loves for us to worship him communally in public services - and of course you know the amazing thing about that, John?"

I paused - uncertain if I did!

"As we worship our Living God, creator of all things on earth and in heaven - WE are lifted up together and WE are blessed even as we bless Him! How wonderful is our God, John! How wonderful - and how wonderful also that we, you and I John, are invited to be a fellow worker with Him to share with people and help everyone – all peoples of the earth – understand this amazing good news."

"So I follow this simple formula, John – you know how I love an orderly formula!" he announced. "Prayer, often and everywhere; daily mediation on Scripture, to engage with His Living Word (in a language of your choice!); and of course regular collective worship in public services. These three things together – no one sufficient alone – allow me to continually seek the Lord. And, most wonderfully of all, to find Him!"

He paused this time, I sensed not to interrupt and fill the space with my own words, but rather that he was about to say something significant.

I was right.

"John," he said, "I don't think you appreciate how VERY much the Lord loves you and glorifies in the labours you have already completed for him!" He grasped my arm earnestly which gave greater effect to his words. I felt the Lord was speaking through him directly to me.

"The Lord cannot love you any more than he already does, John, and yet ... I believe you have important, truly important work still to do for the Lord." He paused again, closing his eyes as if to listen to some unspoken voice. He grasped my arm still firmer. "My goodness, John, I sense through the Holy Spirit this work of yours will have impact for Him beyond your or my comprehension right now. Beyond our imagining! It will be a wonderful blessing for you John – I am even envious of you, truly! – to do such an important work for Christ!"

He let go of my arm. And looked away. And then back at me again directly.

"But it will come at a cost, John. I think you know that."

I looked at him and nodded slowly. I had a sense of it, but not yet a full understanding.

"Thank you, Philip", I replied earnestly. "May God bless you for your candour and for your kindness in sharing this. If what you say turns out to be even half true – that I can play some part at all in our Lord's great plan – then no cost will be too high. No cost too high."

I meant it then.

And I mean it now.

And as I spoke, the fire cracked loudly and startled us both.

And we laughed together.

***

Just as I felt like I was coming increasingly into the light of understanding the true heart of God, so too it seemed that England was receding back into darkness.

King Henry's brief and disastrous marriage to Anne of Cleves quickly dispelled our hopes of the promised deeper alliance between England and the Protestant states. The drawbridge across to the English isles seemed again to draw up as the King looked inwards for his marriages, first to the young Catherine Howard – who quickly betrayed her husband and paid the ultimate price; and then Catherine Parr. We hoped and prayed for both a stable marriage to bring King Henry happiness in his declining years as well as praying that Catherine's sympathies with Reform might influence her husband for the good of our cause.

But it appeared rather that the devil was gaining a further foothold in our homeland, with some of the victories for Christ that we had won being reversed by a recalcitrant Parliament. Thus even the reading of the Bible in open assembly – which we had rejoiced over so greatly on the publishing and authorisation of our Thomas Matthew Bible – was prohibited with further restrictions applied on who might be permitted to read the Bible.

Sadly, all women were forbidden from so doing.

How could the people of England be expected to know God and to nurture their relationship with him if they are to be starved of His Word? Our Saviour himself said 'Man cannot live by bread alone, but by every word that proceeds from the mouth of God'. And what is the Bible if not the Living Word of God?

I complained to my friend Melanchthon about these things just as I cried out to the Lord that he would save England. I was reminded of my friend William Tyndale's last words as he faced strangulation and the faggots, "Lord, open the King of England's eyes!". It was as if the Lord had heard him and acceded to his plea – only for King Henry to fall into a devilish slumber once again to turn his back on true Reform.

But my friend Melanchthon would faithfully console me. "John, have faith. The Lord promises to complete the good works he starts in our hearts as men and women. So too he will complete the turning of the hearts of the nation of England. But our ways are not His ways and our timings are not His. You must just trust in Him to bring the nation to Himself when he is ready and when the time is right."

In my last days at Wittenberg, which would have been Spring 1543, this promise seemed further off than ever with the publication and sanctioning of The King's Book. Such superstitions as transubstantiation were affirmed (as if the Lord's flesh and blood could be both at the communion table and at God's right hand in the heavens!). And the church was dragged back into claiming that rather than salvation being wholly the work of our holy Lord by his infinite Grace and compassion, works were required as well. As if anything we frail mortals could do could bridge the chasm between us and God caused by our great sin!

Even my friend Melanchthon found this hard to bear. Together we had journeyed into the wonder of this truth, that the Lord has done it all through the sacrifice of His son and made us co-heirs with Christ! Such wonders! Such Grace! Such life changing and life affirming truths – to be found clearly spelled out in His Word!

How desperately sad that the church in England sought to rob its people of this wonderful gift from God.

Surely God would not allow that situation to prevail!

***

My years at Wittenberg were amongst the happiest of my life so far.

The intellectual and spiritual stimulation of studying and working with some of the finest minds in Europe was a wonderful luxury, particularly in the relative safety of a tolerant environment. I was able to build upon the understanding the Lord had given me in Antwerp and in particular to explore the theology around His Grace. What better employment might there be!

Meanwhile my domestic life benefitted from this greater security, with Adriana much happier that we were safe from the ravages of revengeful Papists, despite being away from her homeland. Many of her family had also fled to the Protestant states which softened the sense of missing her country of birth.

Our three sons became five – with the arrival of Samuel and Philip (named after my now dear friend Melanchthon, of course).

"Do only males come from that womb of yours?" I teased, when I first held our healthy fifth son.

"Well you're the one who puts them in there!" she replied with a smile and a feigned frown and we laughed together as I held this new miracle of God in my arms and prayed protection and prosperity over him.

With five children under the age of six years, ours was a household full of love and laughter and tears and screams and noise and adventure! Such a wonderful antidote to the cerebral nature of my work, I loved the simplicity of family life when no deep thought was required, all that was needed was our presence together and our love and tolerance of one another.

This was something else I shared with my good friend Melanchthon, who knew also the simple and deep pleasure of family life and the honour of being a father. We discussed many a time how our love for our children – our unconditional love, unrelated to what they would achieve or accomplish – gave us a more real and deeper insight into the depths of love God has for us. And we marvelled that in order to pave the way for the fruition and continuation of that love into eternity, he would sacrifice his own and only son to pay for our sins, the sins of all of us, my very own sins.

But so great was His love, He would not leave His Son in the depths of Hell, but raised Him up – raised Him to sit forever at His own right hand.

How marvellous is our loving Father !

We were blessed indeed with good health for all of our children, which we continued to take as a gift of God's Grace and affirmation of my decision to marry. Although as our friends Philip Melanchthon and his wife Katharina had lost several children in the womb or in infancy, we were careful not to boast.

Who can know the mind of God when such young ones are taken so early back to Him?

We can only trust in Him that they will rest in peace until the day they can be re-united with their families.

***

It was the summer of the year after Philip was born – when Adriana was pregnant once again with what would be yet another son, Bernard - that I was invited to take up the role of Superintendent of the Lutheran Church in Dietmarsh in North West Germany. I was at first reluctant to leave the comforts of Wittenberg which had become so familiar to us now. Melanchthon, however, was enthusiastic for me to take up the role.

"But Philip," I protested, "would you so soon be rid of me?"

"I believe I shall never be rid of you, John, so great is our friendship!" he replied. "But you have a gift for explaining the truths we have discovered together in a way that the most common type of man or woman can grasp. The Lord can use you powerfully to spread this Good News we hold and to help good, ordinary people live good, Godly lives. There can be no greater calling."

"So will you be doing the same, Philip? Would you give up your academic studies and contributions to policy impacting all of Europe for the sake of ordinary souls in the country?" I asked.

"Those ordinary souls are God's children, John and he's entrusting you – you, John Rogers – to look after His sheep. Will you be Jonah and refuse the call? I know that you will not!" Melanchthon was gently chastising me, but I welcomed his directness and had valued the accountability to which he held me. I deeply respected his opinion.

"So be it." I acquiesced, with a nod, although in my heart of hearts I had already made up my mind to go. "I will go and put into practise all that we have studied here together – but on one condition, Philip"

"Name it" he replied.

"That our friendship shall indeed endure and that I may write to you to share with you how it goes leading a flock of country folk in the truths we now hold dear. Will you do that for me, Philip? May we correspond so that I can continue to have the benefit of your good counsel? And so that I can tell you with honesty how it goes working with God's Grace in reality on the front line of life with ordinary folk?" I looked at him pleadingly, but confident our bonds of friendship were already strong enough that this would be so.

"Of course, John. You do not even need to ask such a thing. I look forward to receiving your despatches from the front line. And I know that God will honour your obedience and bless you – and Adriana and all of your wonderful little boys!"

All that was needed then was for me to tell Adriana of my decision. She was sorry to leave our comfortable life in Wittenberg, but she knew my heart had now already moved to Meldorf where we were to settle and she was ever good to her marital oath of obedience to me.

And so we made the trip north to Meldorf.

***

It was with some trepidation that I took on the ministry at Meldorf, having been apprised of the history of that parish. Some twenty years prior, there had been a heinous tragedy when my predecessor – a certain Henry of Zutphen - had been lynched by his very own congregation whom he had been called to serve.

There had been a day of celebration and the monks of the nearby abbey had sought to ingratiate themselves amongst the community by providing great quantities of their locally brewed beers and spirits. Henry had sought to bring some sobriety and Godly order to proceedings as the celebrations began to descend into debauchery. But scandalously those same monks that had initiated the depravity goaded the rabble into a red mist of anger and evil intent such that Henry was mobbed, kicked and beaten: and then held aloft by the crowd and carried across to the great oak outside the church itself.

There a large rope was slung over a low hanging bough and the other end tied roughly around his neck. Henry himself was a stout man and it apparently took a group of five men and (shockingly) one woman to heave him up by his neck to the cheers and jeering of the whole, wild and maddened rabble.

Only afterwards, when Henry ceased resisting and hanged limp from the tree, his shadow thrown onto the pathway of his own church, did a quietness finally fall over the crowd. Henry's wife, who had witnessed the murder from the kitchen window of the vicarage adjacent, came running now weeping to clasp the feet of her lifeless husband. She let out a guttural roar of anguish, whether directed to the Lord or to the crowd no one knew, but it jolted the crowd out of its madness and pierced the heart of that crowd-beast.

The brawny men and one woman who were still holding the rope to keep poor Henry aloft finally softened and gently released the tension to allow him to fall lifeless into the arms of his grieving wife.

Shame fell like a mist across the mob.

And the mist remained even to the day I arrived twenty years later.

Six pairs of hands may have hauled Henry's body into the fearful embrace of that oak tree, but the sin was on the entire community. And it lingered strong still when I began my ministry amongst them.

But God's Grace was sufficient even for this! What Good News I had to tell even this community, who collectively literally had blood on their hands and who so clearly needed the forgiveness only available through the blood of Christ!

I saw many come newly and freshly back to Christ as a result and shared in very many tears of pain, of relief and of gratitude for His forgiveness.

What a privilege to be used by the Lord for such divine purpose!

As if my task were not already made complex enough by this awful history, matters were compounded by the language barrier that I found on arrival. I have always had an ear for language and enjoy its musicality as well as structures and rules. I had mastered German with reasonable ease on moving to Wittenberg and had expected that to stand me in good stead in Meldorf.

But that was to misunderstand the degree of regional variance in the use of that rich and beautiful language across the large expanses of Germany. The local dialect was heavy and slowed my progress in establishing a deep rapport with the people of Meldorf, my congregation.

But I persevered and with the support of my patient wife who had to listen to my frustrations and complaints, by Christmas of that first year I felt I had mastered it. I venture that a visitor to my services would no longer know that I was not locally born and bred - which I use as my yardstick by which to determine my language mastery.

And most of all I have learned that the language of Christ's love is universal.

***

Adriana and I loved our time in Meldorf. We led a quiet life, but enjoyed belonging to a community – who welcomed us warmly once they got to know us and to understand that we were there to serve them, not to exacerbate their already significant sense of guilt nor to judge them for their sin.

It was good to serve the people and to serve God at the same time and I had a new sense of fulfilment in walking in step with God's purposes. Our family flourished and the Holy

Spirit flourished in me, my family and in our congregation.

How can I make such a bold claim? I do so –
as I do for all of my arguments in matters of
faith – based on the truths revealed through
Scripture, in this case Paul's identification of
the Fruit of the Holy Spirit in Galations. I can
affirm and acknowledge that we experienced
and enjoyed each of those in Meldorf. Allow me
a list (I am partial to the orderliness of a list!) to
unpack each – the completion of which will both
enable me to transcend my current imprisoned
and reduced circumstances and to witness again
to the all surpassing Grace of our Lord.

- **Love** – we felt in abundance in our still
  growing family, with Bernard arriving on
  Christmas Eve in the first year we were in
  Meldorf, Augustine joining us in the Spring
  of 1545, followed by little Barnaby in 1546 (he
  was born some weeks prematurely, but the
  Lord sustained him and although weak, he is
  as bright and characterful as his siblings)
  and then - FINALLY ! - a sister to the
  siblings and our first daughter, Susan, the
  following year, the year before we returned
  to England.

- **Joy** – characterised our times together as a
  congregation, not only during our services
  when we together worshipped the Lord in
  Spirit and in truth, but also whenever we

were gathered together – for prayer, discipleship or fellowship. Truly our hearts were united in the joy of knowing the Lord and knowing that whatever daily tribulations we faced we could rest secure in His loving embrace.

- **Peace** – our hearts were at peace in union together across our beloved congregation, even whilst we faced earthly challenges within our community. Despite threats and dangers from the ungodly in our town, our certain hope and security in the everlasting love of our Lord and of the inability of anything in all of the world to separate us from that love, gave us a peace which passed worldly understanding. During our time there, there was a spate of murders most awful in our region – perhaps the devil himself moving against the positive growth of the Word of the Lord in this land. I myself sought to encourage the authorities to clamp down on these murderers and round them up – and not to countenance them buying their freedom when they had taken a life. They had forfeited their right to life by taking another's – but so too I exhorted my congregation not to take matters into their own hands as they had done with such disastrous effect twenty years prior with Henry of Zutphen. They heeded my pleas and we retained a peace in our hearts as a result.

- **Kindness** – as a family we experienced great kindness, strangers in a foreign land, but welcomed as brothers and sisters in Christ. Our home was an open one and we enjoyed countless happy suppers together with numerous members of our congregation and received boundless hospitality and kindness in return.

- **Goodness** – was expressed by our never wanting for anything we needed, be that clothing or shoes (endless shoes!) for our already large family or help with our vegetable garden or the provision of tools for managing the same. This largesse, the outpouring of a goodness of heart amongst our people, became a way of living for our church and it seemed the more we practiced goodness, the more we were receiving of it too.

- **Faithfulness** – ours was a faithful congregation in every way, with only illness preventing anyone attending our services (no one wanted to miss out on the sense of blessing to be found there) and with our people voluntarily coming together in prayer for those that were ill or in need in any way.

- **Gentleness** – demonstrating the transformation and deliverance of these people from their angry sin of twenty years prior, when poor Henry was lynched, gentleness now characterised our church. Differences of opinion in matters of church organisation were listened to respectfully and matters debated calmly based on reference back to Scripture (which I was happy to guide).

- **Self-control** - Even when attacked from outsiders, I have righteous pride in saying that our congregation did not rise in response, but learned to turn the other cheek and overcome their assailants with the love of Christ. No greater example was there than one Anna Fischer, who was set upon outside an ale house one day when returning from one of our services. Anna was the one woman who held and hauled the rope that heaved poor Henry of Zutphen up into that oak tree that fateful and hateful day he was lynched. Anne's assailants delighted in reminding her of that night and threatened the same fate for her now that she had joined the ranks of the righteous – and the verbal attack became physical as she was punched to the ground. But she did not rise to the assault but instead muttered prayers of forgiveness over here assailants even as the kicked and beat her. And her assailants tired and became bored of their attack and perhaps even their hard hearts were ashamed by the loving witness and self control showed by this transformed soul.

May the Lord bless Anna for her self-control
that day – I wonder how she fares today?

Truly those were blessed and happy days.

Whatever becomes of me now, I am grateful to
the Lord for this experience as a shepherd
amongst his people and for the simple pleasures
that afforded me.

**

Peace was far from King Henry's mind when he
invaded France in the summer of 1544, with a
reported amassed army of fifty thousand
Englishmen. It was reported also that this was
intended to be in alliance with the Emperor
Charles V of Spain – which confirmed our
suspicions that Reform continued to be on the
retreat in England.

The invasion came to nought – except very great
expense for Henry – as Charles most typically
reneged on his commitment to the alliance and
courted Francis once again. One wonders at the
folly of kings in matters of warfare – but perhaps
the Lord provides insight to those who lead their
nation in ways that we ordinary folk cannot
fathom.

A further sign of the tide of Reform retreating in
England was the martyrdom of Anne Askew, a
true Reformer with access to the court of the

king's sixth wife, Catherine Parr. King Henry was by now married to Catherine Parr, whom it was reported had sympathies with our cause and was seeking ways and means to influence her husband Henry toward us.

Anne Askew was, by all accounts, a remarkable young woman to whom the Lord had revealed Himself via the Holy Spirit and who loved, knew and understood the Scriptures. It is said that she held and used frequently our Thomas Matthew Bible and had found the truth of the Lord from reading it in her own tongue. Further that she would read aloud to visitors to her home, despite her husband being an unrepentant Catholic, who in due course was to eject her on account of her holding firm to true Reformist beliefs.

Demonstrating the depths of depravity to which the church of the Antichrist will sink, Anne Askew was arrested and even tortured in the Tower of London. It is said that the Constable himself could not in all Christian conscience continue with the torture, despite her refusal to name other true believers. Disgracefully the Lord Chancellor himself, Thomas Wriothesley and Privy Councillor Sir Richard Rich themselves took on the torture without skilled hands to complete the task.

The poor woman was subjected to the rack, but due to the cack-handed amateur torturers her limbs were drawn from their sockets – arms from shoulders, legs from hips as well as elbows and knees dislocated too – leaving her alive but immobilised and in pain most extreme. Her screams could be heard in the Constable's garden where his wife and daughter walked.

Pity them.

They will surely never cease to have those cries ringing in their ears to haunt them in the quiet stillness of night.

Still she would neither name other Reformers nor recant the truth of her understanding (she had a good understanding of all of Scripture and understood the Papist lies regarding the body and blood of Christ supposedly and superstitiously being present in the sacrament).

So she was ultimately led out to the faggots of Smithfield as none could break her will or separate her from the truth and Freedom she had found in the Lord.

May I show such resilience and faithfulness should my day come.

Such was the severity of her injuries that she had to be carried to the stake in a specially prepared chair – she could certainly not walk, nor even crawl to her final earthly place. Wearing only her undergarments, not changed since her torture, she had to be carried to the faggots – yet still was chained hard to retain her. (What! Were they afeared she would up and run away?!).

Three other good men were to face their execution with her for holding firm to their Reformist beliefs – but not before they faced a final, forlorn attempt by a Papist preacher to turn them back to the lies of that rotten church.

How wonderful that Anne stood firm – in her faith at least, even whilst she could not stand in person – and whilst listening attentively to her final sermon did voice her assent or dissent to what was being said, even drawing on the Scriptures as we had translated them in the Thomas Matthew Bible.

And so the faggots were lit and all four – including the young woman in her enfeebled frame – met their end bravely and boldly, trusting in the Lord to the last.

As it transpired, they were to have mercy at the very last, for one of the three men had managed to receive gunpowder from a supporter in the crowd as they were led to their final fate and had hid it about his person within the pocket of his breeches. As the fires rose up and the first flickers of the flames reached waist level there was a loud and violent blast and the souls of those four good folk were immediately transported into the loving hands of our Lord.

The victory was theirs for eternity, but for England the times remained dark and bleak.

* * *

And then everything changed in an instant.

The tide of Reform that had been receding apparently irreversibly in England, all of a sudden surged back to new highs.

I dare say that many of God's people had been praying either, like Tyndale, that Henry's eyes would be opened and heart turned toward our cause or, if he would not soften his heart, the Lord withdraw him to His presence and place on the throne a king with the Lord's heart. I was not one such. Despite the temptation to do so, I held that the Lord's anointed King of England was under the Lord's authority only and whilst I would join with Tyndale in imploring the Lord to open the eyes of the king, I would never utter, even in the privacy of quiet and personal prayer, the treasonous appeal to end his earthly life.

Whether in response to the prayers of some or more likely because the Lord decreed it time, King Henry VIII of England passed away in the January of 1547.

To the great expectation and excitement of us Reformers, his successor was his one surviving legitimate son Edward, becoming King Edward VI of England. The Protestant world hailed this boy king as the new young Josiah, sent by the Lord to reclaim the kingdom of England for God's kingdom and re-institute the victories for Christ won in the middle of Henry's reign and indeed to complete the holy work of Reform.

When, in the Spring of that same year, we heard report of the abolition of the Six Articles, or The Bloody Act as we had named it, we celebrated and gave thanks to the Lord. We heard further news of the purification of the churches in England and our thoughts turned to an idea that had lain long suppressed in the back of our minds, scarcely spoken about until now.

The possibility that we return to England, my home country.

But Adriana was naturally cautious and wary.

"John, I know you would love to return home to live the life you had always hoped to live in an England turned to face the Lord. But it is still dangerous. The new King Edward is reported to be as weak as he is young and whilst God has placed the right sort of counsel to steer him now, we know all too well the volatility of the hearts of man and of royal courts in particular. Shall we now wait a while to see whether Reform truly takes root this time?" she asked me, pleading really for the safety of her family.

"Adriana, you will ever be my wise counsellor by my side and I know that you have the care and love of our family at the very core of your being", I replied. "And I know how much you love Meldorf and our people here – and how well the children are growing here, with such good witness to Christian life as our church provides. But I sense the Lord is calling us on once more – back to my homeland this time."

"You know I will always follow you, John, to the ends of the earth. And I will always be an obedient wife to you, once your mind is set. Do not doubt that" she replied. And I did not. "I just think we would be wise to wait on the Lord for His timing in this. To take stock of the changes happening in England and to ensure that when we do travel to make our home there we can be sure that the Lord has prepared the way for us?"

I saw the wisdom of her counsel.

"My dearest Adriana, my life is so enriched by having you by my side!" I declared, as I took her hand and gave her a gentle and loving kiss on her right cheek. "And you are right in this, thank you. Let us draft up a list ..."

She laughed as she interrupted me, "Not another list! You'll have a list to present at the gates of Heaven to declare your fitness to enter, I'm sure!"

I smiled. She was right, I do love the orderliness and structure of a list!

"Hear me out," I implored, "this list will itemise the criteria we need to be met in order to make the decision to move back to England. And we shall prepare it together, so you are as satisfied with it as me." And so we did.

It was a little like our own manifesto of beliefs, covering the core elements of our faith and the supporting environment we believed we would need for our family to survive and prosper back in England.

It comprised:-

1. Services in English, plainly spoken so that the common man and woman can understand.
2. English Bible available and used in every church, with readers available for those that require it and acknowledged as the source of all Truth in matters of faith.
3. Communion in both kinds allowed for laity.
4. Transubstantiation refuted.
5. Icons and pictures of saints, apostles and other superstitious idols removed from churches.
6. Similarly, superstitious lighting of candles, kissing, kneeling, adorning of images and processions to shrines forbidden.

7. Orderly services with appropriate sobriety, with roaring, howling, whistling, conjuring and juggling forbidden as well as ribald and inappropriate music.
8. Clerical marriage permitted and encouraged as Godly and appropriate.
9. Justification acknowledged to be by faith alone, with good works a consequence, but in no way seen to be earning salvation.
10. Parish and diocesan oversight and supervision in place to ensure all residual Papist practices are wiped out to ensure the spiritual health and safety of all English peoples.

By the end of 1547, we had report from England that many of our criteria had already been met. Cranmer, whom the Lord had protected through the dark days of the latter period of King Henry's reign, was now able to move Reform forward once again. The Lord had blessed him with the appropriate sensitivity to steer England through those dark times and now on toward the light.

The Book of Homilies he produced for churches to draw from were sound and based on biblical truths. He also made attempts to establish the oversight and supervision we had identified as so key to ensuring that Reform took root this time around. Visitations were performed across six 'circuits' identified and established across the country to ensure the new injunctions were being followed.

A failing, however, was to conduct this as a once off exercise rather than to establish a permanent, hierarchical structure of oversight which I remain convinced is a requisite – and biblically sound – foundation for ensuring the devil cannot gain a foothold as the frail human heart is so quickly drawn back to superstition.

Meanwhile the more practical obstacles to our return to England were also be removed by God's Grace. Parliament recanted it Papist catholic legislation, not only abolishing The Bloody Act but also removing the Act for the Burning of Heretics that had been the scourge not only of our brothers and sisters in Christ in recent times, but also of our holy Lollard predecessors some two hundred years prior.

Two hundred years ago – faithful servants of Christ being martyred for standing firm on His truths and facing the fire as a result!

Which brings to mind for me that the Lord's will WILL be done – but in His own timing and not according to the will of sinful mankind! Ours is not to know His timings, we are called simply to do His bidding and to stand for Him in our own times.

So by the end of 1547 – just one year after Henry's death – I felt confident that our list of key criteria for a return to England had been met (with the exception of entrenching Number 10).

But I had had an idea, that I hoped would respectfully ease the mind of my darling wife. I spoke to her one evening over the Christmas-tide.

"Adriana, I believe the Lord has prepared the way for us to return to England ..."

"I have never been to England, John, as you know ..." she retorted, clearly tense about what I was about to announce.

"I know dear," I sought to placate her, "but it is my homeland and you are my wife and as such it will ever be our country. I can't wait to show you the beauty of the land and the excitement of the city of London! You will love it, I know! But I also know, my dear, that you are rightly cautious about whether we can build a safe life there for our wonderful family there. So I have an idea ..."

"Go on" she replied tentatively.

"Well so far we have relied on reports from England on the state of affairs and of the church there. We have been fortunate that my brother Will has been so faithful in sending us reports of progress at home. But for something so important as the safety and wellbeing of our family I believe we cannot rely on second hand reports – even from my blood brother." I paused.

"So ...?" prompted Adriana, with a tilt of the head and holding my gaze firmly.

"So," I replied, "I propose that I return home alone .." I had to put both my hands on her shoulders as she leaped up in alarm. "Peace, my love ! I propose that initially I return home alone to see for myself the lie of the land and the conditions in the church; to see for myself whether the land is now a safe one, in which case I can call for you and you can come to me with the children. If I sense danger for you or our children, I will tell you so and I will return here to you at Meldorf."

She was quiet for perhaps a full minute.

Then she spoke.

"I shall miss you."

"I know" I replied. "But it will not be for long."

"How long?" she asked me.

"Perhaps a month, maybe two. Within three months you will either be with me in London or I shall be returned to you here" I promised.

"I shall miss you" she repeated. We had not been apart one night since our wedding night over ten years prior.

"I know" I replied again, honestly. "And I you too. But we shall soon be reunited – imagine our joy!" I teased her.

"Imagine!" she replied, sarcastically. "But it's a good plan, my husband. You may go to England and make sure it is a place for your wife and our nine children ..."

"You mean eight children ..." I interrupted, but she smiled back at me coyly.

"No, John, nine!" she replied as she rested her right hand onto her stomach in the manner to which I had become so familiar.

And I leaped up and hugged this wife of mine that the Lord had provided to me and who had filled my life and our home with children and love, so much love.

***

Chapter 6 – London, The Promised Land

London appeared the same as I had left fourteen years prior – the same riot and assault of noise and smells and activity and vibrant life on every street. And yet beneath the appearances were differences: the poor were more evident on the streets, with women haggard and babes in arms hanging from them limply. The 'price revolution', as I learned to call it, had ravaged the people of England – the coinage had been debased with base metals, driving up the cost of goods.

Food prices were high – with the size of a loaf of bread half that I recalled when last on these shores and yet priced the same.

Wages were low – with an abundance of unwanted labour.

But despite this, the spiritual temperature of the country was good. I had retained correspondence since the publication of our Thomas Matthew Bible with my friend and publisher, Edward Whitchurch. Despite a spell in prison under

King Henry five years prior, he had since prospered handsomely. He and his long-time partner, Richard Grafton had stuck together through those times of trouble and had been rewarded after that by securing the monopoly on printing the English church service books.

The misgivings I had had about Grafton's desire to make a fortune from being the sole printer of the Scriptures had found expression in this related, but to me importantly distinct venture.

I was glad to see that they – and especially my friend Whitchurch - had prospered.

And it was he who had agreed to give me boarding on my return to London – without Adriana and the children, as we had agreed – so that I could assess for myself the possibilities for us to make home there together and with the children.

Whitchurch had a large and comfortable house on Cheapside, in the shadow of St Paul's. Whilst I was residing there, I was able to undertake the commission to write the translation and Preface of my friend Melanchthon's authoritative Weighing and Considering the Interim, relating to the infamous Augsburg Interim.

As the reader may recall, this was Emperor Charles V of Spain's attempt to bring the German states and church back under popish control. Melanchthon gave the ideas proposed short shrift and skilfully dismantled the theological arguments they had offered with sound reference to Scripture.

I was relieved he did so – comparing in my Preface the idea of good Protestants returning to Papist Catholicism as proposed in the Interim as the same 'as a dog does to that he has spewed out or a washed swine to the mire'. I acknowledge the language was colourful, but I felt it warranted to convey the full disgrace of such a proposition. Once you have come into the light you cannot return to darkness.

I was able also to defend my friend Melanchthon and announce his continued service to the Reformist cause – there having been rumours that he had back-slidden to Popery. This was demonstrably not the case, but the gentle demeanour of my friend and his desire to seek reconciliation and unity with the Romish church was such that his manner was misunderstood to convey also his meaning. As his works made clear, this was not so and I am honoured to say that my friend stood firm in this chapter and indeed throughout.

We had oft discussed and prayed together over those wonderful verses in Ephesians written by Paul exhorting us to be prepared for such times of attack: "Therefore put on the full armour of God, so that when the day of evil comes, you may be able to stand your ground, and after you have done everything, to stand."

I can bear witness to the fact that he did indeed in these times stand firm – and indeed, as I stated in my Preface, I believe that the answer to the Interim itself bears sufficient witness to this also.

I hope and pray I will similarly stand firm when it is my time to be tested.

I was able to work speedily on the English translation and Preface given the comfortable accommodation afforded me at Whitchurch's house – such that we were able to get the Weighing and Considering the Interim publication out just two months after the first issuance of that erroneous edict. It was important to us to act swiftly so that we could speedily rebut this dark scheme, the work of the Antichrist that could have jeopardised the progress of Reform, before it took root.

Staying with Whitchurch also afforded me the opportunity to assess the level to which true Reform had been established in London and more broadly in England. There was, in fact, a mixed level of acceptance of the Truth versus the old, Papist lies. King Edward VI vindicated our nickname for him of the new Josiah and was clearly a true believer. His treatise on Papal Pretences demonstrated wisdom beyond his years that spoke well of his spiritual maturity as well as the sound guidance of his Council.

But amongst the broader nobility and even in the higher ranks of the church, amongst the bishops, there was a surprising diversity of opinion, with some still holding on to the old ways (with the general exception of papal authority being secondary to the King's, which no one any longer would vouch for openly – at least not if they valued their life!).

Much of this insight I received from my friend Nicholas Ridley, now Bishop of Rochester. We had been contemporaries at Pembroke Hall together – he just a year ahead – and indeed he had gone on to be Master of our College in the intervening years. He was close to Cranmer himself and shared his patient and pragmatic view of the timetable for the Reform of England (unlike many other of the Reformers – especially those returning from exile, although I could see the merits of both sides of the argument). He had helped Cranmer in the production of the Book of Common Prayer now mandated for use across the land – and had himself used the influence of his position to direct the removal of superstitious altars and their replacement with plain tables to celebrate the Lord's Supper (as had been used on the very first occasion in the Upper Room).

Whilst residing with Ridley, I took the opportunity to seek his counsel on whether

I should bring Adriana and our children back from Meldorf and make a home here in London.

"Nicholas," I asked "do you consider it safe for exiles such as myself, given the opinions you know I hold?"

"John, you know there is no safer place than in the protective embrace of our Lord" he answered, "but I know you have concerns for your family too and I understand your wariness. You were always a cautious man and I know you do not take decisions lightly. I cannot foresee the future, John, any more than you can. But my judgement is that with the new King there will be no turning back in matters of faith. His faith is earnest and he has good and Godly men around him. **So unless there is some catastrophic event which I cannot foresee, the cause of Reform will only grow in this country.** You and your family will be welcome and safe here, John, of that I'm sure."

"Thank you Nicholas," I replied, "my sense is the same. And I feel the Lord calling me back here now. I feel I can contribute to embedding His truths here amongst his people. I have never lost my love for England and our people and I would love to return here and play my part, whatever that might be."

"I'm delighted to hear that, John. Send for your wife and children," he instructed, "and come and join me as Chaplain in my household whilst we find a more suitable position for your talents. England needs people like you right now, John, you know that. I feel the Lord has much good work for you still to complete here."

And so it was.

I wrote to Adriana and instructed that she should come to me forthwith with the children. And it was not long before she had made the arrangements to close the house in Meldorf, had said her farewells to our beloved congregation there and made her way with our eight children – and carrying our ninth in her womb still – to find me in London. Ridley provided us with temporary accommodation whilst I acted as Chaplain in his household and the transition was smooth.

I was home.

***

Meanwhile the tide of Reform was rising in England.

As if to symbolise the collapse of Papistry in England, report reached us of the physical collapse of that icon of Papist practice, the spire of Lincoln Cathedral. The tallest structure in Christendom was brought down during an exceptionally violent storm and the cathedral which had encouraged gullible pilgrims to part

with their time and riches at the shrines of St
Hugh and Bishop Grosseteste now faced financial
ruin as it surveyed the rubble and physical ruin
in its midst. For over two centuries that spire
had stood sentry over central England, but just
as the Roman Catholic church was corrupted
and went rotten from within in that time, so too
did the foundations on which that spire was
built. The spire had come down, now we felt the
whole rotten Romish Church might do likewise.

Within a year there came into effect an Act of
Uniformity, which brought some much needed
discipline and commonality to the practice of
religion in our land. I heard from Ridley how
there had been considerable debate in the House
of Lords as to the merits of bringing such
standardisation, with the Papists seeking every
opportunity to hold back the tide. But our Lord's
will was not to be blocked and Cranmer's most
excellent Book of Common Prayer became the
standard and unique basis for services across
all England.

However, we also knew that the cause of Reform
was not yet sealed.

Although there was now the legal backing and
structures in place to enable true religion to
flourish, it remained true that perhaps the
majority of Englishmen had not yet truly
grasped the fundamentals of the Gospel. Rather,
many still clung to the familiarity of their

superstitions and the comfort of the cloak of Romish Papistry.

Whilst the majority of those folk quietly disagreed, but grudgingly followed the new regulations, there were some at this time that went further and brought their objections into the light in open rebellion.

From Devon to Norfolk and up to York there were uprisings seeking to hold back the true will of God in freeing His people of our land from the grasp of the Romish Church. It is not difficult to see this as the deep spiritual battle for the souls of Englishmen spilling over into the flesh. As Paul writes to the Ephesians, "For our struggle is not against flesh and blood, but against the rulers, against the authorities, against the powers of this dark world and against the spiritual forces of evil in the heavenly realms'. It was vital therefore that God's true people prayed into these conflicts for our victory not only for the physical forces of Somerset and Dudley leading the armies of the state against the rebels, but also for the victory of the angels and the Lord over the powers of darkness.

And so we did pray for them. And the Lord was gracious unto us with victories, sustaining His cause during this time.

We were not to know then that these victories were not to be lasting.

Elsewhere the battle was fought on a more personal level – and related to the devil seeking to corrupt the momentum of Reform by bringing heresies that would shame the name of the Lord and His people. One such poor soul that the devil chose for this purpose was one Joan Bocher of Kent. The devil seeded in her mind abominable ideas relating to our Lord Jesus's parenthood – disgracefully intimating that He was in some way not truly of the flesh of the Virgin Mary, but in some superstitious way born of the spirit only.

Many good souls - even Archbishop Cranmer himself, Ridley and Lord Chancellor Rich - sought to disavow her of these lies, but the devil had such a grip on her that she would not be moved. Even I became entangled in the controversy, with my friend and colleague John Foxe seeking my counsel once this wretched woman had finally refused to recant of her folly and had been condemned and handed over to the civil authorities to face the punishment of burning.

Foxe, a tutor at the time to the Norfolk family, was of a gentle nature and sought to intervene to see pity taken on Joan Bocher.

"John, you have influence with Ridley and with Cranmer himself – can you not plead for mercy for this poor, unfortunate woman?" he exhorted me, having come to visit me in our lodgings.

"I think you overestimate my influence,"
I responded, "besides which, she is already
convicted."

"But not yet dead," he pressed. "She is likely mad
and unlikely to influence many or even any with
her strange views. Could she not be imprisoned
to remove even that small risk? Then perhaps in
time she will see the error of her ways – more so
if Godly scholars such as yourself might visit her
and provide her with true teaching – and repent
of this madness. Does God's Grace not extend to
that?"

"God's Grace might" I replied, "but she is in the
hands of the civil authorities now and already
condemned to face the fire. There's nothing more
that can be done."

"Nothing more that can be done? Would you so
idly stand by and see a poor, weak woman
subjected to the tortures of the flames? Surely,
in God's name, if she must die she should at least
face a gentler end? Has our Protestant cause
come to this, that we should emulate our
forefathers whom we disavowed for their violence
and lack of Grace?" He grasped both my hands
with both of his to convey the depth of his
imploring.

"John," I replied gently, "firstly as I said, you
attribute me more influence than I fear I have in
reality. And secondly, is the fire such a fearsome

end? Likely smoke fumes will bring an end to her before the burning bites – or her frail condition will in any case bring a swift end. Given that it has to be done, this means is as fair and gentle as any."

At this Foxe lifted his right hand away from mine and came back at it hard with a slap which startled me.

He stared hard at me and pronounced, as if by way of a curse, "**If that is your final word, Rogers, then perchance you may yet find that you, yourself, shall have your hands full of this gentle fire.**" I was shocked at the brutality of his retort and his words have lingered long with me when, often in the depths of the dark night, I have revisited the conversation we had back then and the sad predicament of Joan Bocher.

But I am confident that the blood of this woman was not on my hands.

She was already condemned by others, my superiors and by the authority of the land which must be respected, via the Privy Council itself following examination by the Archbishop of Canterbury himself. There was no denying the heresy in her proclamations and she was given every opportunity to recant of them: But she would not.

These are torrid times, in every sense of the word. Reform was not yet rooted in the land

and was readily corrupted by he who prowls around seeking to devour us. Ultimately there was nothing to be done, but to burn away this heresy to ensure that it did not corrupt the cause of Reform and destabilise the truths beginning to take root in the hearts and souls of Englishmen.

She therefore faced the fire as her body and flesh needed to be burned away along with her foul ideas. It was sad indeed that she could not be brought around and although I would normally only condone taking a life as a result of taking another life, in effect it was required to take her life to ensure that she would not corrupt the souls of others thereby thwarting their opportunity for eternal life with the Lord.

And as for my part, I do not in reality think I could have influenced any different outcome in any case.

And so the issue is academic.

As I sit here now in the grim darkness – in every sense – of Newgate prison, awaiting my destiny with my own faith tested in the literal sense and with others in the position of power over me now and seeking my downfall, my mind turns back to Joan Bocher. Was it wrong to dispose of her life and body in order to maintain the purity of Reform in our land?

I still think not.

Was Foxe's declaration over me prophetic such that I am now facing the punishment thereof?

Again, I think not.

I rest all that I own and all the I avow on the sound foundations of the Holy Scriptures.

By that alone may I be judged.

As such, my own case is unrelated to that of the heretic Joan Bocher and I cannot fathom that my unfortunate circumstances now relate in any way to that moment in the past.

Although the fire may, in the end, be the same, I will go to it under very different circumstances to Joan Bocher – standing on the truth and standing for the true Christ, not any foul heresy.

But it was a sad state of affairs to see her burned, of that there can be no doubt.

And I **regret that it had to come to that.**

May God have mercy on her soul.

***

It was just after this that I was to receive my two livings from the Crown of St Margaret Moyses

and St Sepulchre's, both in London of course.
Whilst both provided a good living by which
I could readily support my large family of
dependents, this latter provided also a large
parsonage house which proved comfortable
accommodation for us all.

I took to my pastoral duties with great
enthusiasm and diligence, although it was
harder going than it had been in Meldorf where
my congregation were more humbly settled
into the truths of the Gospel and more eager to
live them out.

Many things were still being settled in England
as Reformers from Europe returned with their
practices and insights to challenge the vestiges
of Papist Catholicism and superstition.

So it was that John Hooper, who had been exiled
to Zurich under Henry, bravely raised the issue of
vanity over vestments in a sermon directly to the
King Edward. He rightly rallied against the self
aggrandisement of those of us in senior church
office wearing fine and fancy cloth. This brought
him into conflict with my own sponsor, Ridley,
now Bishop of London – when Hooper was to be
elevated to the Bishopric of Gloucester. The
requirements were clear that in such a position
he was expected to wear the traditional
vestments for the supposed edification of the
people and to convey to the congregation the
solemnity of his office.

Hooper had been enlightened as to the fallacy of such arguments when on the continent and took a stand to demonstrate – as much to his fellow bishops as to his congregation – that such practices were at best adiaphora (that is, superficial to matters of true faith) and could at worst possibly be considered to be idolatrous. He stood firm and refused to buckle (if you will pardon the pun!).

I can report that, having sympathies myself with Hooper's arguments – having seen for myself the benefits of the simplicity of garments used on the continent – I was able to find compromise and bring reconciliation to these two great men of the Reform. To Ridley, I made the case that as long as Hooper conceded to wearing vestments at his consecration, which would serve to acknowledge his support of the Act of Uniformity to keep all in good order, then perhaps he could be permitted thereafter to adorn himself as he saw fit. I argued that Hooper could not well argue against this small compromise without being seen to be unbending and not open to finding reconciliation.

Ridley I think was much irritated by Hooper – for reasons I have never got to the bottom of: sometimes I think men, even of such similar temperaments, can simply have differing tempers, although I have ever been able to get along soundly with most men I've come across. But he saw the wisdom in my argument and eventually put it to Hooper such that it became a way out of the deadlock.

Not much later and in no small degree inspired by Hooper's stance, I myself made a similar case against the wearing of foolish headwear. Again, the root of my case was the vanity and pride that it might lead toward, together with a Papist style idolisation and inappropriate elevation of the priest.

Some people might wonder that there be more important matters of state and faith on which to stand than the wearing of a hat. But that would be to miss the point I was seeking to land and secure – that any vestige of pride or idolatry had to be wiped away, especially from a people so ready to seize and fall back on any superstitious and Papist habits.

And so I refused the square cap that had become the customary garment of priests in England and foreswore instead to wear only ever a simple round cap.

This seemed to me to deliver the appropriate level of conformity whilst still making my stance and seeking to secure another win for the Gospel in our land, which has been my life's intent. But I encountered resistance and condemnation from our bishops and so offered them this compromise: I would conform to their decree for uniformity of attire for priests, but only on the condition that, in order to retain a distinction with the still Papist priests, those should be required to wear upon their sleeves a chalice with a host upon it. I knew this was an impossible condition and so it proved, the bishops at that time still not bold enough to place even such a slight restriction and identification on the still Papists.

And so it has been that I have since that day only worn my round cap.

I think it is fair to say that I have become somewhat known for it.

And I hope thereby that the root of my purpose is also known and lands in the heart of more Englishmen.

Every battle that can be won for Christ is worth fighting.

***

Does the physical world foreshadow the battles in the heavenlies?

Sometimes I think so.

Certainly in the years 1551 to 1553 there was such tumult in our land that suggested that the spiritual battle was severe.

As for me, in some ways these years saw the pinnacle of my service in the church. My good relations with Ridley and Cranmer – and I hope my good bearing and sound scriptural teaching – led me to having the honour of being granted the prebendary of St Pancras at St Paul's itself. This placed me at the heart of the religious life of London and provided a platform for me to share the theology I had established over many years of study and prayer and with the teachings I had received from innumerable disciples of Christ. Very soon after I was additionally granted the title and role of Divinity Lecturer, with which came the privilege and, for me, pleasure of preaching regularly at this most august and revered of sacred places.

The position also provided me with living quarters at St Paul's where I spent some of my time, whilst we retained the St Sepulchre's parsonage as our family home. My days were long, but fulfilling as I worked hard to make a difference for the Lord and for Reform in London and thereby England.

Finally, I had the blessing to be granted the Rectory of Chigwell, in Essex, which blessed me and my family with a further income – collectively we had monies incoming now about which we could previously only have dreamed – although I confess that the pressures and demands of my London roles kept me from spending as much time as I would have liked with my parishioners there. But I ensured that my curate was well chosen, one Adam Johnson; and as a solid Reformer, he ensured that the congregation there received the appropriate instruction in the Lord.

So for me, these times represented the high watermark of my career (to date at least! Only the Lord knows what future challenges and opportunities He has for me; whatever they be, I stand ready to serve).

But England was a troubled land at this time.

The economic climate was bad, with repeated harvest failures due to inclement weather, with the debasing of the currency continuing to drive price increases. Families grew hungry and it was difficult at times to convey how blessed they were to have the love of Christ and that they should therefore fill the collection plates, when the plates of their children were empty.

Even the cloth industry on which so much of England's trade had depended was now in decline, with reports from my friends still in Antwerp that warehouses were full with English cloth for which they could no longer find markets. Knowing the scale of the industry in that city and the capacity for marketing English cloth to Europe, this surprised and saddened me.

And it was not only in the economic sense that England was under attack.

Physically too, the land was blighted by a type of plague we named the Sweating Sickness. What was the purpose of the Lord in sending this to our land at this critical time of trial in our collective faith? Was it to test us? To create urgency in the choices of men on where they stand with the Lord? Having seen this dreadful sickness close up I find that hard to settle alongside my knowledge of the Lord as all loving and caring for us.

Was it rather the lion who prowls finding an opportunity to devour us? The devil himself destroying the will and hearts of the English people just as they were turning back to the Lord?

Perhaps.

But I would not give the devil the satisfaction of attributing anything to him that may not have been within his limited powers.

Rather I focussed myself on dealing with the impact and consequences of this awful plague – that played so much on the fears of my congregations and all the peoples of London and England as well as taking away so many dear souls.

One such was a certain William Tomson, parishioner of St Sepulchre and gaoler at Newgate Prison. He was a large, imposing man

with a booming and deep voice and yet with a
gentleness of spirit and a heart for the Lord. He
was a family man also, with his dear wife
Elizabeth and six children.

It was the eldest of the children, Bethany, that
knocked on our door early one evening just as we
were finishing our supper, around 7pm. I say
'knocked', it was more that she battered the door
as if fleeing advancing demons.

She cried out as she did so, "Help, help me please!
Make haste, there is no time to lose ..."

Our maidservant Alice answered the frantic
knocking, "Peace child ! What ails you so!"

The poor Tomson girl was weeping so much she
could scarce make herself understood. Hearing
the commotion, Adriana went to the door – she
has always had a kind way with children and they
respond well to her.

"Bethany, peace my child" she calmed her as she
knelt and placed her hands upon her shoulders in
reassurance. "Take a deep breath, dear. That's
right. Now tell me calmly, what is wrong?"

"It's ... it's ... it's father ..." she managed to get out
between sobs. "He was fine when he came home
and my mother bathed him, but as he dressed
and joined us to pray before supper he began

to complain of the cold ..." She broke off with further sobs.

I had joined by Adriana's side by this time.

"Go on, my child" I encouraged her.

"And I fetched him his coat to help keep him warm, but he could hardly put it on as he began to shake and shiver with such violence .."

I caught Adriana's eye. We already knew what this meant and where it was likely leading. But we needed to know how far things had progressed.

"Oh poor you, Bethany" consoled Adriana, "that must have been so scary for you! And what happened next?"

"It was awful !" Bethany replied, wide eyed and heartrendingly fearful. "And then ... and then ..." It was clearly so hard for her to recall and recount. "As soon as he had his coat on he said he was too hot, much too hot! He cast off his coat and shirt and pulled at his vest as if to get air to his body ...." She lowered her voice. "Then he was very sick. Everywhere. It was so awful!" She broke into weeping once again.

I had my coat on already by this stage and headed out of the door. "I don't know what time

I'll be back" I said to Adriana. "Best you look after
Bethany here, there's nothing more she can do
for her father now. Bethany?" I sought to get
her gaze.

She looked up at me with wide, scared eyes, red
stained from crying.

"You are a very brave girl and you have done very
well to come to me and to explain everything so
well. Good girl. Now you stay here with Mrs
Rogers and she'll find you something to eat." At
that I turned on my heels and hastened to
Tomson's house, just a few hundred yards from
our own.

I knew I had to get to him with great haste. I had
already heard of the pattern of this evil plague,
which proceeded at such a pace that no one had
ever experienced from any other plague or illness.
I needed to get to William Tomson fast to pray
over his soul a final time, as his death was likely –
perhaps inevitably - nigh.

I burst into his house, the front door left ajar by
the fleeing Bethany. This was a house of tears
already, as Tomson's wife, Emma and small
children wept over their husband and father.

I found them upstairs and he was lain on the
marital bed. That scene burned itself onto my
mind and will remain there forever.

He was stripped now to his undergarments
and groaned as he writhed slowly in a tormented
world of his own. Those garments were soaked
wet with his sweat – as if he had been plunged
back into the bath. His sweat had exuded
from his plagued body and through the
undergarments to create a pool of acrid
soaking on the bed.

"William, William – it is I, John Rogers, your
Pastor" I sought to break through his stupor.
He groaned which I hoped was some response of
recognition. "William, stay awake my friend.
Fight this thing! You must stay awake to fight
this. Fight it for your wife, now! Fight for your
children!" He groaned again, I think he had heard
me, but he was clearly growing weak. I shook his
shoulder in an attempt to rouse him and
encourage him. But he only continued to loll
his head from side to side.

Still the sweat poured.

Still the tears poured from his poor wife and
children.

I prayed over him, asking the Lord to save him,
but acknowledging too that His will be done and
beseeching Him to receive this dear man's
spirit if his time was now.

As I prayed William quieted and became still.

"Is he dead?" asked Emma, fearfully between sobs.

"Not yet, Emma" I replied.

I saw her eyes flicker with hope.

A hope I had then to dash.

"But it will not be long now ..."

She interrupted me, "But look, his breathing is eased! He is sleeping! Perchance he will sleep it off now! He's a good, strong man my husband ..."

My turn to interrupt, out of kindness I needed to tell her the cruel truth. I grasped her arms, "Emma ... Emma, he will not return to you now. Thanks be to God he will suffer no more, but with this plague once sleep comes, eternal sleep surely follows. God will receive him soon."

She looked at me wild eyed, then beat my chest with her fists in frustration and rage and mourning as the tears came, angrier and more violent than before. I held her as her sobs eventually subsided. In time we knelt by his soaked bedside and I led her and her small, frightened children in prayer.

By the time I had completed my prayers, William Tomson had passed away into the comforting embrace of our Lord.

It was 9pm.

From falling unwell around 6pm, poor William Tomson was deceased by 9pm.

Such was the devastating power of this awful Sweating Sickness.

Thousands died from it that year. And not a soul in London went untouched in some way by it, losing a loved one or a friend. Such is the powerlessness of man.

And yet, mysteriously – thanks be to God – it passed as quickly as it had arrived.

And the Lord spared me and my family.

***

Meanwhile further progress was being made in the cause of saving souls in England through the Reform of the church. In so many other ways this was a time of excitement and hope, with major victories being won for Christ!

The tide of Reform was rising further – I did not know it, but perhaps to its highest mark. (Will the Lord ordain its return to flood the land? I can only hope and pray so now).

Cranmer drove a second Act of Uniformity through Parliament which removed further superstitious vestiges from the church. This included the prohibition to mention the Romish lie and delusion that was mass, being replaced with the plain descriptor, The Lord's Supper. To me this was a significant victory and severed a key hold that the Papist priesthood sought to hold over the people, casting themselves as conjurors in a mummer's exhibition. Further, it was wisely clarified that the habit of kneeling at that Supper was in no way any acknowledgement of any mystery or power in the elements, rather it represented a right and Godly respect for the majesty of Him whom we remembered and the mystery of what He has accomplished for us.

Similarly the fabricated powers of the saints and the Virgin Mary was declared to be fallacious and their ceremonial invocation were henceforth prohibited. With that went the felonious industry surrounding these superstitions, with the endless and grotesque body parts absurdly venerated and attributed supernatural powers.

What rot!

As if our Lord would need such old bones through which to declare his majesty when all around is the creation come into being simply from the utterance of His voice !

Of equal sound sense was the prohibition of prayers for the dead. What need the dead of our prayers when their fate be already determined by our Lord? And their future already fixed to be with our Lord in heaven forever or forever to suffer the torments and tortures of hell? No, once dead they are separated from us here on earth and we can only hope that they had made their peace with our Lord through the blood of Jesus Christ before they passed. Rather, the sole beneficiaries of such prayers had been the Papist priests who charged handsomely for such services, praying rather on the superstitions of the people to fleece their flock of funds to be used for their own depravity.

My mother had been right to question such practices, all those years ago on the death of my grandfather.

I like to think that my own, small stance on the matter of appropriate head garments for a priest had an impact on the new standards declared for vestments with which a priest should adorn themselves. With the Papist church practices pulled down, the priest should now dress for the role which he clearly now held – that of bridge from the people to the Lord, inviting his congregation to get to know our wonderful Creator personally and to develop their own relationship directly with Him, through the blood and sacrifice of our Lord Jesus Christ and through his unsurpassing Grace!

All that is required to be reconciled with our Maker is to repent and acknowledge this truth. This faith alone can save us! And always will. Everything else is superstition and lies.

Thus, similarly, sound scriptural foundation was henceforth rightly required for prayer and any church activity. Naturally, this gladdened my heart, such is the veneration with which I, of course, hold the Living Word that is Scripture. On it all things can rest and all human answers may be found, if we would but scrutinise and understand it. It is for this reason that I believe so passionately in the need to present every man with God's Word in the language that they themselves speak. My Thomas Matthew Bible testifies to that, if anyone would doubt me.

And with the church set aright at last in the eyes of God and man, there therefore was no longer the need for the physical paraphernalia that was the evil fruit of these sinful practices. All of the riches wrongly accumulated by the Romish Church were expropriated – the gold and silver chalices, candlesticks and cruets as well as the sumptuous carpets, cushions and tapestries that had no place in the Bible and therefore, of course, had no place in our churches. I long argued with Ridley that the proceeds from this expropriation could do such good works to ease the pitiful state of the poor and fatherless. But I never saw the fruit of those expropriated funds used so freely and with such Grace. I cannot tell what became of those funds, which is a shameful scar on us all.

Finally, it was rightly decreed that attendance at church on Sundays was compulsory for all, with heavy imprisonment sentences the result of non-compliance. In practice, even in my own parish, this ultimate sanction was rarely resorted to, but it gave us at least greater strength to our rebukes of the recalcitrant. And it is sad to report that the recalcitrant were larger in number than I would have hoped by this stage. Whilst Reform had been decreed at speed from the highest authority in England, winning the hearts of Englishmen was a more labour intensive and time consuming matter.

I recall that even Latimer, by now chaplain to King Edward himself, complained of the lack of constancy of his congregations at this time. He decried that folk should be walking up and down in the sermon-time (which it is true, they did) and 'would make such a racket with buzzing and buzzing in the preacher's ear that it makes him oftentimes to forget his matter'. I could certainly vouch for that too!

But the sound foundations for the turning of English hearts were finally in place and I anticipated eagerly the movement of his Holy Spirit across our land.

But it was not yet to be so.

***

With the tide of Reform risen so high in England, I had purposed to secure the lives of my foreign born wife and our children in England through their naturalisation. Our family had grown further with the arrival of my little girl, Elizabeth, soon after Adriana and the children had re-joined me in London.

With ten children now in our care, nine of whom were born abroad, I felt that I could signal and affirm my commitment to the cause in England as well as provide them with the security of belonging in England and no longer being seen as aliens. Other preachers who had been exiled under King Henry found themselves in the same position, having been liberated from the unholy constraints to marry by receiving the truths of Scripture and enjoying the Godly fruits of family life.

And so I took it upon myself to arrange a petition from amongst us that would beseech Parliament to recognise those amongst us who had married and had been blessed with children born abroad. And to request that our wives and children be reputed to be taken as the king's natural subjects as lawful persons born within this realm of England. My friend Ridley ensured that this petition was read in the Lords and although I heard report of some critical debate (to be expected from a body with such a history of Papist pockets), our petition was supported and our request passed in to law by Royal Assent by the middle of April.

I believe this was the proudest day of my life.

The partnership I had formed with my beloved Adriana was thereby formerly recognised in my homeland and the family we had made together acknowledged as legitimate and embraced by my compatriots. John Rogers, son of the loriner John Rogers from Doritend, recognised as married to Adriana with their beautiful ten children, now fine English girls and boys.

By order and on the signature of the King himself!

***

And then suddenly everything changed.

Reform experienced an unforeseen reversal and we have yet to see the full outcome.

Rumours of the poor health of King Edward had been rife for some time. I chose not to entertain any such gossip in our household – indeed I forbade it - nor to involve myself in the controversy over the succession of the King.

I have already shared with you my theology of authority whereby I willingly and loyally bow to those the Lord has put over me in civil matters. I therefore considered it ungodly to participate in debates concerning the succession as to whom should succeed on the demise of our current king.

But others were so engaged.

Much good it did them to try and interfere with His divine will.

So that when the event came, so did crisis for Reform in England.

On 6th July 1553 the young King Edward VI died and went to be with our Lord.

And it appeared that Reform in England might then die with him.

I prayed that it would not be so.

Adriana prayed with me also, for here was her greatest fear come to reality - being settled with all her family in a land foreign to her and now potentially turned hostile to our faith.

What would become of me, now that I had established myself in a central and highly visible role in this work of the Lord? How should I now respond to the new uncertainties around the succession? Who was now legitimately the Lord's anointed ruler of England?

And what was the future now of my newly English wife and family?

Our trials had only just begun.

***

John Rogers,
Prebendary and
Lecturer at St Paul's
Cathedral
*Engraving of John Rogers
(c. 1500 -1555), possibly
by Willem van de Pass*

William Tyndale, translator of much
of the Thomas Matthew Bible that
John Rogers went on to publish after
Tyndale execution in 1536
From Foxe's Book of Martyrs

Strangulation and
burning at Brussels
in 1536 of William
Tyndale, Bible
translator and friend
of John Rogers who
went on to complete
his full English Bible
from Antwerp and
have authorised in
England as the
Thomas Matthew

Bible in 1537. The King of England's eyes were
indeed opened!
*Engraving from John Foxe - The Horizon Book of the
Elizabethan World (which credits the Folger Shakespeare Library),
American Heritage / Houghton Mifflin, 1967, PD-Old*

Frontispiece to the Thomas Matthew Bible, edited by
John Rogers and translated by William Tyndale and Miles
Coverdale 1537; the first authorized Bible in the English Language,
under licence from King Henry VIII
From the British Museum

Philip Melanchthon's house in
Wittenberg
Photo by A. Savin

Philip Melanchthon 1537,
Lutheran reformer and
friend of John Rogers
when in Wittenberg.
*Painted by Lucas
Cranach the Elder*

Inside Philip Melanchthon's house in Wittenberg, where John Rogers
would surely have spent time with his friend when there between 1540-44
Photo by Torsten Schleese

Bradford calming the crowd at St Paul's Cross on the preaching
of Gilbert Bourne on 13th August 1553
Painting by Joseph Martin Kronheim (1810-1896) - [From Title page]:
Book of Martyrs by John Foxe Condensed from the Larger Editions
With Original Illustrations PD-US

174

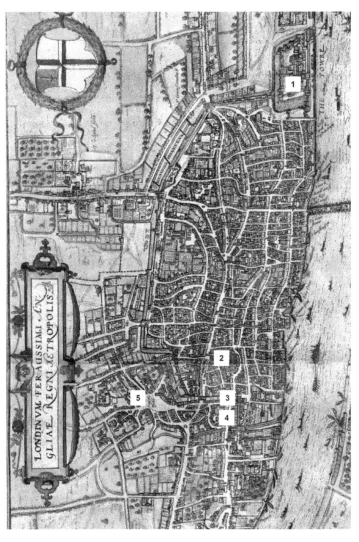

Map of London 1572, near contemporaneous to John Rogers, showing key locations in his time in London – including the (1) Tower of London, (2) St Paul's / St Paul's Cross, (3) Newgate Prison, (4) St Sepulchre's Church opposite and (5) Smithfield

Thomas Cranmer,, Archbishop of Canterbury 1533-55 , martyred March 1556 having finally recanted his recantation
Painting By Unknown artist
Chris Skidmore, Edward VI: The Lost King of England, London: Weidenfeld and Nicolson, 2007

John Hooper, Bishop of Gloucester 1551-4, tried by the same court as John Rogers, who expected to be burned together with him. He was burned a month after Rogers,
Portrait by Henry Bryan Hall, after James Warren Childe 1839

Edmund Bonner, Bishop of London 1539-49 and 1553-59 and co-prosecutor of John Rogers
By Engraving after 16th-century portrait

Stephen Gardiner, Bishop of Winchester, Lord Chancellor under Queen Mary and lead prosecutor of John Rogers
By Quinten Metsys

Burning of John Rogers, first Protestant Martyr under Queen Mary
4th Feb 1555
Woodcut from John Foxe's The Third Volume of the Ecclesiastical History
By Artist unknown

Memorial to John Rogers, John Bradford,
John Philpot and other Martyrs burned during
Queen Mary's reign, close to where they took
place at Smithfield, London.
Photo taken by author

Chapter 7 – London, Defending the Faith

Lady Jane Grey was of excellent character, the granddaughter of the older King Henry, VII, and recently married to Lord Guildford, son to Lord Northumberland who led the Privy Council for King Edward. She knew the Lord and had a purity of faith that doubtless was attractive to Edward and the reason behind his attempts, with Northumberland, to change the line of succession to the throne.

But for reasons I would not dare to presume upon, her path to the throne was blocked.

What was immediately clear to me and to Adriana was that we had entered the most dangerous of times – for Reform and for us personally. My friend and patron Ridley was quick to declare his hand – as ever, quicker than me to determine his opinion and share it forcefully. On 9th July he preached forcibly on the merits of Lady Jane Grey and her godly character and against the Papist preferences of Mary Tudor.

My spirit was deeply disturbed by this.

On the one hand, I knew this characterisation of Lady Jane to be true and could see the benefits for Reform should she succeed rightfully to the throne. And yet I did not possess the luxury of certainty over his views regarding that succession. My instinct and preference for deference to authority led me to be uneasy about the eldest remaining daughter of King Henry being removed from the line of succession. Did not Paul write to the people of Rome, "Let everyone be subject to the governing authorities, for there is no authority except that which God has established"? I had never been convinced of the illegitimacy of King Henry's marriage to Queen Catherine despite the ongoing debates and declarations in that regard.

Furthermore, I could sense the innate loyalty of the plain English people to this daughter of the great Henry – some motivated by loyalty to the strong King himself and others drawn by the attraction of a return to the familiarity of the old, Papist and disgraceful superstitions that her succession was thought to bring. Reform had not yet taken firm root in the land – much seed had landed on stony ground.

So when I witnessed the pronouncement of Lady Jane Grey as the new Queen of England on 10th July, at St Paul's Cross just near my own lodgings there, I had a deep sense of unease.

Lady Jane herself took residence in the Tower of London, whilst her prime sponsor Northumberland took to the country to seal by force that which he had sought to decree by royal command.

As for me, I focussed my prayers on the soul of Mary Tudor.

It was she who demonstrated her royal character in her response to the weak equivocation of the members of the Privy Council. Exactly at the time that those men could not make up their minds on who truly should succeed the throne, Mary herself was resolute in her conviction and declared that if no man would stand and fight for her rightful inheritance, then she would stand, take up sword and fight alone.

I admired her conviction which was suggestive to me of the Lord's hand upon her.

And yet I continued to pray that the Lord would use her strength of character for good and open her eyes to the truths of Reform and the lies of Papist Catholicism. Of course she had long been rooted in those lies and antichristian superstitions, although she had made peace with her father and so had shown herself to be open to correction. Am I still naïve to think that this daughter of the Holy Roman Empire could have her eyes opened by the Lord and see the wonderful truths of his true Gospel? Some may say so, but I know that our Lord Jesus Christ taught us "With God all things are possible".

And my prayers were much required. Word began to reach back to London that Northumberland's military endeavours were being thwarted, with the navy switching allegiance to Mary and parts of the country rising independently to take arms for Henry's daughter. So it was that East Anglia (long a Papist stronghold), Sussex and Bath rose up. Perhaps it was this – together with Northumberland's absence from the heart of government - that persuaded the Council to switch their allegiance firmly back to Mary.

It was in the midst of this upheaval and as I was wrestling with these very issues that I received instruction from the Privy Council to preach myself the following 16th July at St Paul's Cross.

I felt the Lord's hand on these events, calling me to take a stance.

But Adriana was deeply concerned about the danger this might place me in.

"Is it wise to take such a public spectacle in these most turbulent of times?" she asked me as we sat before the fire in our comfortable St Sepulchre's parsonage. The children were all in bed, I have always treasured these precious times when it was just me and my dear wife and when we could speak openly, earnestly and lovingly with one another.

"Wise? I don't know about wise," I replied, "but what I do know is that my name is on the rota and I must fulfil my duty."

"Fulfil your duty ... or your destiny?" she asked, piercing me with those emerald green eyes.

"Perhaps both, Adriana" I replied. "But either way, this is a sermon I cannot evade."

"I understand", she acknowledged, and I was grateful again for her obedience as my wife. "But perhaps there is room for wisdom still? Have you yet determined your message?"

"I have thought of little else since Ridley's outbursts last week" I replied truthfully. His candour had shocked me, but perhaps also the venom directed at Mary Tudor, arguably the true heir to the English throne. My spirit was disquieted and I found it difficult to put my finger on exactly why. "But right now ..." it was the Tuesday evening this fireside discussion took place, "I remain in prayerful consideration of all of these matters."

"Then why not choose solid ground, John?" Adriana asked me, a hopeful glint in her eye.

"Your meaning?" I asked, knowing there would be thoughtful wisdom to my wife's counsel.

"Meaning ..." she leant forward and held my hands in hers, "preach as you must, but preach the wonders and truth of the Gospel only. Why should you comment on politics and worldly matters – as Ridley chose to – when your calling is to preach the good news of freedom in Jesus Christ? Surely no one could hold that against you?"

I looked back at her and let the words sink in. I squeezed her hands back in loving thanks. "The day I married you, Adriana Rogers, was the wisest day of my life!" I declared and leant over to kiss my darling wife, counsellor and partner to my soul through life.

And so it was.

On that Sunday 16th July, there was a buzz and hum in the congregation as I took the pulpit at St Paul's Cross. I had already preached there many times and loved the sense of centrality that St Paul's brought. What a privilege to preach the true Word of God there at the centre of St Paul's , in the centre of London, the great capital of our England. Preaching outdoors only exaggerated this sense that one was speaking to the nation.

That day was exceptionally hot with not a breath of air, for me adding further to the sense of tension. And yet I felt myself becalmed as I strode up into the pulpit, clasping my Thomas Matthew Bible. I would speak of the Love held there in those Scriptures, of our sins as men that separate us forever from a perfect and pure God; and then of the Gospel, the all surpassing good news that this same God, whom we have wronged beyond measure, Himself should reach down and set us aright with Him again. Doing so by sending his only Son, Jesus Christ, to live amongst us as a man and yet a man – the only man – who never sinned; and such a man we sinful men could not abide and cast him down to the most horrendous death. But the grave could not hold him nor could death itself! He conquered death and so gave certain hope to us all!

And I preached again that day, as I had done numerous times both from that same pulpit, but more so in my own parishes in London and Meldorf, that this demanded – demanded! – a response from us all. To stand before our Creator God and to repent of our sins, to acknowledge our risen Lord Jesus Christ and in the power of the Holy Spirit to accept His offer to be born again into the life of a saint! Forever to be reunited with our Creator and to know our future beyond death praising His wonderful name for a thousand and ten thousand and ten thousand times ten thousand years and more!

THAT is the Gospel of our Lord Jesus Christ.

And it was that that I declared – purely, clearly, firmly – that day at St Paul's Cross.

And nothing else.

I could see small groups of those that favoured the old ways, favouring Mary Tudor whom they hoped would restore those rotten and idolatrous ways – they muttered, whispered and gossiped one to another, sweating under the heat of the summer sun. And yet I knew that, as I had agreed with my wise counsel - my wife – nothing I had preached could bring any reproach.

As I closed and stepped back down from the pulpit and back into the sunshine, the congregation murmured, mostly in approval and affirmation, but some I knew felt thwarted.

Both groups disbursed and I returned to my rooms to pray that His Gospel would land in the hearts both of my brothers and sisters in Reform as well – and especially – in the hearts of my enemies.

The Lord had allowed me to pass safely through that testing.

But His plan was not to remain the same.

***

It was on 19th of that month that the inevitable events began to transpire. Mary Tudor was declared Queen of England, with Northumberland's military endeavours come to nought and his desperate attempts to switch allegiance at the last. There was no one that would stand for Lady Jane Grey now, her Tower residence become immediately a place of imprisonment rather than power.

Queen Mary's proclamation was met with acclamation by the large majority of the English people. Was it in response to relief that the horrors of reverting to civil war were now averted? Or excitement at the prospect of a return to the comforts of Papist superstitions the people had grown so used to, smothering them in the warm blanket of the devil's lies?

Whatever the cause, the sense of celebration was real and tangible.

When finally she processed into London, early the next month, church bells rang out along her way and reportedly across the land in one loud, clanging acclamation as bonfires were lit in celebration and cheers and shouts of joy rang out amongst a frightened people.

My own feelings were torn.

I was glad God's will was being done with regards to the succession – with Godly order restored to the civil authorities to reign over us.

And yet I knew that this represented the moment of greatest danger for Reform in England.

I could only continue to pray now for Queen Mary's soul that the Holy Spirit would stir her heart and open her eyes to the true Gospel, as I had preached that very same week at St Paul's Cross.

And then came my true test.

I received instruction, from the Privy Council itself, that I was to preach again at St Paul's Cross – just three weeks since I had previously mounted the pulpit.

Even as the Registrar, who had called me into his office to advise me of this significant news, was giving me my instructions I became aware that the Lord was providing a new and transcending test for me.

Was this a second opportunity provided by God to speak his will into the current state of the nation? Was my first sermon simply a prelude to this next? Was I being called to be bolder for Him and His cause of Reform in these historic and most turbulent of times?

I hastened back to the parsonage to share the news with Adriana, with a mixture of a sense of excitement at being in the wake of the Lord's work and trepidation about the consequences: And of having to share this news with Adriana.

She was busy with the children, but I managed to draw her away and find some privacy up in our bedroom.

"What is it, John, that is so pressing it brings you from your work? How rare that I should have the pleasure of seeing you midday!" she sought to jest, but I could tell she sensed the tension in my presence.

"I have news" I began. "I've been asked – by the Council – to preach once again this Sunday."

"Again?" she protested. "But you did so just three weeks ago! Surely you're not already on the rota ..."

"I am called to preach, Adriana. The Registrar himself told me so" I ecplained.

"Is it a trap?" she asked. She quickly saw the jeopardy in the situation and recalled the gossiping gaggle from my previous preaching at St Paul's Cross.

"A trap it may be, I don't know. But what I do know, my dear wife, is that preach I must." I tried to say it gently, but knew it came out firmly.

She was quiet a moment, staring at the floor as I held her hands gently by her sides.

She lifted her head and looked directly into my eyes and I wondered again at the beauty not only of her eyes, but of the wonderful spirit that they conveyed. Truly I have been blessed to have such a lifelong companion and friend.

"I know you must" she replied. "And I pray to our loving Lord that he will give you guidance on what to preach – and what not to say – so that you can be obedient to Him and His Word. I pray His protection over you also, my darling husband. But you must be true to yourself now and stand on His truth. May He be your refuge, stronghold and strength!"

And I felt my love for my wife surge again and thanked the Lord once again for my blessings and His provision of her in my life.

And at that moment also, I knew and understood what needed to be done.

I was not frightened, not scared in any way – but rather felt the presence of the Holy Spirit right there in my own chamber and with my own wife.

Now I would stand.

I would stand firm on the truths the Lord had shown me.

And if needed now, I would seal my stance with blood.

"It will be dangerous, you know that, dear husband" she offered.

"That I do know" I replied. "and my dearest, marvellous, most wonderful wife ... so it must be. You know I love you, Adriana" I professed. "I love you more than I knew a man could love a woman. And I love you even more because you love me – and you know my heart, my heart for the Lord and my eternal gratitude for His mercy and Grace. We must trust in Him. We CAN trust in him, with the most precious of our earthly treasures, our very own children. For He loves each and every one of them every part as much as we do – indeed in His perfect love, he loves them even more."

She was weeping now.

Silently and in dignified control of herself, but the silent tears were real and spoke of the depths of her fears for the future that she sought to supress by offering them back to the Lord and trusting in him.

I hugged her and held her awhile.

Then stepping back, but holding her still, I made the following commitment. "If this I must seal now with my blood, then I trust in the Lord to strengthen me through my trials. But this I promise to you, Adriana: I will not court affliction. You know that I bow to the authority

now granted our Queen Mary and I will not in
this sermon nor ever speak ill against her as our
Sovereign Queen, as some have done – including
even Ridley. But in God's name I will speak out
against the deceits and lies that a return to
Papist ways would bring. Standing in the light,
I cannot commend nor stand silent to see
darkness fall again on this nation."

My wife nodded, even as the tears still fell,
knowing both the truth of my words as well
as the strength and depth of my conviction.
I hugged her again and then, together, we knelt
before our bridal bed as we had done every night
in the quieter, more pleasant times, to pray to
our Father God.

I led us in prayer.

"Lord, I give you thanks for Adriana, my most
dear and precious wife and your gracious gift to
me to sweeten my life beyond my expectation
and measure. I pray your protection over her
now and over each and every one of our dearest
ten children with whom you have blessed us both.
I promise now, my Lord, to stand for you and not
to take a single step backwards for your precious
name. Guide me, Lord, provide me the wisdom to
know when to speak out boldly for you and when
to stand - and when to hold my tongue. And may
every word that I speak for You be rooted in
your Word, which speaks truth and life over

us all and one which we can depend upon beyond all else. Amen."

"Amen" echoed Adriana – with a strength and confidence which surprised me.

As we rose to our feet, she smiled at me and kissed me on the cheek.

"You seem at ease, dearest?" I queried.

"I believe I am, John. I have this strong conviction that the Lord will sustain us – all of us – through whatever trials we may now face."

I felt confidence surge through my veins. I had already set my face to this task, wherever it may lead, but with the full commitment and backing of the person most dear to me in all the world, my lovely Adriana, I felt indefatigable and wonderfully courageous.

"He will, my love, He will" I replied. "And now I know what I must do. I have a sermon to write! Perhaps the most important of my life!". I leant over and kissed her on the cheek again, simultaneously squeezing her hand – then turned and took myself back to my quarters at St Paul's to write.

Twenty years of learning and understanding and being brought into the light by the Lord had led me to this. I had an absolute clarity now about the truths of the Gospel and of Scripture and therefore a crystal clear eye for the deceits and lies poured onto the English people by the Church of Rome. These I laid down and identified in my sermon, as if calling them to light could in itself weaken their grip on our people. I did not hold back – this time – on warning those that had ears to hear of the dangers of falling back into idolatrous, superstitious and deceitful ways.

I railed against the idolatry of the icons of the saints, decrying them as breaking the second commandment. I condemned the misappropriation of the wealth sequestered from the Papist abbeys and overly ornate churches – pointing out the good those funds could have been put to in alleviating the lot of the needy and poor, as Jesus instructed.

Equally, I also trod carefully. In the sense that the exigences of the Papist church of Antichrist I condemned wholeheartedly whilst extoling the Victories in Christ we had achieved under King Edward.

But I never – not once – showed any disloyalty or disrespect to Queen Mary herself. I preached on the sound foundations of Scripture, but did not stray into things politic.

I directed my ire most directly at those in our priesthood who should have known better as they knew the Scriptures and yet chose to ignore

them for their own profit and gain. Whereas in
my previous sermon I had felt directed to speak
to the common people of England and conveyed
the message of hope that is the Gospel, now
I sensed the anger of the Lord that those called
to be the shepherds of his flock should abuse
and afflict them so with their lies and falsehoods.

As I prepared my sermon, I had in mind Jesus'
own righteous anger overturning the tables in
the Temple of Jerusalem. As I preached that day,
I sensed the same righteous anger and felt at one
with the heart of God Himself in so doing.

I had a small hope that my staying loyal to the
Sovereign Queen Mary, speaking not a word
against her, might provide me with some degree
of protection from recriminations from my
boldness to speak out for the cause of Reform
and against the pestilence of Popery.

But my small hope was quickly thwarted.

I had stirred the hornets' nest of the modern
day Pharisees and I quickly faced their wrath and
retribution. No sooner had I returned to my
official residences than there was a knock at the
door – it was two servants of Bishop Gardiner,
summoning me forthwith to the Tower to
explain myself before the Council.

My stomach turned, but this was not
unexpected and so I placed my round cap back

on my head and stole myself to make a stand
before the highest authorities in the land – but
knowing I stood on a higher authority still. I
headed out of St Paul's and headed toward the
Tower – the glistening white of these formidable
and ancient buildings appearing soon within
my view.

As I walked I rehearsed my defence and my
confidence grew. I approached the Tower from
the banks of the River Thames and announced
myself to the guards at the gate. I was expected
and was then escorted by two burly and
unspeaking guards into the inner sanctum
of the Tower.

As I entered the hall, there arrayed before me
were the most powerful persons in the land –
all now known to be Romish Church supporters
and arrant Papists. Norfolk, restored to full
power under his patron Queen Mary, sat
imposing in the centre and was the first to speak.

"Ahh, Rogers, we've been expecting you" he
bellowed (although I think his normal volume of
speech). "What a disgraceful scene you've created
in the heart of our capital! What have you to say
for yourself?" He pointed with a quill pen he had
been using, as if aiming an arrow dart at my
very heart.

"I am at a loss, my Lord. I come only from
preaching the Word of the Lord to my

congregation, per my calling and in accordance with your very own instruction." I kept my voice calm, seeking both to show my steely confidence whilst also ensuring I showed due respect to this august company.

"Our instruction? OUR instruction?" Norfolk bellowed. "Did we instruct you to spread insidious sedition and throw unfounded accusations against some of the finest and most Godly men of our land? Did we ask you to dishonour her majesty our Queen and incite rebellion against her?"

"None of these things have I done," I replied calmly but speedily so the list of unfounded accusations would cease. "I simply preached in accordance with the very laws of this land."

At this, Norfolk looked to Gardiner, as if I had touched some nerve they hoped I would not find. Gardiner took the cue.

"Rogers, you know that your preaching was inciteful, inspired by the hatred of true Catholicism and intended to stir up your supporters against the restoration of the true faith now made possible by the accession of our Queen Mary."

"On the contrary, my Lord, I know no such thing" I countered. "All I know is that I preached on the sound foundations of the Scriptures in accordance with the laws of this land as established under King Edward in recent years ..." I paused and scanned the eyes of each man arraigned in front of me. "... and still extant today. I preach within the laws of this land today and on the foundation of Scripture itself."

"Is that so?" Gardiner asked, sarcastically. "Is that really so Rogers, or should I call you Matthew?" This resulted in a ripple of sardonic laughter around the room, as if the pseudonym I had used for my Thomas Matthew Bible was something to be ashamed about and now a badly kept secret.

Gardiner himself sneered at me.

"It is so" I replied simply, needing no oath on which to stand when I could simply stand on the truth. "I spoke no ill of our Queen Mary and never will, nor will incite any person against her Godly ascension to the throne. On this you may be sure – if you should require witnesses there were enough today at St Paul's Cross, I should think."

A disgruntled muttering from the group.

"But my Lords, you may also be sure that I will with full vigour continue to preach the Word of our Lord on the basis of the Scriptures whilst there is breath in my body ..."

"Which may not be long ..." someone muttered, I could not determine who, to much ribald laughter amongst the group.

I waited for the hubbub to die down and continued calmly.

"I will preach the Word of our Lord according to my calling and call on as many hundred witnesses as you require to vouch for how today I did preach only within and according to the limits of the laws of this land."

I paused – but no further question was forthcoming. I felt embolded and so went on.

"Unless you have had some other report?" I challenged.

The group seemed as one to look toward Gardiner. He shifted some papers before him and then glanced at Norfolk, who – I think, but cannot be sure – seemed to give the slightest hint of a shake of the head by way of communication. Gardiner seemed to receive the message.

"Consider yourself fortunate, Rogers, that your insidious sedition and heretical lies have not caught up with you today." He looked up at me menacingly and paused, before holding aloft his right forefinger in front of me and adding, "But rest assured catch up with you they will,

I – WE ..." he waved his finger around the room to encompass all members of this most powerful council in the land, "... we will make sure of that."

And then, somewhat to my surprise and a little unbelief, he shouted out "Guards!"

In came my two burly companions who had clearly been waiting outside the door – they stood attentively by the door.

"Take this man out of my sight and escort him from these premises. He has no place here unless he return in chains." At that, Gardiner turned and spoke in a low voice to his follow members of the Council, providing clear indication that the questioning was over.

I turned and headed out of the door, as my accompanying two guards fell into step behind me. They were silent again as we made our way to the gate and simply stopped at the gate itself as I proceeded on through and back home along the Thames.

Once clear of the Tower, I drew a deep breath and looked to the skies, which were cloudless and with only the slightest of breezes exhaling up the Thames. I exhaled so my breath joined the breeze and I closed my eyes for a moment to give thanks to the Lord for His deliverance. I paused and listed to the whisper of the Lord on the wind. I felt that this was only the beginning of my trials, but the Lord's presence was near and real, and, perhaps strangely, I felt a strong sense of His love and reassurance.

As I strolled back home along the Thames, my mind mulled over the exchanges I had had with the Privy Council. A righteous anger rose in my heart. I recalled the injustices I had called out earlier that day – which I knew to be true and I knew equally to be heinous in the eyes of the Lord. And it occurred to me that never a Catholic of those I had just stood before had ever done as much as I had done that day in calling out those sinful behaviours.

And I resolved once again in my heart and before God that never would I renounce these truths, never back down – whatever the provocation or consequences – but would ever stand on the truths of Scripture, of the Gospel and of our Lord's instructions.

As I did so I felt my spirits rise. I surveyed the flurry of London life around me, along the Thames, along the banks of the Thames and in the lanes and by-roads of London itself.

And I found myself whistling a cheerful tune all the way to my door.

***

Gilbert Bourne was already a prebendary at St Paul's when I arrived. During Edward's reign, he appeared a Reformer, but with the winds of change that Queen Mary's ascension to the throne brought, his true colours were soon to be seen.

Bourne was chosen to preach at St Paul's Cross the week after I had done so early in August 1553. Perhaps as a result of the noise and fuss over my own preaching there the week before, the congregation that Sunday 13th August was swollen even larger. In particular our Reformer supporters came out strongly in order to show their support.

And therein lay the seeds of the drama that then unfolded.

No sooner had Bourne stepped up to the very same pulpit from which I had preached from Scripture the week before, than he embarked on a sustained and shocking recantation of Reform and defence of Papist Catholicism. Where I had sought to ground my every declaration in the truths of Scripture, Bourne had no such scruples, but spewed such lies and vitriol that so baited the Godly congregation that they began to stir and react.

I saw the same huddles of Roman Catholic sympathisers smirking and chattering amongst themselves as this scene unfolded.

It was clear to me that this was a predetermined act of provocation to bait and stir up the

Protestant congregation to the point of violence and disrepute. Cries of 'shame' and 'lies' began to be shouted out and men and women in the congregation began to stand and shake their fists at this Papist in their honoured pulpit.

Bourne would not be deterred nor waivered until his full work was done. On he went, using the most inflammatory of language to decry Reform and call for a crawling return back to damnable Papistry.

Inevitably, the congregation – a living beast itself by this stage – began to express their anger with actions, launching missiles at Bourne comprising anything they could lay their hands on.

Turmoil and uproar followed, with tussles in the congregation between Protestants and Roman Catholics.

John Bradford was a sound Reformer and a Goldy man, whose character I much admired. He was respected amongst all at St Paul's and amongst us Reformers generally. So it was no surprise to me that it was he who was first to act.

He leapt to his feet and headed up to the pulpit, calling out 'Rogers, with me!" as he did so. I responded immediately, understanding he meant for us to create a human shield between the baying beast of a crowd now and its tormentor. Whether he had singled me out for my physical attributes (I had retained my strength, though not tall I was and still am of stocky and sturdy build) or for my reputation amongst the Reformists most agitated by this onslaught – or indeed simply assured of my stout support, I know not.

Despite the disgusting language this man had used, I knew the violent response was not the way of our Lord Jesus and it saddened me to see His people tempted and provoked into sinning this way.

No sooner had we reached Bourne in the pulpit, with the beast in full war cry now, than events escalated. Where the missiles had comprised sticks, stones, rocks even – there then hurtled through the air from a source unknown a dagger, clearly intended to cause injury to Bourne. Fortunately, perhaps for all concerned, the aim amidst the boiling hurly burly was awry and rather than piercing the prattling Papist (cowering now), it caught and pinned the sleeve of his protector, Bradford.

Those closest to the front exhaled a gasp of shock at this escalation of provoked agitation to outright physical violence, which seemed to reverberate back down the back of the beast as the occurrence was relayed.

Bradford calmly used his free hand to pull out the dagger and raised it above his head.

"Church!" he shouted (he had a strong voice which was able to carry above the commotion). "Church, this is NOT the way!" he yelled, waving the dagger aloft.

I waved my arms alongside him to help tame the beast. "Blessed are the meek!" I called out, seeking to connect their hearts back with the heart of our Lord. "Blessed are the peacemakers! Do not choose the way of violence!" (Here I quoted Proverbs which the Lord brought to my mind). "Do not give the Enemy a foothold!"

At this the beast – the agitated congregation – began to subside. Seizing the moment, Bradford whispered to me loudly, "Now, John – let's go!" and together we bundled Bourne physically down the stairs of the pulpit and headed toward the nearest exit from the thronging crowd.

The congregation continued to be subdued, some praying aloud now for forgiveness (whether for their own actions or the heinous lies pronounced from the pulpit, I am not sure). "Move aside, move aside" I called out and indeed the sea of people and faces in front of us divided so we could escort Bourne toward safety.

He cowered under our protection, hiding his face until we were safely away and into an empty lane leading back into the ordinariness of London on a Sunday. If we expected Bourne to be grateful for our intervention to save him from physical violence having stirred up that very reaction that he had seemed to court, then we were to be disappointed. Once safely into the lane, he did not even speak to us, but rather straightened his cloak, then smiled over our shoulders. It was Bourne's brother and several of his priest acolytes together with Bonner himself, Bishop of London, who had followed us away from the now humming crowd and who now seemed to wear a satisfied smile.

Bonner walked straight past Bradford and myself, ignoring us, and put his arm around Bourne as he led him on down the lane and into the streets of London, chatting apparently amiably as they went.

I looked at Bradford and he raised his eyebrows at me in response.

"I fear we have been played" he said to me, with sadness in his voice.

"I believe you're right," I responded "I think our well meaning brethren may just have fallen headlong into a carefully laid trap, taking our cause for Reform with it."

"I think so, John, may the Lord protect us all. I think we've just witnessed the lighting of a touch paper that will lead to a fearful fire for Reform."

"May we be ready, my brother" I replied.
"May we be ready."

***

Reaction from the Council was swift, adding to our suspicions that there was pre-meditation to the provocation and subsequent proceedings. That very day – even though a Sunday – the Council again met at the Tower and instigated the clampdown on the freedom of us Reformers to speak out, thereby halting the cause and pushing back the Protestant tide once again.

By order of the Council, any preacher was thereby forbidden to preach or even read aloud from the Scriptures unless they had received special licence from the Queen to do so. With the Queen's religious temperament and preferences clear for all to see, we understood that this in effect silenced the voices for Reform and True Religion from the pulpits of every church in every parish across the land.

This was swiftly followed, just a few days after the event itself, on 16th August first by the disgraceful arrest of Bradford himself. The utterly spurious and outrageous charge was of inciting the crowd at St Paul's Cross to riot and attempting violence to Bourne, the harbinger of the Papist rotten rallying cry.

What lies and deceit the Roman Catholics would stoop to in order to bring us down! Having witnessed and been a party to the proceedings, I can testify that nothing could be further from the truth than this travesty of telling. Far from inciting any riot – for which the blame lay and lays so firmly on Bourne himself and any other members of his cabal – Bradford had striven only to bring peace and protect the perpetrator of the provocation.

But by now truth was a foreigner in our own land and it would not stand in the way of the will of the Council, hell bent as it now was on seeing the restoration of Papist Catholicism, the downfall of true Reform and, along with it, true Reformers.

And next it was my turn.

On the afternoon of that same 16th August, another blisteringly hot summer's day, there was a firm knock at the door of my official residence in St Paul's. I was summoned again and forthwith to stand before the Council – the same servants of Gardiner that had delivered my summons just ten days prior.

I retraced my steps to the Tower and was escorted once again to the hall where the Queen's Privy Council were expecting my presence.

In the centre, again, Norfolk – menacing and brooding. "Rogers!" he bellowed. "Back so soon?". The others laughed, but Gardiner was quickly to the point.

He stood and stated formally, "You are summoned before this Council for your continued sedition and disloyalty to the Crown, despite our previous warnings. You stand accused of preaching heresy and of inciting riot. What say you?"

The attack was swift and direct, but I was prepared.

"My Lord," I replied calmly, but firmly, "I deny any such charge and remind you and the rest of this august Council that we have been over these issues just ten days ago, when you saw fit to let me leave and return about my business ..."

Gardiner interrupted me then, "The Council did no such thing! It is typical of you to seek to misconstrue our encounter and telling that you choose so arrogantly to defy us."

I deemed it best to remain silent.

Gardiner seemed disappointed not to be able to continue the duel, that was so weighted in his favour with the power and bias of the Council behind him.

"Do you deny that you were present at the disgraceful scenes at St Paul's Cross three days ago on 13th August when poor Bourne was prevented from fulfilling his duty under Queen Mary to preach the repentance and return to Catholicism of the English people, as now decreed by this very Council?"

"I do not deny that I was present, that you know" I replied, turning slowly to look Bonner directly in the eyes, knowing he had witnessed both my presence and active, pacifying role. I continued, "But I categorically deny any involvement in incitement to riot – your envoy Bourne needed no help with that."

At this the room erupted in uproar, with so many calling out and shouting I could not make out any particular sense, although I sensed the meaning.

"No involvement? No involvement?" it was Bonner himself this time. "And yet it is strange, is it not, that the crowd – so animated, so angry, so violent – should at just a few words from yourself and your co-conspiritor Bradford become becalmed, quiet and acquiescent?" The rest of the Council nodded and mumbled their approval for this direction of enquiry.

Emboldened by the peer support, Bonner warmed to his theme. "It would seem to me, sirs ..." he was playing to his audience now, "... that Matthew here ..." – much guffawing and loud hilarity at my expense – "... that Matthew here had that baying wild crowd of ruffians and heretics very much in his own pocket! How quickly they responded to your direction, to your instruction – as if, almost as if ... you had pre-arranged every over-reaction, every jeer, perhaps even every missile – who should throw what,

210

when, even until the last throw of the dagger, so skilfully aimed to cause drama and effect, but not harm! Was it so, Rogers? Was it so, Matthew?"

I could barely hear the final insults as these men – holding he highest offices in the realm – banged the table in delight, in anger (mock or authentic, I could not tell) and shouted their condemnation at me.

Bonner, who had risen to his feet as his verbal assault on me ascended, sat back down, apparently spent and satisfied that he had landed the lethal blow.

"A compelling vision," ventured Gardiner, complimenting his fellow collaborator, "so Matthew ..." – more subdued chuckling this time – "... do you deny it?"

"I do" I replied simply.

And let the simplicity of truth speak for itself.

This angered Gardiner, but seemed the trigger for what had clearly been predetermined as he snatched some papers and began to read from them. "John Rogers, alias Matthew, as a seditious preacher you are ordered by the Lords of the Council to keep yourself prisoner in your house at St Paul's, without conference of any person other than such that are daily in your household until such time as a contrary commandment is received. Now get out of our sight."

And so it was that my confinement began.

At this stage I was effectively placed under house arrest, confined to my official residence at St Paul's – ironically virtually opposite the residence of my now enemy, Bishop Bonner.

I was relieved – and a little surprised – that I had not been instructed directly to prison, as had happened to Bradford. Such was the summary nature of the injustice being committed in the cause of returning the land to the pestilence of Roman Catholicism that it seemed any crime could be accused and forthwith determined by the Council for that purpose. The law barely could keep up with the evil crusade – but little did that matter.

For the time being, I committed myself to praying for steadfastness and thanked the Lord for the relative freedoms afforded me. One such was to be able still to see and speak with my dear wife, falling within the definition of my household.

It was several days later, in the evening, that we were again able to share our inner most thoughts by the hearth in privacy, to take on and digest recent events together.

"But it's just so unfair!" Adriana cried out,
when I relayed the conversations of the Council
proceedings to her and in particular Bonner's
version of events. "How could he say that when
he saw what happened with his own eyes? We ALL
did! And you did nothing wrong, only helped to
save the skin of that wretched man Bourne and
PREVENT further discord!"

"I know my love," I sought to placate her, "but we
know what's really happening here, don't we?"

"Do we?" she asked, not at all sure.

I reminded her of Paul's letter to the people of
Ephesus, "Paul spoke for us all when he wrote 'For
our struggle is not against the flesh and blood,
but against the rulers, against the authorities,
against the powers of this dark world and against
the spiritual forces of evil in the heavenly realms'.
Bonner, Gardiner, Norfolk – all of them are pawns
in the devil's game to lead us astray and away
from the light. Their eyes are blinded to truth,
even when it is right before them."

"That talk scares me, John", she replied, tears
welling in her eyes. "If it be so then our situation
is even more terrifying than having the entire
Privy Council against us!"

I took her hands in mine and looked at her
directly, loving everything about her all over
again. "No, no, Adriana" I comforted her, "don't

you see, it's quite the opposite! If it is only the devil who stands behind this then we know – we KNOW, Adriana – that our God stands so much greater and stronger than he! We just need to do as James tells us and 'Submit ourselves to God, resist the devil and he will flee from us!'"

"You make it sound so simple, John ..." she began.

"It IS simple, darling," I jumped in, "that's what is so wonderful about this Good News we have!"

"But is there another way?" she asked, looking at me with pleading eyes.

"Another way?" I asked, suspicious of what was coming next.

"Rather than waiting for the devil to flee from us, what if WE were to flee from HIM?" she asked, a glint in her eye of hope.

I had to smile at her quick wittedness. But I shook my head slowly, although before I could speak she continued – sensing perhaps that this was her last opportunity to seek escape from the oncoming storm.

"Just think about it, John!" she implored. "Bradford was sent to prison, directly, yes?"

"Yes," I replied, "but ..."

"And Hill, Green, Johnson and numerous others of our Reformer ilk have been sent direct to prison, yes?" she continued, breathless.

"Yes ..." I replied hesitantly.

"And yet others, John ..." she looked at me coyly, seeming to be starting to lose her confidence, " ... others have already fled this country to the safety of the continent, where believing the true Gospel is no crime and does not get punished!"

I sighed, "Adriana ...." I began, but she cut me off for her final attempt.

"Think about it John! Why have they only put you under house arrest, without even a guard at the door? Does that mean they would be content, really, if you DID just remove yourself from their sight – for good this time? Could THAT be the Lord's hand, husband dear, offering us a chance of escape from this nightmare? Imagine ... imagine, John, the good work you could do for the Lord back in Meldorf! Imagine the welcome you would receive on our return!"

I was silent a moment.

She drew breath.

And then the devil lay down his final card.

"And imagine the good life our children could have under the free skies of Germany!"

At this I stood up and released her hands.

"Get thee behind me Satan!" I declared.

I was not speaking to her at this point and I
believe she understood that and did not mistake
my meaning. "I renounce the lie that the
protection of me and my family is in my own
hands only and declare that the Lord's will be
done in all of this! I have stated the truths
revealed to me by the Lord and by Scripture and
on those I will stand. I have preached His Word
and renounced the lies and deceits of the Papist
Church – this is my life's work! **And I am ready to
seal this with my blood!"**

Adriana was crying now, but acquiescent. I
looked down at her and my love for her was so
very great.

"My darling wife!" I said softly and lifted her into
my embrace. "I am sorry to speak harshly in front
of you, but I think you know why. The devil has
followed me from the Tower and is tempting me
to take the easy path with the very things I hold
most dear in all of this world. I must stand firm
against him and stand up for what I have
preached and lived for since my rebirth in Christ.
All is not lost. I will be obedient to the direction of
the Council and stand ready to defend myself by
arguing my cause based on the Scriptures when
given the chance. And if justice is to be served in

this world, then I may yet be freed again and we'll see our happy, family times return."

She nodded whilst not leaving our embrace. "I know, my husband, I know. Forgive my weakness – you know my failing is the very strength of love I have for you and our beloved children. But I would place them all under the protection of the Lord our God. I put my trust in Him, as I know you would have it."

She looked up at me, tears gone now.

"We will do as you require, dear husband. I love you so very much. Ever have I loved and admired your strength of faith and it is my life's work to emulate that. Whatever we face now, we face together."

And we sealed that agreement with a kiss.

***

It was not long after this that Queen Mary herself made a Proclamation, the tone of which might have led us to hope, were it not for the actions of her Councillors that we saw with our own eyes. Her Majesty called on both parties – Roman Catholics and Protestants - to exercise tolerance with one another, not to accuse the one of idolatry nor the other of heresy, but to allow Parliament to settle the fiery and inflammatory

issues (as if they were spiritually and
academically equipped so to do!).

Beneath the royal velvet glove, the steel fist
of her Council, as they ensured that their own
declaration the previous Sunday prohibiting
the preaching or reading of the Scriptures by
Protestants was formalised.

By this time I was shackled by my containment,
but my Protestant brethren too were silenced by
the force of those now wielding the reins of power
in the land. Even to discuss the actions of the
Queen or Council was then prohibited by royal
proclamation.

**Truly the voice of Reform in England had been
silenced.**

But actions can speak louder than words!

For some the testing proved too much. I was
sorry to hear report that Northumberland, who
had so boldly championed, defended and led the
cause of Reform under King Edward, failed at the
last. Perhaps he hoped, in a moment of weakness
of the flesh, that he might be pardoned and save
his earthly body by recanting of all truths that
the Lord had revealed to him and crawling back
to the vile embrace of Papist Catholicism.

But even that did not save him in this world.
And in that moment of weakness he had

jeopardised his security in the next. May God have mercy on his soul.

The blood was up for these Papists and they would take their revenge.

It was a lesson I noted well.

Meanwhile I bided my time in the constraints of my official residence, occasionally seeing the comings and goings of the other prebendaries and of Bonner himself. Whenever I saw him I forced myself to pray for his soul, that the Lord would soften his heart and reveal his love truly to him. But I found it hard to pray with conviction, knowing the hard heartedness of the man and the degree of rancour that had accumulated in his soul due to the manner in which he himself was treated during the high tide of Reform.

I knew that his hatred of me was great, perhaps especially because of the role I had played in unleashing the power of the Word in our native tongue with the Thomas Matthew Bible. I was saddened that a priest could so misunderstand the Gospel that they should take such a stance, but reminded myself constantly that 'our struggle was not against flesh and blood'. Bonner and even Gardiner – all of the Privy Council, chosen for their weakness and superstition - were but pawns in the devil's schemes.

But I was shocked that autumn when the devil's
hand seized not just the Privy Council – a
relatively small group of men, hand picked for
their proclivity toward Papism – but Parliament
itself. It was as the leaves of the hornbeam trees
in the courtyard outside my rooms were turning
a burned amber and beginning to fall that I had
message that, true to Queen Mary's word, the
core matters of faith had been put before
Parliament for debate.

I would have hoped that enough seed by then
had fallen on fertile ground that a robust
scriptural argument for Reform could be made
(oh how I wish I could have been given the
platform to make it!). But it transpired that
Parliament itself had been stony ground and
weak hearts and feeble minds quickly fell into line
with the political pragmatism of following the
religious leanings of the new monarch and her
Council.

So it was that of 350 men, only 80 stood firm
against the abolition of all of the Victories for
Christ scored under King Edward, pushing the
tide back to the low ebb of King Henry's last
years. Soon the vile mass had returned as had
the unscriptural use of Latin used to deceive
congregations and mask the true heart of the
Romish Church.

The irony was not lost on me that Adriana and
I would never have come to England and brought

the children to my land of birth under such a
regime – not meeting as it did our own criteria
for safe passage.

But that was then and the Lord's ways are not
our ways.

It is perhaps worthy of mention at this stage
how I come to know details of the proceedings
in the nation during this time when I was not
allowed to convene with anyone outside my
household. I was careful to be scrupulously and
visibly compliant to this, not wanting to provide
my accusers with anything that they could in
future hold against me. This did not stop me
getting news from my wife and household
servants, however – and in turn there was no
apparent prohibition on Adriana speaking feely
herself with my friends and other Reformers to
provide me with news and updates on the state
of affairs outside the four walls that now
constrained me, albeit in relative comfort.

There were several such trusted souls who took
pity on my plight and furnished Adriana with
the news I craved, although for the most part
that pained me to hear. These generous folk,
although not directly contravening any law or
proclamation, were risking their reputations
in so doing – and indeed now, more so than ever,
continue to do so now that my plight has
worsened and I no longer have contact with my
dear wife (but have found other means to

received their information). I am deeply grateful to them for this and ask that the Lord bless them for it and protect them and their families.

I will not now divulge their names in order to maintain their anonymity and in their anonymity their safety. Nor shall I divulge the names of the prison guards who now sympathise with me and act as the conduit for the same now that my contact with my wife has been forbidden. For although I am deeply cautious with this manuscript and have plans to keep it from those that would do supporters of our cause harm, I cannot be sure these writings will not fall into the hands of my enemies.

I pray that will not happen and that this record of events that occurred to me under the Lord's will shall survive and enlighten and encourage future true believers.

***

It was around this time that two of my boys – Samuel and Philip, respectively our fourth and fifth children – sought in their own, misguided and childish ways to strike a blow themselves for our Reformist cause. This brought a mixture of amusement and pride to me, but shock and distress to Adriana and our girls, especially.

I tell the tale to give you an insight into the intimacy of our family life – and, if truth be known, for some light relief for me in the retelling of the tale in my current, constrained state here in Newgate prison.

It was our little girls, Susie and Lizzie who first raised the alarm. They had heard a commotion in the street outside our family home not a hundred yards from St Sepulchre's. They pleaded with their mother to be able to go out and see what all the commotion was about.

"We'll go together mother, we promise!" pleaded Susie, who would have been about six years old at the time (but was always mature for her age, perhaps the result of being the eldest girl).

"And I'll hold Susie's hand the whole way!" promised little Elizabeth, no more than four at the time and very much Susie's shadow.

"Neither of you are going anywhere unescorted!" replied Adriana.

"John can take us!" replied Susie, quick as a flash.

"What's that?" replied John, hearing his name being used and coming into the room.

"The girls are desperate to see what all the fuss is about outside." Explained Adriana, at which point a great surge of laughter came in through the window.

"PLEASE!" cried Lizzie, grabbing her older brother's hand and hugging it tight. John was always close to the girls and had a kind heart.

"Come on then, I'll take you," he said, "but on the strict condition we come back when I say so!"

"Yes, yes!" cried both Susie and Lizzie in unison as they rushed to the door.

"Take care now," admonished their mother, "and girls, you do what Johnny tells you!"

"We will, mother! We will!" they called out and their voices disappeared with them out of the door.

John later explained the scene that they came across virtually outside our front windows. A crowd was continuing to gather, with ribald laughter intermingled with lone shouts of "Shame!", "Lord, forgive us!".

The girls had run on ahead of John and slipped between the adults crowding around a crab apple tree that grew alongside the road. The next thing John heard was high pitched screaming, in unison. It took a moment for John to register that the squeals emanated from his sisters – but when he did, his heart raced and he sprinted toward them, pushing aside the onlookers.

When he caught sight of his sisters again, tears were streaming down their faces and the screaming had evolved to weeping. John swept them up in his arms before taking in the scene before them.

Hanging over one of the lower branches of the tree was a thin rope, on the end of which was a dead cat.

It was a black cat, with white front paws and a white tip on its tail.

John recognised it as a stray that was often seen around St Sepulchre's – he'd even had occasion to shoo it out of the church on his father's behest in the past. The sight of this dead cat hanging would in itself have caused more disgust than amusement, but it was what had been done to the cat that caused the merriment for some.

The cat had been carefully dressed in the garish garments of a Papist priest.

White handkerchiefs had been sown together for a cassock, with space for little front legs and little white paws to come through, giving the appearance of white gloves. A thick red material with golden embroidery made up a tiny cape for the front and back. And adorning the cat's head, with some additional wooden sticks in support was a miniature mitre – with cuts made to allow the little black ears to pop through giving a most comical appearance.

"Come away girls" John encouraged his sisters as he led them back toward the rectory. As he did so, he saw two of his younger brothers duck their heads below he wall of our next door neighbour. Whilst he could no longer see them, he could hear their uncontrolled giggles ... and his suspicions were confirmed.

The girls ran to their mother for comfort as soon as they came in the house.

"Whatever is the matter?" asked Adriana, looking to John for explanation.

John explained calmly, "Some fools have thought it funny to kill that poor black cat with the white front paws, dress it up in Papist garb and hang him from the Grangers' crab apple tree." Adriana raised her hand to her mouth in disgusted alarm. But the three younger boys, Bernard, Augustine and Barnaby, on hearing this each dashed for the door to go and see for themselves. (Boys will always have a ghoulish interest in death and animals, it strikes me!).

"Boys, no ..." Adriana called in vain, as the boys were already out of the door and running at speed down the pathway to see for themselves.

Daniel, our eldest, and Ambrose (son number three), came ambling in from the adjoining parlour. "What's going on?" asked Daniel, casually. The girls weeping had subsided by now and their eyes were wide with the dreadful thrill and excitement of it all.

John repeated what he had told his mother.

"But mother ..." John began, then hesitated.

"Yes, John, what is it you want to say?" prompted Adriana, already with a sense of foreboding.

"I saw Sam and Philip hiding behind the Granger's wall." John stated, unsure how much further detail to provide.

"Oh yes," replied his mother, "is that so strange? I'm sure they're interested but a little anxious, with all of those people crowding around." Ambrose laughed at this, knowing his next two younger brothers to be made of tougher – and more mischievous – stuff!

"No, mother" explained John, "it's not that. The red embroidered material the poor cat was dressed in ..." - he paused again, knowing emotions were about to escalate - "... it's the same material as our old curtains you replaced just last week."

John watched as his mother's eyes grew wide with realisation.

"They've gone too far this time!" she exclaimed through gritted teeth. "Daniel, fetch your younger brothers back this moment, I will speak to them in the parlour".

Daniel disappeared immediately out of the door, followed by Ambrose, perhaps keen to warn his younger brothers to beware their mother's wrath. Daniel had each younger brother by the scruff of the neck as he presented them to his mother, who was seated straight backed at the head of the table.

"You will sit here and explain it all to me" she stated, ice cold and seething with anger.

"Mother, mother, it's not what you think ..." started Philip. But his mother interrupted him, "You have no idea what I think, young man! With your father confined in his official residence, here I am left to try and hold house and home together. To keep up our good standing in the neighbourhood and amongst our congregation ..."

Samuel saw an opportunity, "But mother, that's exactly ..."

"QUIET! While your mother is speaking!" barked Adriana. She really could be quite fearsome when riled – but then I think she has had to be with such a large brood as ours and with so many boys. "Here I am, doing my best to hold the household together in these most trying and dangerous of times, with your father detained for a righteous cause and you ... you ..." She turned her head away and sought to compose herself.

"What were you thinking?" picked up Daniel, ever the diplomat. "Sam, Philip? Why did you do this?"

Sam took his opportunity. "With father shut away we thought we could take up the Cause!" he began. Adriana looked at him and gave him the chance to speak. "If father can't explain to people how rotten the Papist church is – and if no one can as it's not allowed in church – then we thought we could find another way. And it's working – everyone is crowded round laughing!"

"But the pussy cat!" cried out Susie, who was crowding in at the door with her siblings. "You killed that poor cat for a stupid joke!" she accused her brother, and then began to sob again.

"No!" countered Sam, "No, we didn't kill it! Honestly mother ..." he looked pleadingly at his mother, "... we'd never hurt a living thing! We found it dead behind the Grangers' wall and then had the idea to dress it up to make fun of the stupid Papists! Tell them Philip, tell them!"

Philip was nodding furiously, "Yes mother, honest, we didn't kill it, we just found it!"

Their mother did believe them. She was relieved, but would not so easily let them off for their misdemeanour.

"Well that's something, at least" she began. "But there's still no excuse for treating a dead animal with such ridicule and cruelty .."

"But mother ..." began Sam.

"No Sam, let me finish. It was cruel and heartless and an unchristian thing to do. I understand you meant to make a point and were trying to support your father ..." - she paused as she felt her emotions rise – "... and I thank you for that. But it is also VERY dangerous for you to meddle in things you don't understand. Leave that to the adults. Now go to your room and stay there until supper. Instead of using poor, innocent dead animals to try and be clever, you would do far better to get onto your knees in prayer and ask the Lord to protect Reform and to protect your father. Go on, up you go!"

The boys turned and scampered out of the room, relieved their punishment had not been worse. Adriana instructed Daniel to go and remove the cat and to see it buried – without it's Papist garments.

Adriana told me all of this when she visited me at St Paul's that evening. I tried not to laugh – she was still not amused. So I tutted and shook my head at the appropriate moments and sought to console her and acknowledge the burden she was under maintaining our brood alone.

But all the while, secretly, I was SO proud of my boys !

***

Chapter 8 – London, Newgate Prison

I heard report of other small acts of resistance such as that staged by my Sam and Philip, but apart from providing some short respite of cheer and hope, it was becoming increasingly clear that the tide was fast receding for Reform in England. Greater structural shifts or Godly interventions were required if that tide was to be turned before Romish Catholicism rose yet higher.

One such opportunity appeared briefly to come in the form of the uprising led by one Thomas Wyatt from Kent. It was never quite clear to me how much this uprising was truly in the cause of Reform and how much a reaction to the likelihood that the Mary Queen of England would marry Philip, heir to the Spanish throne. Mary met this threat from within with strength and dignity, which no doubt played a significant part in her ability to raise a significant army of London citizens to defend their sovereign.

Was she at any point tempted to flee for her own personal safety?

If she was, she showed no sign, which so inspired Londoners – naturally suspicious of Kentish men in any case – that they stood firm alongside their queen. London Bridge was closed off to Wyatt, who circled around to the south to attack from Kingston. But the Queen's cavalry split his troops and whittled down the attack until their cause was lost.

Any hope that armed resistance might bring back Reform was lost. That was not to be God's will. I had not dared hope too greatly that God would use Wyatt to overturn the threats of Roman Catholicism in England. I could not reconcile opposition to the Lord's Anointed Monarch for such a Godly cause.

But it was still hard to contemplate that my own predicament was not to be alleviated.

Retribution followed for the treacherous rebels, with countless hangings. Although Queen Mary further endeared herself to her people – and Londoners in particular – by pardoning many hundred rebels also, thereby switching their allegiance and that of their families back in Kent.

She showed herself to be a wise monarch at that point – which gives me some small hope that Her Majesty may yet show me mercy.

But first my situation significantly worsened.

Was it as a result of the increased anxiety of the Council following Wyatt's rebellion, so that I am a victim of the broad political sweep of history in this land? Or was it something more mundane and personal?

I had noticed that Bonner had grown increasingly agitated at seeing me watch him as he moved in and out of his own lodgings at St Paul's. I was in the habit of sitting by the front window of my lodgings, to give me some sense at least of what was happening outside my doors. This gave me a clear view of the Bishop of London's own lodgings diagonally across the courtyard – and I admit to finding it of interest to see who was coming and leaving his home, speculating what reason each may have to visit. Perhaps that was inappropriate, but with so little else to occupy me I had little else to do.

It was two days prior to my move that I had been watching Bonner arrive with Gardiner and several of his entourage that he caught my eye through the window – not for the first time. He immediately became agitated and gesticulated toward Gardiner, who also glanced in my direction, as did his colleagues. Having been held under effective house arrest for nearly six months and having done so honestly, diligently and sticking to the restrictions placed on me, I was beyond embarrassment by this point. Indeed, I perhaps invited them to hold my gaze and let my situation rest again on their consciences.

But rather than lead to any alleviation of my predicament, instead my circumstances took a turn for the worse.

On 27th January of this year (1554) around eight in the morning, there was a loud, aggressive and insistent banging on my door. I was at prayer, but rose to answer the door myself, with a sense of foreboding. At my door was a small guard of four persons, dressed in Gardiner's livery.

"John Rogers?" barked the leader of this small gang, the smallest by a fair distance, holding a staff, perhaps to increase his sense presence and obviously the source of the racket on my door.

I nodded and stated simply, "It is I".

He seemed to push out his chest and take a deep breath as he thrust a paper before me. "By order of the Privy Council you are to accompany us with immediate effect to Newgate Prison" he announced loudly, whilst the three guardsmen shifted uneasily behind him.

"On what charge?" I replied, feeling the blood pulse through my veins, but seeking to conceal my natural alarm.

"For the protection of the realm, Mr Rogers" he replied.

"I am but a priest, living quietly at my home as instructed ..." I began to protest. But the captain interrupted, thrusting the paper into my chest for me to take a hold.

"I am not here to argue your case, Rogers, only to escort you to Newgate by order of the Privy Council. You may come with us peacefully now, but I must tell you that if you do not I am authorised to take you there by whatever force is necessary."

He was reddening in the face now, uncertain of my reaction and perhaps anticipating conflict. I saw that there was no merit in arguing with the man, who was after all simply carrying out his duty. I held my hand up with my palm before him to give myself a moment as I glanced at the paper he had handed me that now held such power over my future.

I could not take in the full text, but the words "Newgate prison", "forthwith", "danger to the realm" leaped out at me – as did the flowing signature at the bottom of the page. "Stephen Gardiner, Lord Chancellor".

I nodded.

There seemed little point in that moment disputing the legality of such an arrest.

And the captain seemed to relax a little.

"I shall collect my things", I conceded. The captain tensed again.

"I am instructed to take you forthwith, sir! You are to come with us now" he insisted. At this point, little Susan appeared from behind me, clutching my leg and peering up at these intruders.

"Who are these men?" Susan asked, innocently, but with a hint of alarm in her voice.

"You go back and fetch mummy, Suzy"
I instructed her gently, as I peeled her off my leg and nudged her gently back toward the parlour. "Daddy needs to go with these men for work now, but I need to speak with mummy before I go." As I said this I glanced at the captain, hoping he would concede this last dialogue and the chance to say farewell to my wife.

Suzy ran off to fetch her mother, who came hurrying to me at the door. She had a quizzical look on her face, seeking reassurance from me, but beginning to fear the worse.

"John? Who are these men?" she asked. The captain began to speak, but I raised my hand again to quieten him. I wanted her to hear from me rather than this unknown guard.

"It's time." I stated simply. We had discussed how things might turn out and knew there was a real possibility that my relative comfort in house arrest might soon be replaced by more formal imprisonment. Still, Adriana's eyes widened in alarm as she immediately grasped my meaning. "I have to go with them now. Newgate." Adriana's eyes widened further and she looked as if she was about to protest. But I raised both hands and rested them on her shoulders, looking her directly in the eyes.

"It's alright, darling" I sought to reassure her. "The Lord is with me and I am prepared for this next stage. These men have said that I may accompany them freely, but I do need to go with them now." Adriana nodded, holding back the tears.

"Please fetch me my Bible ..." I began, but the captain pushed forward his staff and announced. "No Bible! I am under strict instructions to bring you as you are to Newgate. You can discuss with the warden there any particulars you need."

"But he is a man of God ..." began Adriana, seeking to defend me and argue my cause, knowing my reliance on the Word of God for my daily sustenance.

"Shhhhhh", I calmed her. "Adriana, it's fine. I'll arrange for my things to be brought to me once I've settled in my new lodgings. I have enough knowledge of His Word to carry me through the coming days. And Adriana ....?"

She looked back at me, with the same love in her eyes that she had carried for so many years – and my heart leaped again with my love for her and gratitude for the life we had had together.

I smiled.

And she smiled weakly back.

"You know who to tell" I said. We had discussed how to spread word of any developments in my situation so that we could receive the prayer support we needed and our friends and supporters could be rallied to help in my defence.

"Yes, my dear" she replied. She glanced at the captain, but then returned her gaze to me. "I love you, John Rogers" she stated simply. And she leant over to me, grasped both of my hands in hers and kissed me briefly on the cheek, as if I was simply going to matins.

"Time to go!" announced the captain.

"And God bless you all too" she managed to say to the group of guards, without a hint of irony – and I was proud of her for her Christian sentiment.

"Goodbye my dear. I'll send word" I promised. And then to the captain, "Lead on then sir, I am at your disposal and will comply fully with your instructions." He nodded and led the way, with two of the guard holding back nonetheless to follow me from behind, ensuring that I could not slip away even if I had been minded to do so.

Adriana waved at me from the door, with Suzy and now Lizzie too wrapped around her legs. Such a pretty picture and one I had seen so many times as my wife would wave me off to some mundane appointment.

And yet this appointment was far from mundane.

I knew not then and still know not how this story will end.

Although I am beginning to suspect the outcome.

***

It was but a short walk from my lodgings at St Paul's to Newgate prison – a walk I had done myself a hundred times or more as I would travel between my official lodgings and our family home by St Sepulchre's.

But it had never felt like this.

I was more alert to every person we passed, aware of the hustle and bustle of the street and of the traders shouting out in advertisement of their wares. Life seemed to be continuing just as before, as if my long five months in house confinement had passed unnoticed by anyone.

But I also felt the eyes on me, bringing me an unwanted and unwarranted sense of shame – what a strange sight it must have been, a man of the cloth escorted by an armed guard. I wonder how many of those we passed stopped to think what cause there could be to treat me so? I did pass one or two of my parishioners, who looked both surprised and alarmed to see me in such bizarre and changed circumstances. One managed to get his wits about him and called out to me, "God be with you, John Rogers – be strong in the Lord, Pastor!".

I was deeply grateful to him for that and returned a smile, seeking to convey that I was indeed strong in the Lord and trusting in Him.

But I did not speak, out of respect for the task of my guard to bring me to Newgate safely and without incident.

I had visited Newgate on numerous occasions in my pastoral role at St Sepulchre's, being in such close proximation as it was. Indeed several of the gaolers were parishioners - and indeed friends – of mine (which in due course was to prove a great blessing).

So it was strange indeed to be arriving under guard and as the prisoner, not the visiting priest.

Although the gaolers I was handed over to by the captain and his guard were not known to me, it was obvious that my gaoler friends had informed their colleagues of my standing ahead of my arrival.

I was treated well – as well as could have been expected in the circumstances – and escorted to the room allocated to me. It was dark, cold and damp – but I knew, having visited other parts of the gaol as a priest, that it was relative comfort compared to other parts of the prison where the poor, destitute and seriously criminal convicts were herded together.

I said a prayer of blessing as I entered the room and waited on the Lord for any sense of what He wanted from me whilst I was here. I did receive a sense of calm and was reminded of the many times the apostle Paul faced prison and how his joy and passion for the Lord never waned.

I asked the Lord to give me such resilience and that I should be as his light to the others in this dark and dismal place – gaolers and prisoners alike.

I was provided with meals twice daily, in a hall where other prisoners of my standing, kept in the same wing of the prison, were allowed to come together to eat. Thus it was that I learned that even if my gaoling was personally motivated by Bonner, it was also part of a broader crack down on us Reformers. Thus over the coming days and weeks I was to meet many others gaoled for their stance and refusal to bow the knee to the Roman Church.

We were able to share news of mutual acquaintances and I learned of many, many others who had opted to escape this land to the relative freedoms on the continent, just as I had done some twenty years ago.

I did not blame them for leaving.

Each person must follow their own conscience and the Lord's guiding, just as I had done.

But I had – and have – no regrets in not fleeing myself this time.

I felt the Lord's presence strongly with me and felt his purpose for me – not only as Reverend John Rogers, of St Paul's and St Sepulchre, but also as Thomas Matthew, complier of the first authorised English Bible – to make my stand in His name.

What an honour to do so!

The more I spent time in my cell, in prayer and in the presence of the Lord, the greater this sense of mission – this privilege of mission! – grew.

Gradually my gaoler parishioners were able to speak with me, as our paths crossed due to their allotted duties and with their help I was able to hatch two plans.

Firstly, I felt convicted to demonstrate the love of Jesus to ALL who were in this dreadful place. Knowing how much worse were the conditions for my now-fellow prisoners in the other parts of the gaol, I collaborated with my fellow Protestants to forego one of our two meals a day so that the food might be shared instead with those poor, wretched souls.

Initially I met with some resistance from some who pointed out what great sinners these people were – truly thieves, vagabonds and even murderers. But I pointed out that before the Lord we are all sinners, with no crime so great that Jesus' forgiveness could not be ours, all of ours. Indeed, it was exactly for that purpose that I was proposing this act of sacrifice, so that the message of the love of Jesus, demonstrated in this simple act, might break through into the lives of these wretched people and that they might know salvation, before it was too late for them.

With the cooperation of my gaoler parishioners and their trusted colleagues, we began this new routine. And although there was indeed sacrifice in having an empty stomach for much of the day, we sensed the Lord's blessing over us for our small act of kindness.

The second, more risky endeavour – for my gaoler parishioners especially – was none other than the notion to write up these memoirs of my life. I will not name who helped me with this plan, in case this manuscript falls into the wrong hands. But it was only a few weeks in to my time here at Newgate that a good, dear friend here was able to procure me paper, pen and ink to commence this task.

I will forever be deeply grateful and indebted to him for that, because this exercise had helped me greatly both in passing the hours and in seeing afresh how the Lord has worked in my life – such a blessed life! – over so many years.

I knew that if certain parties in the prison were to find out about my privileges, they would not only be confiscated from me, but also the manuscript destroyed: and perhaps worse, those that aided me found out and punished accordingly.

In order to avoid the loss of the manuscript I had laboured on to date, at least, we devised a plan whereby I would hide the latest sheaths in my sleeve when taking air in the courtyard on the occasions one of my supporters was on sentry there. I had noticed some loose brickwork when strolling there one morning and had managed to remove several of the bricks and find a cavity behind that would be perfect for housing my manuscript until such time as we could find a way to release it into the world, perhaps on my release. Or should that not be God's will, via my supporters collaborating to bring it out into the world.

Thus I embarked upon the work you are reading now, starting with the Foreward and working my way chronologically through my life, as you will have read.

So now I write to you in the present.

My tale may become rather less expansive, restricted as I am now to these four walls, although the privilege I have still to meet with my fellow prisoners, mostly Reformers, gives me some rich encounters to pass on to you. And I plan to share my reflections with you on what limited information we are receiving about what is happening outside these walls.

***

It was with great sadness that I heard report of the execution of the poor young Lady Jane Grey, very soon after my own imprisonment at Newgate. Whilst I deplored the manner in which she was used for traitorous ends against the true Queen Mary by those powerful men, she was surely but an innocent pawn in the grand game

of national politics, power and greed. May the
Lord grant her peace now as she rests with him. I
hear that as she approached her death place with
braveness beyond her years, she held fast to her
faith and held firm in her trust of the Lord,
reciting the 51st Psalm, the Psalm Miserere.

I was prompted then to re-read that Psalm using
the Bible that one of my congregants had
managed to smuggle in to my cell, thanks be to
God. Although I already know the Psalm
verbatim as it is already committed to my heart
and I could recite it, I find that reading it from
the Scriptures allows the Holy Spirit to speak to
me afresh about new depths to its meaning.

I wept as I read it.

Thinking of that trembling girl preparing to
meet her maker at such a tender age and before
her life had been able to blossom and bloom.

**And all too aware, that I myself might soon face
that same moment of testing and truth.**

PSALM 51
Have mercy on me, O God,
    according to your unfailing love;
according to your great compassion
    blot out my transgressions.
Wash away all my iniquity
    and cleanse me from my sin.

I pray that the Lady Jane Grey went to meet her Lord confident that her Saviour Jesus Christ had done everything necessary to make this cleansing complete and real. So she would be presented to our Lord unblemished and clean, fit to spend an eternity of bliss in the comfort and wonder of her creator.

I thank God that I have that same outrageous claim on forgiveness through Christ.

> For I know my transgressions,
>> and my sin is always before me.
> Against you, you only, have I sinned
>> and done what is evil in your sight:
> so you are right in your verdict
>> and justified when you judge.
> Surely I was sinful at birth,
>> sinful from the time my mother conceived me.
> Yet you desired faithfulness even in the womb;
>> you taught me wisdom in that secret place.

Although it was the Papist Catholics currently wielding power in England that put Lady Jane to the sword to meet her end, her sins were against the Lord only, as are all of the sons and daughters of Adam and Eve.

If my time comes to face my death at the hands of man, still I shall claim that it is only the Lord I must answer to for my sins. Everything I have done in His name, for which I am prepared to offer up my life, in the name of Reform and bringing His truth to the people of this land I neither regret nor renounce. And through the Lord Jesus Christ I will be presented to our Father not as a Sinner, but as a Saint who sinned and whose sins are wiped clean by the blood of Christ. Amen.

> Cleanse me with hyssop, and I will be clean;
>> wash me, and I will be whiter than snow.
> Let me hear joy and gladness;
>> let the bones you have crushed rejoice.
> Hide your face from my sins
>> and blot out all my iniquity.

May the Lady Jane meet her maker whiter than snow, pure and untainted by her sins thanks to the saving and unsurpassing Grace of Jesus.

And I, who have lived many times the lives of Lady Jane, child as she was – may I also know that unearned privilege of having my numerous (too numerous to count or list!) sins hidden from our Father God when I come into his awesome and fearful presence. I am reminded at this time – perhaps it is the prompting of the Holy Spirit? – of Jesus's parable of the lost son. And how, after the younger son had squandered his inheritance, rejecting his father, dishonouring him and disgracing him, finding himself utterly lost and without hope, he finally came to his senses, repented and returned to his father's estate in the hope of living out a life as a lowly servant. Did his father reject him? Did he send him away or have him beaten? NO ! Rather, while the son was still a long way off, the father - clearly constantly scanning the horizon in hope and love - tucks up his garments and runs – RUNS! – to greet his beloved son with the warmest of embraces.

So the Lord will have greeted the Lady Jane.

Oh, may he so greet meet me!

> Create in me a pure heart, O God,
> > and renew a steadfast spirit within me.
> Do not cast me from your presence
> > or take your Holy Spirit from me.
> Restore to me the joy of your salvation
> > and grant me a willing spirit, to sustain me.

I thank the Lord that he so sustained the Lady Jane through to her final end on this earth and pray that she knows now the full joy of presence with the Lord and the full wonder of being able to see our Lord Jesus Christ finally face to face.

What unsurpassing joy that will be! How wonderful that He should have suffered so much, have given up everything – even He, the Son of God! – to face such shame and pain and horror and disgrace and anger and hatred, he faced it all ... to be able to meet us face to face in the presence of His loving Father! He did it all to meet YOU face to face.

He did it all to meet ME face to face!

What joy awaits!

> Then I will teach transgressors your ways,
>   so that sinners will turn back to you.
> Deliver me from the guilt of bloodshed, O God,
>   you who are God my Saviour,
>   and my tongue will sing of your righteousness.
> Open my lips, Lord,
>   and my mouth will declare your praise.
> You do not delight in sacrifice, or I would bring it:
>   you do not take pleasure in burnt offerings.

May the example of His daughter, the Lady Jane encourage and inspire all true Christians and indeed inspire sinners still to repent yet and turn to the forgiveness of our Lord. How sorrowful she should have been sacrificed to the vanity of man and to the purposes of the Antichrist.

The Lord needs no such sacrifice of his true believers, having already made the ultimate sacrifice Himself.

And now, to me, how these words jump off the page!

'He does not take pleasure in burnt offerings.'

Would he take pleasure in mine?

> My sacrifice, O God, is a broken spirit;
> > a broken and contrite heart
> > you, God, will not despise.
> May it please you to prosper Zion,
> > to build up the walls of Jerusalem.
> Then you will delight in the sacrifices of the
> righteous,
> > in burnt offerings offered whole;
> > then bulls will be offered on your altar.

What dreams and hopes did poor Lady Jane forego in meeting her end so early in life? Whatever they were, and she would surely have as many of those as any young woman on the cusp of adulthood, they will surely pale when she sees the enormity of her contribution to rebuilding the new Jerusalem of God's Church in this land.

And then if my end is to come soon also – which it may well do, I sense – then may it be that the Lord DOES delight in my very own burned offering.

For I would offer my whole, my everything - my blood, my body, my mind, my soul, my ALL - for the love of my Lord Jesus Christ! Amen!

***

With the untimely demise of the Lady Jane comes also the demise of any hope of a speedy return to the Reformist cause.

We are now just past Easter time and I am hearing depressing report from the outside world that much superstition is returning to our churches, as sadly we knew it would without the guiding hand of the Lord's true shepherds, being the Protestant priests.

The Lord's Word that had adorned many a church in lieu of the idolatrous images of saints have been wickedly washed away, the magic trick that is mass has made a return, palms are waved absurdly on Palm Sunday and even creeping to the cross is reported to have made a return. What terrible but apt imagery, the nation brought back to its knees in superstitious practice under the heavy yoke of Roman Catholicism to curry some kind of favour from our Lord – as if everything had not already been done for them by our Lord Jesus on the cross itself!

More and more I am also hearing report of honest, Godly priests being deprived of their livings by virtue only of their being joined in matrimony to their dear wives. How wicked that men should separate these shepherds from their flocks despite their innocence and obedience only to God's instruction to man to wed and procreate.

Even bishops are not exempt, with a wholescale removal of the Godly men raised up during the halcyon days of King Edward's reign and their replacement by Papist lackeys bent only on returning the country to the servitude of Popery.

It saddens me to hear such reports. Barely do we receive any news of encouragement during these days.

But I keep my eyes fixed on my Lord.

And he is my refuge and my strength.

Joy still resides in my heart knowing as I do the unsurpassing goodness of his love that will sustain me whatever might occur in this fallen world.

Even in the deepest black of night when I have no sight and the sounds and smells of this hellish imprisonment threaten to overwhelm me, I make myself recall the greatness and the wonder of my Lord.

A low groan floats through the air, the sound of utter despair and despondency from a soul in an adjacent cell for whom all hope is lost. I say a silent prayer for them that they too can know the comfort and security of the Lord. A waft of reeking, wretched air passes over as if carried by the groans, a stench that would earlier have made me retch, but I am accustomed enough now not to flinch physically, only to feel the attack on my spirit.

And then the Lord prompts Psalm 23 to my mind, "Even though I walk through the darkest valley, I will fear no evil for you are with me: your rod and your staff comfort me. You prepare a table before me in the presence of my enemies. You anoint my head with oil: my cup overflows. Surely your goodness and love will follow me all the days of my life and I will dwell in the house of the Lord forever." Amen! Amen! And Amen!

**

The weather is turning now, with strength returning to the sun such that I can feel its warmth through the rays that pierce through my high cell window. I find myself in a strange limbo, one day passing much as another and with little or no word about what is to become of me and my fellow Reformers.

But now a turn of events that perhaps signals the climax of our struggle.

The Papists appear to be making their move, initially with a denunciation of the catechism which had been produced in the last years of King Edward's time. John Philpot, archdeacon of Winchester and a good Protestant was tasked with defending the catechism and the truths within, which articulated much of the core elements of Reform. I was humbled and grateful to hear that he had sought to bring both myself and Ridley to defend the work and underpinning theology alongside him – but for whatever reasons (are the Papists so afraid of God's faithful and true servants?), this request was declined.

Despite assurances from the Queen herself, Philpot was then disgracefully condemned by his own words in defence of true Protestantism, by Gardiner especially. I understand that he has been excommunicated, deprived of his living and imprisoned at Southwark, much like myself.

Then I hear news that the bishops Cranmer, Latimer and Ridley have been coerced into a show trial, believing they might have opportunity to defend the cause and provide the intellectual case for Reform. They had apparently been moved from the Tower to Bocardo prison in Oxford, perhaps to lend this mumming trial a sheen of intellectual rigour. But I hear it was far from a free or Godly debate. Rather my fellow Reformists were accused of heresy on the grounds of refusing to admit to the deceit of the mass, were publicly disgraced and baited like bears in the pit by the Papists, the whole event seemingly a ruse with which to ridicule and discredit them.

Nonetheless this has been hailed as an academic victory for the Roman Catholic cause, such is the disdain with which truth and academic and theological rigour are now held even in that great seat of learning, Oxford.

Fortunately we had report of this before I was asked to join a similar 'debate' in Cambridge along with my fellow Reformers Hooper, Bradford, Philpot, Saunders, Taylor and others (a dozen in all). We were permitted to convene and discuss the matter (our being kept in various prisons across London) which we did amongst ourselves and also brought the issue to the Lord in prayer together. We met here at Newgate, with the others not being kept here brought under guard to us.

Through these discussions and prayer together (what a joy to be re-united with likeminded men of God and what a privilege to be able to pray with them to our Lord!) we concluded and were united in our view that the conditions of the 'debate' were so heavily and unfairly stacked against us that we would not get a fair hearing and that it was therefore more likely that our cause would be damaged then strengthened by agreeing to it.

However, Bradford – as brave a man you ever could meet – raised a concern.

"Will we be seen as cowards to decline the opportunity? We might understand the reasons behind our decision, but will others not take it that we have no robust arguments with which to defend our cause under scrutiny?" he asked.

Hooper picked up the theme, "There is that risk, John, yes. Whilst our fellow Reformist leaders will understand, it is possible that the main body of the people – even our congregations – will be disheartened that we appear not willing to make a public stand and argue the cause on which we have preached."

"It is not the arguments and defence we lack, but the opportunity to present it fairly and openly" I added. "Somehow we must make that clear. We cannot simply refuse and do nothing, or the Papists will publicly deride us and claim their own victory."

"I agree" said Hooper. "Then why don't we lay down our arguments in simple fashion in writing and let them be published just as they are".

"Let truth speak for itself, you mean?" asked Bradford.

"Exactly. We are united in our thinking and can sign a common declaration. One that explains clearly and simply why we reject the public show they want to put on and goes on to state the plain truths of our faith and the simple proclamation of the Protestant cause."

We were agreed and I immediately took up a pen as we began to list our grievances against the public show trial and then our articles of faith. Bradford took the lead in proposing the statements, but we collectively refined and ordered them and I captured our agreed wording. It was a great encouragement to have these men of God around me and to spur one another on in the truths we had received from the Lord.

And so we produced our Declaration to which we could each sign our names and make public our unity, both in our reasons for declining the debate as well as the Articles of Faith to which we could all subscribe.

I summarise here both aspects of the Declaration, with several annotations added for further clarity.

Declaration of the Preachers in Prison

We are only prepared to dispute these matters of faith in writing, unless we may be heard before the Queen and her Council or before Parliament, for the following reasons:-

1) Everyone knows that both universities hold positions in the areas of dispute that are directly against God's word and that as such they are our enemies and have already condemned us even before any debate has taken place.

2) The bishops and clergy do not really seek to identify the truth from this debate, but rather to achieve our destruction and their glory.

3) The judges in this debate are therefore enemies of the truth before whom pearls are not to be cast.

4) Some of us have been in prison for eight or nine months with no books, paper, pen, ink or convenient place to study and as such would be reliant on our memory to make our defence rather than making a studied case.

5) We would not be allowed to make our case fully, but would be interrupted and stopped in mid flow.

6) Those that would write up the report and account of this debate would be appointed by our enemies and as such could only record that which would meet with their approval rather than the truth.

We deliberately addressed this declaration to the 'whole congregation and Church of England' and exhorted all God fearing men and women to be obedient to the Queen and not rebel against her or speak out in any way against her. We also included a blessing for Queen Mary, making abundantly clear that our dispute related to matters of religion and theology and in no way presented any rebellion against the Lord's Anointed Sovereign.

We listed then our Articles of Faith, summarised:-

1) We acknowledge and confess all the Canonical books of the Old Testament and all the books of the New Testament as written by the inspiration of the Holy Spirit and as such being the final judge and arbiter of all controversies and matters of religion.

2) We confess and believe in the catholic church (which is the spouse of Christ – and by which we mean the true, universal Church of Christ, not the Papist, Roman Catholic Church in its current corrupted form) as a most obedient and loving wife embracing the doctrines of these books and therefore to be heard accordingly by all people. With any not hearing this church being heretics, schismatics and heathens.

3) We believe in and confess the Apostle's Creed and in the symbols of the councils of Nice, Constantinople, Ephesus, Chalcedon and Toletum; and also of Athanasius, Ireneus, Tarullia and Damascus in the year 376. Anyone not believing in these doctrines errs from the truth.

4) We believe and confess that justification is from God's mercy through Christ and so by faith alone. And so we disallow the Papist doctrine of free will (man cannot of

himself turn back to God), of works of
supererogation (we canot by our works
make God love us any more) and of the
necessity of auricular confession (no
priestly intermediary is required for man
to engage with God, who knows our
hearts and thoughts without us needing
to speak aloud).

5) We confess and believe concerning the
external service of God that it ought to
be according to the Word of God and,
therefore, in the congregation all things
public should be done in an edifying
language (in other words, English in our
land) and not in Latin (which the majority
of people would not understand).

6) We confess and believe that God is to be
prayed to only by Christ Jesus and only
Him called upon; we therefore disallow
invocation or prayer to saints departed
this life.

7) We confess and believe that as a man
departs this life so shall he be judged on
the last day and then either enter into a
blessed state forever or be damned forever.
And is therefore past help or else needs no
help from any of us in this life. For which
reason we affirm that Purgatory, Masses
of Sacred Steps, Trentals (masses said over
thirty days for the deceased) and such
Suffrages as the Papist church deems
necessary, to be the doctrine of Antichrist.

8) We confess and believe the Sacraments of Christ to be Baptism and The Lord's Supper, which ought to be administered according to the instruction of Christ. And we plainly confess that the mutilation of the Lord's Supper and the withholding of one kind from the lay people is Antichristian. And so is the doctrine of Transubstantiation of the Sacramental bread and wine after the words of consecration, as they are called.

We further confess that the prohibition of marriage as unlawful to any person is an Antichristian doctrine. And that by God's Grace we will be able to prove all our confessions to be most true by the verity of God's Word.

We closed with our commitment as obedient subjects to behave well to those in authority, to pray for them that the Lord would give them all, collectively and individually, wisdom and Grace. Furthermore, we once again exhorted all men so to do and declared our desire and prayers that none would rebel against our Queen.

We submitted our manuscript to the Warden, one James Petter, who pledged to see it reach Gardiner. It was a strange anti-climax to our afternoon together, conscious as we all were that there was little chance that our collective declaration would receive significant attention and would likely be brushed aside by Gardiner, Bonner et al.

But we had stood firm on the Truth and for that we were rightly proud.

We bade farewell one to the other in somber mood, conscious that this might be the last we saw of one another. Although each sought to cheer the other with admonishments to hold firm and not to waiver, confident that the Lord only was our refuge and hope and that His Word promised He would forever be with us, both in this life and the next.

They were good men, each of them.

And so we departed.

And, perhaps as expected, that was the last we heard of it.

***

Mid summer now and the streets are alive with celebrations, which we hear from our prison cell windows. The guards inform us that it is on the occasion of the marriage of Queen Mary to Prince Philip of Spain, heir to that Papist state and its empire.

The guards also report misgivings aired in the taverns and inns of London, motivated more by

the concerns of being ruled by a Spanish King
than by matters of faith, sadly.

But the church bells ring out nonetheless
and we are left to contemplate our contrasting
circumstances as London celebrates with beer
and wine and feasting and we are left to our
meagre rations, confined in these most dreary
of settings.

My mind turns to my dear wife Adriana and our
wonderful children. Are they able to join the
celebrations, to revel in simple pleasures of good
company and companionship? Or does my
incarceration reach out and imprison them too
in a dark world of fear and foreboding? I hope
and pray it is the latter. I would hate to think of
my predicament casting such a shadow on their
young lives, especially when, despite it all, I have
so much to be grateful for and to look forward
to! Knowing the Lord will not fail me, even if my
earthly hours are limited now and the sands of
my time here in this world are soon to pour no
more.

I resolve to get word again to Adriana and tell
her this - if I can, via my congregant guards,
although I know I put them and their families at
risk when I do so and therefore seek to keep this
clandestine communication to a minimum.
However, I must try and free her and our
children from the tethers which bind me.

But I know they face hardship.

Back since my first containment under house arrest the income from my livings has been unjustly, illegally and cruelly stopped. We had some small savings on which we could rely in those early months, but since my moving to Newgate it has been impossible for me to provide for my family.

I thank God daily for faithful members of our congregation at St Sepulchre's and for some true, longstanding friends who have provided for the basic needs Adriana and the children have: But I know this must be of great concern to her. I pray that she will be resolute in trusting on the Lord to provide and that he will indeed do so through the Grace, love and charity of His true people.

Even that becomes harder as more and more Protestant Reformers flee to the safety of other lands, so that our supporters are fewer and further afield. Rumours of a thousand fleeing this land abound – a thousand good souls now departed and with them the light they each brought to our country.

Truly England becomes darker by the day.

These reflections embolden me to reach out directly to Gardiner, the Lord Chancellor, to make direct application for justice and mercy, in particular with regard to my financial circumstances. I remain formally in office in each of my livings and yet receive not a penny in income from them. How can that be justice? How can that be the conduct of Christ's church? It is neither – and I shall lay this bare before Gardiner in writing, if the Warden permits me the pen, ink and paper to do so for this specific purpose (he knows not, of course, about this manuscript and the access I have to the tools with which to create it). Surely he cannot refuse me that, given the injustice and inequity of my circumstance, with which he must surely be aware?

I will call the guard now to seek audience with him.

***

I did meet with the warden and he did indeed permit me to write to the Lord Chancellor – on the precondition that I did so there and then in his office and under the watchful eye of his guards. And so I wrote my plea to Gardiner and laid down my claim to income given that I had yet to be proven guilty of any charge, still held office and had committed no crime that might warrant my imprisonment.

I have heard nothing back from him.

Which does not surprise me, knowing him to be one of the key architects of my current circumstance.

I hear report that Adriana had also sought audience with him to plead our cause. Surely the name John Rogers can never be far from his thoughts! Please God may that prompt him to consider our cause – especially that of my family – and bring ease to their sufferings.

Reading back the last few pages of my writing here (before packing this latest set of documents away in my secret hiding place in the courtyard), I am conscious of a degree of melancholy that appears to have come over me.

I have spent some time now in prayer on this matter and wish to renounce that spirit of defeatism or even victimhood. Who am I to complain when so much has already been done for me and so much – such incalculable riches of happiness and contentment! – is promised me by the Living Lord!

I am prompted by the Holy Spirit to recall the imprisonments of the apostle Paul. May he be my inspiration and example.

Like me, held under house arrest.

Like me, imprisoned (and unlike me chained to a prison guard, many of whom came to know the Lord through Paul's example!).

Nothing could stop him professing the Good News and sharing the unsurpassing truth of God's goodness.

And he was executed for holding true to our Lord.

Like me?

***

The seasons are turning again, with the heat of summer giving way now to cold, fresh, misty mornings. Any news I hear seems to be of yet another Reformist families choosing to take flight to the safety of the continent.

With so many leaving these shores and so many also imprisoned, I wonder whether there be any Reformist leaders left in the land to coral and console our flock. May the Lord protect them and keep them and sustain them through these times when the devil prowls and seeks to swallow them back into the darkness of Papism.

One such recently joined me here at Newgate is Robert Smith, a Godly man, tall and slender and of an artistic temperament. We were permitted to sup together and found comfort in one another's company in this dark and depressing place. He found prison life hard to bear, given the joy he took in painting, poetry and the beauty of the world around him – but I was able to bring him some solace in our discussions, which ranged from Scriptures (he had strong interest in the process of translation for the Thomas Matthew Bible and was much admiring – rightly so – of the abilities of my friend and colleague Tyndale), to my experiences on the continent and to our shared appreciation and pleasures of family life.

Knowing his passion for writing, I shared with him my precious quills and paper. He had determined to write a poem to his children as a form of guidance to them that could stand in his stead if he were not to be permitted to see them again, but instead was to be hastened to meet our Lord.

"This is a heavy duty I feel on my shoulders, John. How can I capture a lifetime's guidance to my dear children in a single poem?" he asked me as we ate together in the dimly lit hall.

"Maybe it is not so dauting a task" I responded.

"How so?" he asked, a little taken aback that I was belittling his burden.

"Well, when Moses went up the mountain to get instructions from the Lord for all of humanity for all of time, he returned not with a book but with Ten simple Commandments" I retorted.

He raised his eyebrows, struggling with the truth of my remarks against the complexities and colour and rich shading that he saw in life around him as a man of sensitivity.

"That is true, that is true" he acknowledged. "But I want to convey more than commands, I want

to exhort them to live their lives well and fully
and I wish to convey to them the fullness of love
I have in my hearts for each of them."

I have always had an orderly mind, one that
collates and organises and categorises
information into the elegance of a list – and so
I struggled to understand his fears.

"There is no reason why you can't succinctly
convey your emotion as well as your instruction"
I said, meaning it as an encouragement,
although I was conscious I might be coming
across as callous. "The simple effect of the
words coming from you, their father, will
imbibe the message with emotional depth.
If you were to write a list of the key attributes
you would like your children to adopt, what
would they be?"

He paused a moment in reflection and then spoke
quietly, his gaze not directly at me but slightly
above my right ear as if speaking to someone
standing behind me. "I wish to share with them
my desire that their inheritance from me should
be more than the goods and chattels I leave. It is
my heart's desire that they should understand
that they are also heirs to that which is eternal
and will never decay. That which I am prepared to
give my life for!"

He looked at me directly as he made this last
claim and I returned his gaze, understanding the

depth of sentiment and heart behind this bold claim, one which I too shared with all my heart.

"Go on," I encouraged "and what specifically about that would you convey?"

"I wish that they would keep God always before their eyes and with every sinew of their strength seek his face, eschewing worldly distractions to keep focussed on the wonder and glory of our Lord!" he stated. And paused. Then he went on, "And I pray that they will not be tempted by that whore of Rome, the Papist church, but rather turn their backs on their supercilious superstitions! May my sacrifice be the example to them that they should never drink of her cursed cup nor obey their deceitful decrees!"

"That is a very poetic way of putting it, Robert! You should use that!" I encouraged him. "So what practically do you desire of your children in following this true way? What does that look like for you?"

"Well firstly, of course, they should obey the 5th Commandment and honour their mother by caring for her when I am no longer able to. It would be my deepest regret that I should not be here to care for my dear wife, she depends on me so. But my eldest, George, will soon turn sixteen and will become a man to be be able to care for her in my absence. He is a good lad, with a mature head on his shoulders and with the love and support of our congregation he will make a good head of household. Although I pray also that he and all my children will remember their father who showed them the true way."

"You will be remembered, Robert, not only by your children, but by all of God's true people" I replied. "And more than remembered, rightly revered for your faithfulness!"

"Thank you, John" he replied earnestly, warming to his theme now. "And I would have them work out practically the consequence of their salvation. Not to earn any further favour from our Lord, for He could not love them any more nor any less than He already does. But rather as an outworking of their appreciation and understanding of the Grace they themselves have received. So I would have them, as they grow to maturity, be generous to the poor and those in need. Our world is so full of those in such desperate need, crying out for help in a harsh and heartless world. May they be the help to those in need around them and the Good Samaritan to the helpless."

He paused in thought, as if imagining future scenes of his children, grown to adulthood, lending the hand of kindness to the destitute and needy.

He looked up at me and smiled, still silent.

I prompted for more. "And what would stop the fulfilment of this Godly life in your children?"

He frowned. "They must eschew the temptations of the flesh. And understand and respect that their very bodies are temples for the Lord."

"Yes," I concurred, "lust is the most devious of sins and most aggressive of the fruits of the sinful nature of man."

"And pride," he added. "The final stand of the devil, when all else is going the true way of the Lord, pride can creep in and knock a man off course and into the devil's path. So I would wish for them that they would hold a right humility through all of their days, recognising that we come into this life with nought and leave with nought."

He stopped again.

And nodded, summarising. "Yes, I would have them seek the Lord and know the all consuming power of His love, as the most precious of inheritances from my own life – and not have their head turned by the whore of Rome. That they would take care of their mother, remembering me, but also outwork the freedom found in their salvation to play their part in taking care of the poor and needy. And that they would not be blown off course through the temptations of the flesh or pride such that they can run the straight race and that we can meet again together in the glories of heaven!"

"A fine summary and a worthy legacy, Robert" I encouraged him. "You remind me of Micah's exhortation for us to 'act justly, love mercy and to walk humbly with your God.' Now that was a succinct summary of wise advice!"

"Thank you, John" he replied in a heartfelt way. "And you John? What would you wish to convey to your ten wonderful children from the learnings you have accumulated in your erudite life?"

I had been mulling this over whilst he had been sharing his thoughts and so already had an idea of how I would respond.

"I would direct them to the Word of God, Robert – which may not surprise you!" He chuckled, smiled and nodded and I went on. "Ten verses spring to mind ..." (I saw him smile knowingly again, aware, I think, of both my love of the Word and my habit of memorising the passages dear to me, as well as my orderly mind which readily categorised and organised information) "... which I have held dear and which have illuminated my own life. It would be the prayer of my heart that these verses would similarly illuminate their lives."

"Go on," Robert implored me – and as he did so he drew out paper and quill and wet that quill with ink, ready to take note of what I had to share. I was content that he should do so, knowing myself well enough that I could never encapsulate my thoughts in the poetic form in which he was s skilled.

"I have in mind four verses of spiritual counsel, four of practical advice ..." I saw him supress another chuckle as he saw my orderly mind categorising and organising my thoughts. I continued, knowing that he meant it in admiration, not mockingly. "... I see one verse as a link between the two and a final one as an overarching sentiment which in fact embraces the overall counsel."

"That sounds very well structured," he encouraged me, without irony. "So what would those verses be that you would have your children engrave upon their hearts?"

I continued, warming to my theme. Here is the listing I then provided and the counsel I would myself provide to my children, albeit not in poetic form:-

Spiritual Guidance

1. **Seek first the kingdom of God.**
   From the words of our Lord Jesus in the Gospel of Matthew "Seek first his kingdom

and his righteousness and all these things will be given to you as well."

From this all else flows. Elsewhere Jesus replied to the question of what was the most important of the commandments with the answer that we should love the Lord our God with all our heart and all our soul and all our minds. This is our first purpose in life.

2. **Do not fear for the Lord will hold you in his hand**
From the Prophet Isaiah "So do not fear, for I am with you: do not be dismayed, for I am your God. I will strengthen you and help you: I will uphold you with my righteous right hand."

Too many people spend too long living in fear and anxiety, frightened of what might happen to them or become of them in this world. But the Lord is GOOD and promises to uphold us. And as Paul said to the Romans, if God is for us, who can stand against us?

3. **Be assured of the certain hope offered through Jesus Christ**
From Paul's letter to the Hebrews "We have this hope as an anchor for the soul, firm and secure."

This is no vain nor empty hope, but one upon which we can build our whole

lives and be as certain as certain
can be.

4. **And know that we shall one day see Him
    face to face**
    From Paul's first letter to the Corinthians
    "For now we see only a reflection as in a
    mirror; then we shall see face to face."

    How great and marvellous is this promise!
    To see the Risen Lord Jesus Christ face to
    face and be presented without shame nor
    blemish because of what He himself has
    done out of supreme love for us!

Consequence of this spiritual awareness
5. **So live freely and with joy**
    From Paul's letter to the Philipians "For to
    me, to live is Christ and to die is gain."

    Paul reflects here my own sentiment that
    so wonderful will it be to see Jesus face to
    face and to reside in the marvellous and
    astounding presence of the Living God in
    heaven that to die to experience that can
    only be gain! And if death has then lost its
    sting, we can live with the utmost freedom
    and joy in that knowledge here on earth.
    May each of my children know such joy!

Practical guidance on living a Godly life
6. **Choose to have a thankful heart**
    From Paul's first letter to the
    Thessalonians "Rejoice always, pray
    continually, give thanks in all

279

circumstances; for this is God's will for you in Jesus Christ."

Living with a thankful heart – making the choice daily to give thanks to the Lord in all circumstances, to daily remind ourselves of what he has done for us and the promise that awaits us – that can transform lives, not just of the individual, but also of those around them whom they will subsequently bless. That is how Jesus would have us live, so that is how I have sought to live; and how I pray my children can live also.

7. **Be humble and seek counsel from the wise**
    From the Book of Proverbs 12 v 15 "The way of fools seems right to them, but the wise listen to advice."

    Humility is the antidote to pride and opens our hearts to receive wisdom from those the Lord has placed around us. May none of my children take such pride in their own ability that they seek not to have humble, servant hearts. Rather, may the Lord place wise people in their path to whose views they adhere, as I have done with Godly men such as Tyndale, Melanchton and Ridley.

8. **Do unto others as you would have them do unto you**
    As Matthew recorded Jesus say in his Gospel "So in everything, do to others what you would have them do to you, for this sums up the Law and the Prophets."

The second greatest commandment, according to Jesus – after only loving God with all our hearts – and such practical advice on how to live as God intended.

9. And work wholeheartedly as if for the Lord
   From Paul's letter to the Colossians
   "Whatever you do, work at it with all your heart, as working for the Lord, not human masters, since you know that you will receive an inheritance from the Lord as a reward."

   I do not mind what professions my children take, nor how high they rise in authority in their roles. I only pray that they can adopt this attitude to work at whatever their chosen path might be, as if working for the Lord, to honour Him and to provide a right and good example to all. They can rest their heads on their pillows at night in contentment then, knowing they can do, nor need do no more.

In summary
10. Be an encourager!
    From Paul's letter to the Hebrews again
    "Let us consider how we may spur one another on toward love and good deeds, not giving up meeting together, as some are in the habit of doing, but encouraging on another – and all the more as we see the Day approaching."

If my children would take all of this biblical counsel to heart, I would rest happy – and my final exhortation would be that they would exhort others to do the same! Was not Jesus' final commandment to us on earth to teach others to obey everything he had commanded us, by making disciples? What better way to fulfil that than to live by example and encourage others to do the same!

I finished speaking and realised that Robert had his head down and was frantically seeking to transcribe my every word – which made me smile. He went on writing for a few moments more and then placed his quill down with a flourish.

"Wonderful, John, really wonderful!" he asserted. "You have such a gift to be able to order your thoughts so comprehensively and yet succinctly. I am embarrassed now at my own ramblings. I need time to shape and bring order to my thoughts and then to craft them into poetic form. But with your permission I would love to do that – with both my thoughts and yours? I would be honoured to bring our thoughts together into a poem that I can share with my children – and I will ensure that your children also receive it, if I may?"

"You are most welcome, my dear friend" I replied honestly. "If you are able to create poetry from that – I certainly would not be able! – then you have my blessing. I need no acknowledgement in that, for the content is from Scripture alone and that is free to all men! God willing our children will take this counsel to heart and perhaps in turn our children's children and on through the generations! What a gift that would be to our descendants!"

We shook hands on that and I thanked him for a most pleasant evening. I loved spending time with this man, a family man like myself whose heart like mine belonged to the Lord and whose predicament and likely future was so like my own.

Contemplating this counsel for my children had the effect of girding my loins also for my own trials that I begin to see clearly ahead of me now. If I could not take my own counsel to my own heart, what kind of man would I be?

But I am a man of my word, a man of God, saved by His blood and these things I preach I would seal with my own blood.

***

Winter sets in now, the cold starts to seep into my bones once more and familiar bodily aches do reappear. But I am again engaged with my fellow imprisoned Reformists to make plea – this time to the highest authority in the land - that we may be given fair hearing and cease to be treated unjustly, cruelly and unfairly.

It was John Bradford who moved that we should create a petition addressed directly to our Queen and her King and, with several of us giving our consent, he was entrusted to draft it for our agreement. Despite the silence with which our previous Declaration had been met, we felt we had little to lose by seeking to make our case in plain view and directly to the Queen and King – for we felt that otherwise the Papist traps were closing around us as they drove Parliament to ever stronger sanction against us.

Time was against us.

Bradford penned an elegant petition which was duly respectful to our monarch, but also laid bare our grievances. We made complaint that we had all had our livings, houses, possessions, goods and books taken from us contrary to all laws of justice equity and right as well as being cast into prison. We asked to be granted liberty to answer before our Queen and King – or anyone so appointed by their majesties – either by mouth or by writing in plain English to address the controversies of which we are accused. We promised to defend ourselves with moderation and quiet behaviour – knowing they might be alarmed that we might seek to rabble raise, but rather emphasising that we are each peaceful subjects – we asked only that we have free access to our books and to conference together to be able to make our cogent case.

So confident are we that we can make an unarguable, biblically sound case for our positions that we stated we would be able to prove ourselves true and faithful Christians and neither heretics nor teachers of heresy. Further that we were and are therefore not cut off from the true catholic universal church of Christ.

And to demonstrate that we would stake our very lives on this surety, we offered and accepted to be ready to offer ourselves to the most heavy punishment it would please their majesties to appoint should we not be able to prove our case: That the doctrine of the church, the homilies and service taught and set forth in the time of Edward VI was the true doctrine of Christ's catholic church and agreeable to the articles of the Christian faith.

This time the signatories to the Petition were myself, Bradbury, Hooper, Ferrar, Philpot and Saunders – Godly men all.

It was cathartic to put in plain English our grievance and complaint and to offer boldly to make our defence before the Lord's Anointed Queen of England. Especially so doing it in co-signature and collaboration with others of like mind and suffering the same injustices as me.

But I had slight hope that our petition would be heard, much less granted.

***

It was about this time that I had the pleasure of spending time at suppers with the publisher, John Day. He was a good and Godly young man, who had greatly benefited the cause of Reform in England through his publication of many Protestant works and translations. He and I spoke readily and easily with one another, sharing our passion in the cause and belief that the written word has a vital role to play in spreading His Truth in our land.

But it was and is my belief, that the printed word is not in itself sufficient to ensure the seed planted is nurtured through germination to full bloom. I explained to Day, that I had long held that a system of supervision and governance was required over the priesthood to ensure that the teaching and pastoral care the English people received continued to be based on the True Word and would remain uncontaminated by the superstitions and idolatry of Papist practices.

"I have every faith and full confidence that in your lifetime you will see the alteration of religion in our land so that the True Gospel will again be freely preached" I assured him. He is a younger man than me, by some decades.

"I pray that what you say will prove true," he replied, "and that I will indeed live to see that!"

"Oh we can be sure of it, of that I'm sure John" I reassured him. "Firstly, remember the Word of the Lord, through the prophet Isaiah, 'My word that goes out from my mouth will not return to me empty, but will accomplish what I desire and achieve the purpose for which I sent it." The Lord has begun this work of Reform to awaken His people, and will not cease until it is complete – whatever the cost."

Day nodded quietly in calm consent and I let that reassurance sink in a moment to warm his soul. Then I continued, "And as for you, if Gardiner had wanted rid of you he would more quickly have had you incarcerated, like myself, Hooper, Bradford and the other clergy. It is the clergy that they are keen to purge, not a layperson such as you. You are here temporarily to try scare you into desisting supporting the cause and to teach you a lesson. Mark my words."

"But listen to me now," I continued, "I want you to remember this – and to share this with our brethren when you are released from here and when our cause is – as God will ensure - on the rise again. When Adriana and I were still out in Meldorf and considering a return to my homeland, we compiled a listing of the criteria we wished to see that would truly make a stable Protestant nation. The tenth of those and the only one which at that time – we are talking about the time when young Edward had first come to the throne, so about six years ago it would have been – was this: That there should be a process of supervision and oversight over all of the clergy in England. Even before the recent purge, we did not have sufficient good and true ministers to furnish all churches in the land. In order then to prevent the Papists spreading their lies and deceits amongst our flock, there should be a superintendent over every ten churches. A good and learned superintendent could then oversee their readers and put out any they find whom they consider to be Papists. So too the bishop should review their superintendents to ensure the same purity remains amongst them and the whole structure can encourage and develop sound understanding of biblical truth and teaching so that the people of this country can receive wise and sound instruction in the Lord's ways. In this way Reform can have the firm foundations we need to oust every vestige of the disease of Papistry and the branches of this English vine can remain growing and maturing in Him."

Day acknowledged the wisdom of this and recognised how this could indeed provide the firm foundations that Reform had lacked under the previous king.

But I had one further warning.

"One more thing I tell you, John Day – and I would you pass this on also to our brethren when once again you are a free man. If our brethren do not follow this sound counsel – and

Hooper is in agreement with me on all of this,
you can tell them that also – then their end will
be still worse than ours."

I meant it not as a curse, but only to imbue my
words and counsel with the weight and gravitas
that surely it needs to ensure this becomes
enshrined in the practices of the Church of
England.

**May the Lord carry this word and bless it and
bring it into being, even after I am gone.**

***

Christmas now, and the cold chill of the
mornings has hardened to firm frost and the dull
ache of my bones to chronic pain. But I pray daily
and continue to give thanks for small mercies
– that I still get to converse occasionally with my
fellow prisoners at mealtimes and that I have
still my pen and paper that allows me to keep
record of my plight – hopefully that those I love
can understand what has been happening to me
whilst I have been cruelly separated from them.

I managed to get word to my most beloved
Adriana and asked her again to seek direct
audience with the Lord Chancellor Gardiner to
seek alleviation of our plight.

As feared, we have had no word back in response
to our petition, but hear only of Parliament's

progress removing from statute the victories we achieved under good King Edward and in increasing the penalties of disobedience to the foul beast that is the Papist Catholic Church.

Moreover, I hear that Reginald Pole, Cardinal of the Church of Antichrist and long term conspirer and enemy of Reform, is returned to England amongst great fanfare and welcome. How sad that we were not able to open the eyes of the nation to see the Antichrist for what he is, so that still he holds the innocent and gullible people of England in his deathly thrall.

Could we have done more, in the time we had, to remove their blind superstition and attraction to the beguiling, but empty promises of Rome? I'm not sure we could have done more, we spoke out plainly and scattered the seed in obedience to our instruction.

Is it our fault that so much of England proved to be stony ground? Where the good seed we sowed, if it germinated, could not take hold and was so easily dried out by the sun or strangled by the Antichristian weeds?

I think not.

I hope and pray not.

Meanwhile, Adriana reports back that she did seek audience with Gardiner, boldly visiting his residence in person with half a dozen or more loyal female friends of ours and supporters of our cause. They were brave to do so – not least Adriana herself and my heart swells with pride that she would so put herself in jeopardy for the love of me, knowing as I do her timid spirit.

I envisage the scene, Adriana arriving, with her band of ladies by her side, at Gardiner's imposing residence; sounds of Christmas revelry echoing from within. Her knocking at the door and bravely stating her business to the servant answering the door, his mood switching quickly from merrymaking and gaiety to deadly serious business. His insisting the women stay outside in the cold whilst he confers with his master – and his embarrassment at having to return to face this formidable female force with the news that his master will brook no audience with them.

Adriana pleads her cause further, the servant becomes more forceful in his refusal until eventually Adriana's consorts must intervene to draw her away back into the cold, dark night, distraught and weeping and seeing all hope slip through her fingers along with the sands of time.

How jarring then the sounds of laughter and revelry she must have heard as she made her way, supported by her female companions, back down the driveway home. And how hard it must have been for her to return home to the expectant and hopeful faces of our young children, only to deflate their spirits once more with the fatal news that there was to be no lifting of the dark predicament in which the family's fortune were held.

I'm sorry, my dear Adriana, that you should have to be put through such trials – that I should have asked of you to do so. May God bless you for your obedience and faithfulness to your husband and may He keep you and let His face shine upon you and give you peace, even in these darkest of times.

Bless you Adriana.

***

Chapter 9 – London, Examination

The long awaited day arrives at last.

It is 22nd January and I am summoned formally to appear before the Privy Council and at last to be examined and questioned.

I was not alone in being presented before the Council this day accused of heresy, with perhaps ten others presented also, although we were mostly kept apart and faced our accusers alone.

I have detailed elsewhere my verbatim record of the exchanges I had with the Lord Chancellor, Gardiner and Bishop Bonner as well as the other Privy Councillors in attendance. I found it helpful to seek to recall every aspect of the discussion in that way and I hope that it will help explain to others the truth of how I sought to answer faithfully and honestly to the charges brought against me.

Here I shall outline the themes only of those examinations, by way of summary and precis of the discussions so that the matters of greatest import can be conveyed as part of this broad canvas picture of my life that I have sought to draw.

Perhaps these two descriptions might be bound together to make a whole one day, the detail in an appendix for the more studious reader and the summary here available to those with a more cursory interest.

The Council was sitting at the Lord Chancellor's official residence in Southwark and so we had to make our way on that cold winter's day through London and over the Thames. In attendance, as well as Gardiner and Bonner, were three other bishops, two lords (including William Paget, showing no shame that he should have served under King Henry and confessed the same beliefs as myself and others accused, whereas now he had swapped his opinions as the wind had changed its direction), the secretary Sir John Bourne and Sir Richard Southwell.

The room was not large and the effect of so many men of granted authority closely assembled and directing their gaze aggressively and sneeringly on me was oppressive. But I resolved to guard my tongue so as not to incriminate myself nor do injustice to our cause and conduct myself with due deference to this court.

I knelt before them in an act of submissive
humility, but held my head high to demonstrate
that I was prepared to stand my ground, the
holy ground of God's true Word.

It was Lord Chancellor Gardiner who led the
examination and opened with a general question
about my take on the state of affairs in the
realm. I had to admit to knowing little of that,
given my own state of confinement, but Gardiner
quickly scoffed at my professed and genuine
ignorance and set the tone for the one sided
discourse that was to follow.

The main thrust of their attack was then on the
subject of who was the Supreme Head of the
Church. They wished me to acknowledge the
Romish Pope as such and I would not do so.
Moreover I pointed out that not only had the
Parliament of 1534 concluded that to say so was
erroneous – which Gardiner claimed was under
cruel coercion, without seeming to see the irony
of such a claim given my own circumstance! – but
that they, the bishops, had collectively brought
me to the same position of understanding, which
I could not now give up on without conference.

I went on to point out that not only had they all
acceded to this, but Gardiner himself had written
in its defence in 1535 in his work De Vera
Obedientia. This asserted the royal supremacy
over the church rather than the Pope's.

He did not seem well pleased that I should raise this.

I pointed out also that only Christ Himself could be considered as the supreme spiritual head of the church and offered, again, to make my case plain if they would give me pen, ink and my books to do so.

This was flatly refused.

Further, Gardiner stated that no conference could be offered to a heretic as it was forbidden to engage with such, which belied the fact that they had already determined my status and fate.

Bishop Worcester then attacked me by stating that I did not know my creed, which expresses belief in the Holy Catholic Church. I pointed out that there is no reference to Rome in that creed, but that I did indeed acknowledge and belong to the true church which upheld the Word of God rather than promulgated teachings against His Word. He challenged me to name one – just one! I could have been there all day! – and I cited 1 Corinthians 14 "For anyone who speaks a tongue (I meant here Latin rather than plain English) does not speak to people but to God."

The room erupted in anger.

The anger of deluded fools.

It was then that I realised that these men would neither hear me when I spoke nor yet suffer me to write. And as such there was no remedy but to let them alone and commit the matter to God.

When the clamour died down, Gardiner eventually changed tack and spoke to me of the mercy of the Queen available to me only now. I stated I would have her mercy, but not at the cost of my conscience.

Next came a very personal attack from the Secretary, Sir John Bourne, on my marriage, claiming it broke the law. I calmly, but firmly refuted this pointing out that I had married where it was lawful and had been careful not to return to England until it had become lawful here also, in 1548. Uproar and commotion again, with some saying they knew not of any land where a priest may marry – such ignorance! – and I retorted that Germany was one such.

The commotion was such that I was not able to add that my marriage had been the subject of a specific Act of Parliament in this land, making my wife and children legally English subjects. What further authority did they require? The injustice of it cut me to the core, as much as not being able simply to argue and prove my case with sound reason.

But instead proceedings were brought to a rapid close, I was told I would be summoned again in due course and I was roughly led out of the room as raucous rumblings continued.

I was led back through London to my cell at Newgate, during which time I prayed to the Lord to help me stand firm and to continue to bear true witness to His truth and goodness. And I realised in that moment, quite powerfully, that I needed the prayers of God's true people to sustain me.

So when I had finished writing up the full transcript of my Examination (which I did before writing this synopsis, in order that I should best be able to recall every detail), I wrote also this heartfelt prayer.

I include it here in full as I feel it captures my true heart and feelings right now.

"I desire the hearty and unfeigned help of the prayers of all Christ's true members – the true children of the unfeigned catholic church – that the Lord of all consolation will now be my comfort, aid, strength, buckler and shield and also of all my brethren that are in the same case of distress.

That I and they may despise all manner of threats and cruelty and even the burning fire and dreadful dart of death and stick like true soldiers to our dear and loving captain Christ, our only redeemer and saviour and also the only true head of the catholic church, who does all in us which is the very property of a head – which thing all the bishops of Rome cannot do. And that we do not traitorously run out of his tents, or rather out of the plain field, in the greatest jeopardy of battle, but persevere in the fight, if he will not otherwise deliver us, until we be most cruelly slain by his enemies.

For this I most heartily and, at this present time, with weeping tears, most instantly and earnestly desire and beseech you all to pray.

And I beseech you also, if I die, to be good to my poor wife, being a stranger, and all my little souls, hers and my children; who with all the whole faithful and true catholic church of Christ, the Lord of life and death, save, keep, defend, in all the troubles and assaults of this world and bring at the last to everlasting salvation, the true and sure inheritance of all Christians.

Amen.

Amen."

I have no means of dispatching this, my prayer, to anyone else, here in prison much less outside, but the writing of it gives me comfort and I pray that supernaturally, through the power of the Holy Spirit, my supporters may be prompted so to pray. And that if I am to meet the fire, my parting wish will be both found and enacted regarding my dear wife and beloved children.

And so to bed, leaving all else to the Lord.
Tomorrow will have troubles enough on its own.

***

My first Examination had been on the Tuesday
22nd January and I was uncertain how long it
would be before I was summoned again. It was
clear that Gardiner and Bonner were scheming
and preparing the ground for their next
moves against us, for on the night of Friday 25th
January we heard a great commotion gathering
in volume as we sat for supper in Newgate. All
rushed to the windows to see what was occurring
and we were greeted by what looked like the
Roman Catholic Church in England risen to
arms. They were proceeding through the streets
in great pomp, dressed in their most absurd and
exuberant garb – Bonner and another half dozen
or more bishops at the head, followed by rank
upon rank of priests. There seemed an endless
line, as if the churches of London had been
emptied of them.

Indeed, you could describe it as a swarm.

We learned the next day that there were
apparently 160 priests in number, intended to
equal the number in Parliament who had
traitorously acceded to and acknowledged the
Pope's supremacy.

Gardiner knows how to play to his audience.

Later that night the sound of the revelries outside filled the air and drifted into our cells. As did an eerie orange reddish hue to the light produced by a multitude of celebratory bonfires.

More disconcerting still was the faint, dusky smell of smoke filling the air from those same fires. It was not comfortable having this reminder of my own potential fate in the light and air around me. I drifted restlessly in and out of sleep that night (which is unusual for me) and my mind played tricks on me, seeking to persuade me that Gardiner had planned this whole episode, even the placement of the bonfires, to cause me distress.

I finally woke with a start and centred myself on the Lord again, seeking His presence with me and reminding myself of my security in Him.

***

I finished my write up of the first Examination, my prayer and my description here two nights later, on Sunday 27th January. How true my final words turned out to be! The very next day I am summoned again to St Mary Over the Way in Southwark – very near the Bishop of Winchester, the Lord Chancellor's dwelling - for this Examination to continue beyond the preliminary stage.

I knew more what to expect this time and was strengthened with the solace I found in committing my prayers to paper, reminded as I was by the truth of my cause and the crowd of saints in prayerful support of me. I also resolved to speak my mind more directly to lay down on record the injustice and cruelty with which I have been treated.

I had reflected that I had been too compliant in the first session and too reactive to Gardiner's lead. This time I was determined to speak plainly and clearly concerning the inequity of my plight, even though I held scant hope that it would make a difference to my plight.

But I needed to speak out the truth about my treatment.

There were three of us to be examined that day – Hooper first, then a certain John Cardmaker and finally myself. It was the afternoon before my turn came, which had allowed me good time to pray and prepare myself for the ordeal ahead.

I was led to the Lady Chapel at the rear of the church where a great crowd had gathered in addition to the privy counsellors. Gardiner had clearly had his confidence boosted by the extravagant ceremonies of the Friday previous such that he felt that public opinion would now favour his side. The general hubbub rose as I entered the room and I felt a myriad of curious eyes on me.

I felt strangely calm and assured that the Lord was with me.

I was ready to speak boldly for Ħim.

I knelt, as I had previously, on the cold stone floor and took in for a moment the beauty of the arches and pillars in this house of God. Ϻy eyes then settled directly on Gardiner, knowing he would lead the Examination. Ꞇo his right, Bonner, barely concealing his contempt of me and his disgust at having again to be in my presence.

Gardiner did indeed lead and carried on directly from the previous line of inquiry, asking (foolishly, but necessarily) whether I had reflected and was now willing to come back into the 'one church that he, the bishops, Parliament and the whole realm' had now joined and to come out of schism with the Papist church.

I was ready this time to articulate better where I stood and would always stand. I stated boldly that I understood now the 'mercy' they were offering me was that of the antichristian church of Rome, which I utterly refuted. I declared again that I could prove my cause and doctrine from the Scriptures and the authority of the fathers that lived four hundred years after Christ.

Predictably this was again refused me, this time on the grounds of my private status versus the authority of Parliament. My plea that any authority in earth should be under God's Word in Scripture was swept aside.

The attack then became more personal.

Gardiner stated that there was nothing in me to be heard but 'ignorance, arrogance, pride and vainglory' in my presumption to speak so. I was taken aback at first by this shift to attack my character, but I maintained my composure to respond at first with due humility – that I was indeed ignorant under God, but that by his strength and assistance I could still prove this case.

I continued to look Gardiner directly in the eye as I then spoke out and denied that I had ever been proud nor vainglorious – and went on to state that all the world knew on which side pride, arrogance and vainglory was to be found. What irony that he and the bishops should sit there in their pomp and selfish importance and accuse me thus!

Gardiner ignored my slur, though the truth of it must surely have hit home. He went on to accuse me falsely and blatantly that I did speak out against the Queen at first opportunity – he was referring to my speaking at St Paul's Cross that first time in her reign. I flatly and directly denied this lie – and went on to state my view that the

Queen would herself have done well if it had not been for Gardiner and his ilk's counsel.

Gardiner claimed that the Queen had been the lead in taking the return to Rome to Parliament, to which I stated I could not, nor would not believe it (I still believe with all my heart that our Queen might fulfil the Lord's purpose in Reform if only she had the right counsellors by her side, as her brother Edward had). The Bishop of Carlisle then piped up that all the bishops would bear witness to what Gardiner said – to which I replied, that is something I could well believe!

The watching crowd roared with laughter at this and I noticed the flash of anger pass between Gardiner and Bonner as they felt the pain of being bettered and perhaps exposed by the sharpness of my wit. I think at this moment they determined not to allow the public in to view the proceedings on the following day, for the next day it was only my Examiners who were permitted into the room.

Sir Robert Rochester and then Sir John Bourne interjected at this point – against the process of the court, although there was none to stand up for me on this point – and made some sycophantic remarks regarding the veracity of what Gardiner had said. I did not deign to pick apart their arguments, knowing it would be fruitless before their peers.

Next, Gardiner raised the sacrament. He and the other bishops piously made a great show of removing their hats as they raised this holy subject, demonstrating again the superstitious spirit at the heart of their rotten religion. Gardiner asked me if I believed that the presence of the Lord Jesus was 'really and substantially present' at this sacrament.

Knowing this to be at the heart of their false religion, but also at the heart of the re-enacted heresy laws – meaning my very earthly life was at risk based on how I answered this one question – I drew a breath and looked down a moment to compose myself and my reply, before responding.

In so doing, I knew that I was nailing my colours to the true mast of our Lord Jesus and thereby preparing the way for the burning sacrifice of my body for my cause and Captain.

I stated that just as the most part of their doctrine was false, defended only by force and cruelty, so too was this false. For I could not and cannot understand the words 'really' and 'substantially' to signify other than corporally. But corporally Christ is only in heaven and so Christ cannot be corporally also in their sacrament.

There was a moment of shocked silence – and I seized it for my own purpose.

Knowing that my plight was all but sealed now, I moved onto the attack, to speak out the truths of my treatment and predicament.

I again looked squarely at Gardiner and accused him thus (I cite in full to convey the full force with which I made my accusation: "My Lord you have dealt with me most cruelly. For you have set me in prison without law and against the law and kept me there almost a year and a half. For I was almost half a year in my house, where I was obedient to you (God knows) and spoke with no man. And now I have been a full year in Newgate at great cost and charges, having a wife and ten children to look after and I never a penny of my livings, neither of the prebend, nor of the residence, neither of the vicarage of Sepulchre, which was against the law."

Gardiner was disorientated and wrong footed by my attack, obviously not expecting me to be anything other than compliant with his frame for this mock trial. He blurted that Ridley – then Bishop of London – who had given me these preferments was a usurper and that therefore I was the unjust possessor of them.

I immediately retorted, "Was the king then a usurper, who gave Ridley the bishopric?"

'Yes" he replied – to my amazement and to the amazement of all in the room, for if Edward was a usurper, what then was his successor and sister, Queen Mary herself? He blushed and flushed red and began to seek to justify his specific attack on Edward by reciting the supposed injustices that Godly King had 'inflicted' on both himself and his co-conspirator and lifetime ally, Bonner. He then sought to back track and renounce what he had said, saying that he had misspoken, but I declared that his words were an overflow from his true heart and I doubted verily that he was truly sorry for his comments. I knew him to be an enemy of King Edward and had no doubt that his loyalty to the Queen was now a vehicle only for his own aggrandisement and plans for his wretched church.

I picked up on my original theme – I demanded an answer, "Why have you sent me to prison?"

He said it was because I preached against the Queen – which I again immediately denied vehemently. I admitted that of course I had preached at St Paul's Cross, but could call on all the witnesses that day present that I did preach not a word against Her Majesty. Further, that they themselves had examined me thereafter and had let me go free after the preaching of that sermon. Really, this line of inquiry beggared belief, with no foundation whatsoever in truth.

Bizarrely, he then said I had at that time preached against the commandment of the

Council – when it was on their own instruction that I had preached! I denied this vehemently again – and moved again to attack.

I observed that I had been held in confinement and now a year in prison without their sending for me, conferring with me or having any engagement with me whatsoever until now that they have a whip with which to whip me and a sword with which to cut off my head. I was referring here to the Heresy Laws which they had now pushed through Parliament to be able to achieve the destruction of Reform and Reformers.

And I added bitterly, "For sure, all the world understands this kind of 'charity'."

Gardiner was seething with anger and moved around the papers before him in surly manner. I went to go on, but he raised his hand and stated that the court had 'heard enough of my prattling'.

There was much I would have said more, if I had been able. I wanted to remind him that I had sent my wife numerous times to see him on my behalf, even at Christmas time and with eight ladies in support. That I had written to him on numerous occasions without reply and yet others, good and Godly men, had sought my solace from him on my behalf, all ignored and to no avail.

These things I would have put before him and the Council and all that would hear. And these things declare his antichristian charity and that he had sought and does seek no less than my blood and the destruction of my poor wife and ten children.

But it was around four o'clock now and Gardiner brought the court back to order by stating that the charity of the church was such that it required that I be given a third opportunity to recant and return to his Catholic church. (He knew by then that I would not recant on the third time, nay nor the fourth or fifth or forty fifth, but that I would be steadfast to the end).

I pointed out again that I had never for one day left the true catholic church nor would I ever, but that his church I would never go into, by God's Grace.

He asked if, then, his church was false and antichristian.

"Yes", I replied simply.

And he followed through, seeking for all to hear my self-condemnation under their errant laws, asking again what of their doctrine of the sacrament.

"False!" I replied.

Some wit in the crowd shouted out that I was but acting and I gave him short shrift and returned my steady gaze toward Gardiner and in turn to his henchman Bonner.

Gardiner then summarily wrapped up proceedings, demanding that I come again on the morrow between nine and ten – and I replied that I was ready to come before them at anytime, emphasising again that I had nothing to hide nor of which to be ashamed.

And so I rose and was escorted out of the room and out of the Lady's Chapel, through the main church and back onto the street, with Hooper being brought out before me.

Cardmaker was not with us. I asked one of my guards what had become of him and learned that, sadly, he had not stood firm and had failed the test. I was saddened that he should have forsaken us and had shrunk from the banner of our Master and Captain Christ Jesus. May the Lord grant him to return and fight with us, till we are smitten down together, if that be the Lord's will.

For truly, not a hair on our heads shall perish but it be the Lord's will.

And may this same Lord grant us to be obedient to the end and in the end.

Amen.

But it was good and heartening, at that point, to see my friend Hooper and to know that he too had been faithful to the task. As we came out onto the street a great throng of people had gathered and shouted their encouragement to us when they saw us – which lifted my spirits. I came up alongside Hooper and he too was in good spirits, despite our dire circumstances.

"Come, brother Rogers" he shouted, above the noise and din of the crowd, "must we two take this matter first in hand and begin to fry these faggots?"

His humour and fortitude at such a time was a great inspiration to me and I replied heartily, "Yes sir, by God's Grace".

"Doubt not" Hooper rejoined, "but God will give us strength."

The crowd cheered and roared all the louder in hearing this, but the guards pushed us roughly on. So great was that friendly crowd that we had difficulty making progress.

But that short exchange between Hooper and myself, two men of God true to His Word, was nothing less than a sacred promise one to each other that we would not, like Cardmaker, deny our Master and Captain Christ, but would stand firm in His strength even until the bitter, fiery end.

***

It was to the Compter in Southwark that Hooper and I were taken that night, to spend what I expected to be an uncomfortable night in that small prison. I ate a simple meal and then spent some time in prayer, praying for each of my children and for Adriana that the Lord would comfort them during this time of my trial and protect them thereafter. I then extended my prayers to my circle of friends into whose path the Lord had graciously placed me and I reflected on the blessed life I had been given on this earth.

I thanked the Lord that He had brought me to Godly people who could help me grow closer to Him.

And then I slept remarkably well. I have always done so, but these circumstances and surroundings were certainly a sterner test. Despite the trials I faced now and the potential future ordeal, my spirit was at peace and at one with my Lord.

I thank God for that.

The next day the sheriffs came for us both and we were brought back to the church at St Mary Over the Way and to the Lady Chapel there. Hooper went first and I was kept again in an antechamber, where I waited patiently and spent time quietly with the Lord. The wait was shorter this time. It was clear that today the proceedings were to be of a more perfunctory nature and the outcome already clear.

I later learned that Hooper had already been condemned when I was summoned and brought before the court. The mood was serious and sombre. Gone were the raucous crowd, leaving only the court officials, with the Bishop of Winchester, Chancellor Gardiner still presiding. He was in no mood to tarry and came straight to the point by asking whether overnight I had reflected and was ready now to repent and return to his Catholic church.

I avoided answering the question directly, but requested again that I be given leave to make my case based on Scriptures in writing. This was refused me on the grounds of me being a private man and Parliament being above all private people. Anticipating this response – and having pondered this overnight - I sought to name to examples where this had not been so, where in fact individuals had prevailed over Parliament. I was going to give the cases of St Augustine and Panormitanus and began to cite those cases, but Gardiner crudely cut me off, demanding I sit down and mocking me that I was there to be instructed by them, not the other way around.

I replied "My Lord, I will stand and not sit: shall I not be permitted to speak for my life?"

His reply was brutal.

"Shall we suffer you to tell us tales, prattle and prate?" He then berated and bullied me with similar accusations to the day previous such that I was prevented from speaking. Although I was able to say that he should not make me afraid to speak.

"See what a spirit this fellow has! Finding fault in my accustomed earnestness and hearty manner of speaking!" he exclaimed, performing to his audience, his inferiors in the Council.

"I have a true spirit," I retorted, "agreeing to and obeying the Word of God".

Gardiner had had enough, his performance complete.

He proceeded then to my condemnation and excommunication.

The papers had been pre-prepared and Gardiner read out the condemnation with solemnity. I stood, held my head high and accepted this inevitable consequence of my standing firm to Christ's cause.

As I listened carefully, it was clear that there were just two charges against me – one that I affirmed the Romish Catholic Church to be that of the Antichrist and the other that I denied the real presence of Christ in the sacrament.

In truth there is much else in the rotten Papist doctrine that I would condemn and be prepared to be condemned for standing against. But these two elements would suffice as solid ground on which I would stand and seal with my blood.

The excommunication followed based on their seeing me as a heretic within their church and as such they further placed upon me the sentence of the 'great curse', meaning that I was now cut off from all meaningful engagement with anyone, including my friends and loved ones: for if they were to show me the slightest kindness – even to provide me with food or drink or shelter - the same fate that was to befall me would be cast on them also.

But there would be little opportunity for, or risk of, any such interaction.

For I knew the consequence of my being excommunicated and passed over for punishment to the secular authorities.

The penalty for this is clear.

I am to be burned alive.

Knowing I was now utterly condemned,
I responded robustly and fully to speak truth
and thereby shame my enemies.

"Well, my Lord, here I stand before God and you
and all this honourable audience and take thee

to witness that I never wittingly nor willingly
taught any false doctrine and therefore
I have a good conscience before God and before
all good men. And I'm sure that you and I shall
come before a judge who is righteous, before
whom I shall be as good a man as you; and
where, I do not doubt, I shall be found a true
member of the catholic church and everlastingly
saved. And as for your false church, you need
not excommunicate me from it, for I have not
been in it these last twenty years, thank God!
But now you have done all you can, my Lord,
I pray you grant me one thing yet."

"What is that?" barked Gardiner in response.

"That my poor wife, being a stranger in this
country, may come and speak with me whilst I
still live; for she has ten children that are hers
and mine and I' wish to give her counsel in what
to do now."

**Gardiner's response was cruel, brutal and wrong
in equal measure.**

"No, she is not your wife" he said, almost casually,
but seeming to enjoy this last opportunity for
cruelty to torment me.

"Indeed she is, my Lord, and has been for eighteen
years" I replied directly.

"Should I grant her to be your wife?" he asked, mockingly.

I had had enough and saw that there was no chance that this hard hearted man would allow such a simple request that a condemned man should once more see his wife, having not done so for over a year.

"You can choose whether you will or not," I replied curtly, "the truth is she is my wife, whatever you say."

"She shall not come to you" he stated flatly, evil triumph in his eye at my obvious pain.

"Then I have exhausted all of your charity" I replied, cuttingly. "You make yourself highly displeased with the idea that priests might marry, but you're quite happy they should openly entertain whores. As in Wales, where every priest has his whore, openly dwelling with him and lying by him at night. Just as your Pope allows all the priests in the Netherlands and France to do the same."

He had no answer to this, knowing the truth of it, only averting his eyes from me as I was taken away.

I would have said more, if I'd been allowed. Specifically, I wanted to prove my case that a private man might reason against and write up the case against a wicked Act of Parliament or ungodly counsel: the very same request that had been denied me without explanation.

And secondly, I wish I had the opportunity to show and prove that prosperity and good fortune are not always a token and proof of God's love. It was clear in the smug manner with which Gardiner, Bonner and the Council conducted themselves that they felt God was on their side, as they had the upper hand of power restored to them. But there are numerous examples in the Bible where the opposite is so often true., which I readily would have shared with them, given the opportunity. Indeed, suffering could almost be said to be the badge of the true Christian.

However, these things I was not permitted to espouse, but instead was hustled and bustled out of the room and back into confinement at the Clink in Southwark.

We – Hooper and I – were kept there until after dark. Indeed we were further kept 'in the dark' as to why this was, as to why we were not immediately returning to Newgate Prison. But the reason became clear soon enough.

And what a marvel it turned out to be that night!

What a marvel and what an encouragement to us both to continue to hold fast to our purpose.

Late that night there was a sudden commotion
from a large body of men – heavily armed men,
with bills and weapons enough – and we were
roughly and speedily bustled out of the Clink
and up to the Bishop of Winchester's house
again. For a moment we thought we were to have
audience again with Gardiner, but this time we
were only to pass through it at speed and come
back out into the church yard of St Mary Over
the Way and on into the street.

Hooper and I looked at one another quizzically,
but Hooper then pointed, with a smile, up at the
street light and I noticed what he meant.

The light had been extinguished.

Not only that street light, but every street light
that we encountered as we made our way toward
and over London Bridge. Even the lights on the
stalls of the costermongers had been put out.

I understood in that moment the fear in which
we were held by our captors. Such fear, that they
had gone to the considerable trouble of sending a
party to go ahead of our journey and extinguish
the lights so that their actions could be taken
under the cover of darkness.

**But where there is true light, darkness cannot
overcome it!**

To our delight – and to the initial alarm of our
sizeable sentry guard – as we came across London

Bridge, there was a strong glow of bright light. As we drew near we could make out that this emanated from a great crowd of people lining the street, each holding aloft candles that lit our way. These candles lit too the faces of those carrying them and it was with great joy that I could see again so many friends, colleagues and members of my congregations who had come out to support me in what might have been my darkest hour.

They cried out to us in encouragement, "Be of good cheer!", "The Lord bless you!", "God be with you!", "Keep the faith!" – on and on went the cries as we made our way through London, our pathway to our certain end lit up by the faithfulness of the saints.

Their candles lit up also my heart and in so doing lifted my very soul.

By the time we reached Newgate, we were of such good cheer that my cheeks ached from smiling.

It had been a long while since I had had that joy.

How wonderful – and how extraordinary - that the Lord should arrange it so that I should feel that on this, the day I had been utterly condemned.

And I wondered if I would feel the same contentment on my final journey to meet my fiery end.

By God's Grace, I pray that I will.

***

Several days have passed now since those dreadful few days and that wonderful night. It is Sunday today. I remain so grateful to God and to his faithful peoples who gave us such succour and encouragement that night, for it has given me a calmness of spirit and firm determination to see this thing through now to its bitter end, with my faith placed firmly in the loving hands of my Lord Jesus Christ.

I have been able to write up the full account of all my Examinations – and have hidden them in this very cell – and having written the summary account here, I have little left to share. When I finish this evening, I will stow away these pages of my manuscript (perhaps the last?) with the others, behind the loose brickwork in the courtyard where I am permitted to exercise.

I had hoped to get word to Adriana about their whereabouts – I have not wanted to endanger any others with the knowledge – but my opportunities to speak with her have so far been thwarted.

I wonder who will find them if I am not able to pass their whereabout onto Adriana?

And I wonder when that will be?

I do not know, but I content myself that the Lord knows.

I do not know either when I shall be summoned for burning, no one is able – or willing at least – to tell me.

So I take each day – each hour – as it comes and seek out the comforting presence of my Lord in prayer as much as I am able.

This evening I was able to have supper again with Day, which was an encouragement. Incidentally, we have two meals a day again now, for since we are condemned, Alexander Arnold, keeper of this prison, has decreed that we are no longer permitted to grant one of our meals to those prisoners in greater need than ourselves. I pray that they may be sustained in other ways and especially that our simple act of Christian generosity might spur them on to turn back to Christ and repent of their sinful ways, as all men must.

Moreover, I have not been permitted communication with Hooper since our condemnation – he is kept elsewhere in this prison, below me on a lower floor. So I asked Day – who has more privileges here than us, the condemned – to pass on my message to him, even if via the attendants.

I wished for Day to pass on to Hooper that
I had drank to his health and stated that
there was never a better little fellow that would
stick to a man than I would stick to him.

I am humbled to be joined together with such a
great man as Hooper in my condemnation and
will be proud to stand by him at the very end,
when our time comes to be burned together, as
we surely will.

I wanted him to know and be sure that I would
indeed stick with him in this to the very end: And
do so boldly, proclaiming my confidence and faith
in our Lord, even as the flames lap and snap
around us.

I only hope my physical bravery can match the
intent of my spirit.

By God's Grace, it will!

***

And now, just one more task remains to me.
The hardest task of all. When finally my hour
comes and I am summoned for formal
excommunication and degradation, I shall
make one more plea to be able to speak to my
dearest wife, my Adriana.

But I do not hold out great hope that my
request will be granted, given that the Lord

Chancellor has already so abruptly and utterly refused it. I understand the charity these Papists offer me now, the charity which is nought.

So it may be, then, that these written words will be the last opportunity I have to convey my true feelings and counsel to my dearest and purest wife, my own Adriana.

Tears prick my eyes as I write this.

Much I can bear in the name of my Lord Jesus, even the heat and sting of the flames I feel I can withstand, for it can only burn my flesh and bones.

But the pain of being parted from my dearest wife and from our most beloved and blessed children ... that destroys my heart and weakens my soul and is almost unbearable.

And yet bear it I must.

So, to Adriana, my wife, my love, my beauty, my sister in Christ, my everything and all - who has been my companion and friend through life since first we met some twenty years ago (twenty years of joy!).

I had so hoped - so very much hoped - that I could see you again just one more time to look into your beautiful eyes once more and to see deep into the soul of the one I love so very much.

But it seems it is not to be.

Instead I must resort to committing these last few thoughts and counsel to writing, in the hope that you will discover them when I am with you no longer. I am conscious that other eyes may be upon this and so cannot write as intimately as my heart desires, but I believe you already know well what fills my heart regarding you and our family and so in many ways no further words are necessary.

But there are several things I would share with you whilst I am able.

Firstly, on a most practical note – and I write in shorthand so that you will understand my meaning without my jeopardising the safety of those who may help you: Look to W and our friends there. I have long since had correspondence with our dear friend PM and he is ready to give you and all of our children succour and support, to help you get established again in that place where we were so happy together. The church there is ready and willing to give you the financial support you need – according to JB, whom you should contact - until such time that our elder children are able to provide for you, as surely they will before too long. Tell Daniel he is the man of the house now and that I have every faith in him to fill the shoes I leave.

And make haste in this, my dear. There is no time to waste as surely the devil prowls and is eager to devour.

Next, I pray that you will hold fast still to our faith and not put blame on the Lord for my travails. Believe me, my dear, please believe me when I say that truly I suffer these hardships gladly for the joy of knowing I suffer for our Lord Jesus! Nothing can separate us from His love – nothing! Flames most certainly cannot then. And even if those flames can devour my body and flesh here on earth, they cannot prevent us from being together one day in the very presence of our Lord in very Heaven for eternity! What a hope we have, then!

So please, my darling, please do not weep for me too long. Be glad that I am glad to be with my Saviour and in the full knowledge that in time you will be with me and Him too!

And may my faithfulness and yours be a witness to our children – and then to their children and even their children's children and on through the generations, God willing – such that they might follow the true path and know the all surpassing joy that is to be had in knowing, belonging and being obedient to Him. Amen!

And so then, my dear, my most dear heart and love, Adriana, I thank the Lord for you! For the blessing of our ten children – and for our new little one, whom I pray the Lord will bless and keep just as he has all our other most treasured blessings. And I thank Him for fifty five years of a most marvellous and fulfilling life – and most especially for the wonderful, joyous, contented twenty years of happiness and love and peace that we have had together and brought our children into! Remember me, but remember those happy times rather than this last short period of pain. And when you do recall this time, remember that it was all for our great Saviour who will bless us doubly and trebly for our faithfulness in these, the darkest of hours!

I love you Adriana. I always will.

Auf Wiedersehen.

We will meet again!

God's peace be with you.

Amen.

***

Postscript – The Story Ends and Lives On

And there the manuscript abruptly ends.

So it falls to me to describe the dramatic and most extraordinary events of that next day, Monday 4th February 1555 when the Martyr John Rogers finally met his fiery end in unutterably brave, faithful and truly legendary manner.

I shall describe the events as accurately as I am able, from the sources available to us today. After which I will provide some reflections and perspective on this life most well lived and so impactful down the generations.

An indication of just how much at peace Rogers was with his fate and how great his confidence and assurance of his heavenly future was how deeply he was sleeping the next morning when he was woken by the jailer's wife. She struggled to stir him, so soundly and peaceful was his slumber. Isn't that the most extraordinary thing? Would you sleep so soundly, knowing the horrendous fate that awaited you at any day and any moment? What an extraordinary man and how great must have been his faith in God – embodying the most common biblical exhortation not to worry or fear, in the most extreme of circumstances.

But wake him she did, eventually, and it fell upon that unfortunate woman to inform him that his hour had come. His response then was even more extraordinary.

He did not fret nor panic nor wail nor call out to God to save him nor show any sign of fear or apprehension whatsoever.

No, his immediate response was "If it be so, then I need not tie my points!"

His humour at this most sombre of moments must have made a deep impression on that woman, although history does not record her own story after this.

We do know, however, that Rogers was next escorted to the chapel in Newgate prison to be confronted by the Bishop of London, Bonner and his entourage of eight officials and a sizeable guard, to endure a farcical ceremony of degradation from the priesthood. This required the condemned to don the full clothing of their office, then to be ceremonially stripped of each part of them whilst various incantations and invocations were cited. Clearly intended as a theatrical and complete humiliation for the unfortunate victim, although one imagines that this whole charade would have had little impact on Rogers.

Certainly I think we can be confident that he would have felt no sense of spiritual consequences to the ceremony, so sure was he in his security in the Lord. And in any case, he had already stated – as we have seen – that he had considered he had already left the Catholic Church, from which he was now being ceremonially excommunicated, over twenty years prior. We have also seen how he was utterly convinced that this

Papist Catholic Church from which Bonner believed he was removing him was literally the church of the Antichrist. As such we may be sure that Rogers would have been quite unaffected by the whole process.

Once Bonner had completed his solemn ritual, Rogers – as we have seen he had determined to do – made one more request of his persecutor. He asked of Bonner that he be granted just one thing.

"What is that?" asked Bonner.

"Only that I may talk a few minutes with my wife before my burning" he replied matter of factly, reducing the request he had already made to Gardiner to just a short time limit.

But as he had anticipated, Bonner gave the request short shrift. We have no record of the words used for this cruel and brutal denial, all we do know is that he was indeed denied. One wonders what bitter hatred must have been in Bonner's and Gardiner's hearts to deny a condemned man this simplest of last requests. What harm they could possibly think could have come by this – a man condemned so soon to die to be able to speak his last few tender words to his wife - one cannot imagine.

Rather it seems that their burning desire to see their enemy completely brought down, disgraced and dispatched from this earth was so great that it obliterated any trace of Grace or kindness or compassion. Or maybe their intent was not to give any acknowledgement to his wife of eighteen years lest it give the slightest hint that Rogers could conceivably be considered to have been legally married - which of course he was, with even Parliament sanctioning the union and naturalising their offspring in Edward's reign.

Having been dealt with by Bonner on behalf of the Catholic Church, he was summarily handed over to the temporal authorities, in the form of one of the sheriffs, a certain Master Woodroffe. He felt it necessary (for reasons I also cannot quite fathom, given the circumstances and his immediately prior excommunication and degradation from office, following three days of examinations by the Bishops and Council) to ask Rogers again whether he would now recant of his 'abominable doctrine and evil opinion of the sacrament of the altar'.

Rogers was resolute and eloquent in equal measure.

"That which I have preached I will seal with my blood!" he declared.

Woodroffe's response was to declare – and one imagines him spitting this out in disgust – "Then thou art a heretic!"

Rogers responded meekly and coolly, "That shall be known at the day of judgement"

But Woodroffe was not done.

"Well, I shall never pray for thee', obviously imbued in the idea that prayers for the dead might influence the outcome of the deceased on the day of judgement.

Even in these most extreme, humiliating and terrifying of circumstances, Rogers found the strength to reply with remarkable grace: "But I will pray for you!"

What a testimony to Rogers' generous and truly Christian spirit that was!

He was led then back through the miserable prison that had been his home for the last twelve months and more and, at around ten o'clock in the morning, went out into the street where a large and heavily armed guard awaited him to take him toward Smithfield, with the two sheriffs escorting.

At this point Rogers must have been casting his eye around to find Hooper, with whom it was clear he expected to be burned. But for reasons not recorded, Gardiner and Bonner had determined that Rogers would meet his death alone that day and therefore become forever the sole first Protestant Martyr in the reign of Queen Mary.

If he felt any sense of alarm or insecurity at finding himself alone and carrying the weight of the Protestant cause on his own shoulders only, then he did not show it. Rather, he retained his dignity and composure to the most remarkable degree as he began to make his way up the short distance from Newgate to Smithfield.

He was upheld and encouraged by a huge crowd lining the streets, some shouting their encouragements and blessings and others exclaiming their sorrow and weeping. But the overwhelming emotion, most remarkably, was of praise and thanksgiving for this faithful man of God, bravely and resolutely walking toward the fire and a gruesome death, and yet confident that on that very day he would meet his beloved Saviour in heaven. So great was this atmosphere of rejoicing and celebration that even an enemy of Rogers, the Catholic French Ambassador Count Noailles, stated afterward that he and the scene was more like a bridegroom going to meet his bride at the altar than a condemned man heading toward the agony of the fire.

Rogers would have enjoyed the analogy, I think, although would have pointed out that according to Scripture it is Christ in fact who is the bridegroom and Rogers, with the rest of what he would describe as the true church, His bride.

On he strode through this maelstrom of noise and elation and rejoicing and tears and sorrow – on past the very church he had led, St Sepulchre's. One can imagine his congregation would have been some of the most eager and at the front of the line of supporters to cheer him on and convey their love and respect. The bell of St Sepulchre would toll on the day of an execution and likely that day his own church bells tolled for him. What were his emotions as he heard that resounding gong that so often had heralded the start of a service or a celebration but now tolled for his final death march?

Around this point he meets what was likely the hardest test of both his faith and fortitude.

There, protected no doubt by the most faithful members of St Sepulchre's and the most fervent supporters of Rogers, doubtless right alongside the road respectfully granted the clearest of views and access to the condemned man, was his wife of eighteen years with their eleven children huddled and doubtless fearful and confused around her. Yes, eleven children now, not the ten Rogers had known and loved already, for Adriana had given birth to another little girl, Hester, whom he had not until now set eyes upon. She was cradled at her breast now and must have been conceived when John and Adriana were still able to be together in the confines of his house arrest, before he was dispatched to Newgate prison.

This was not the reunion Rogers had sought and begged from both Gardiner and Bonner. With no privacy to utter final words of love and encouragement and no opportunity or time to share any of the words of counsel he would have imparted had he been able. Surely that would have included the existence and whereabouts of his two manuscripts – the one in his cell detailing verbatim his examinations and the other, the full story of his life, hidden in the walls of Newgate prison.

But no, instead we can imagine only the locking of his eyes to hers, imploring her to be strong in the Lord and to reassure her that his faith in the Lord to sustain him was sufficient and absolute. Perhaps the children cried out to him, perhaps he was able to voice his rock solid certainty that the Lord would be his stronghold now and lift him to a better place in glory. Perhaps she shouted out her eternal love for him.

Or perhaps no words passed at all and a look was all there was.

Whichever it was, Rogers walked on with a steely strength and determination and, according to his definitive biographer from the nineteenth century, Joseph Lemuel Chester, "From that moment, the ultimate success of the Reformation was assured." What he meant was that Rogers' faithfulness and fortitude in meeting his fate without buckling, even when confronted with the pain of his loss of life here on earth was before him in the form of his huddled, fearful and unprotected family, set an example that was to be followed by the other Protestant martyrs.

He was living up to his claim that he would seal with his blood that which he had preached and that steadfastness added immeasurable credence to his words and beliefs.

And so on he walked, taking up now the refrain of Psalm 51, the Psalm Miserere, which Lady Jane Grey had cited which Rogers had so struck and touched him, as we know from his memoirs here. How deeply he must have felt every line of that Psalm now and what a sight and sound that must have been as he held his head high, declaring his confidence of being in the Lord's hands, resting in his death as he had in his life on the Word of Scripture.

On then, as the way opened up into Smithfield itself, where a huge crowd had gathered and where there was ready prepared a pyre of faggots and stake awaiting him. Drawings from this event and others show people crowding around and pressed against every window onto the courtyard in front of St Bartholomew's church where the execution was to take place.

The practice then was to tie the condemned man firmly to the stake around the waist, leaving the hands free. So Rogers was thus tied to the stake with the faggots prepared around him awaiting to be lit.

Rogers continued calmly and assuredly repeating his Psalm.

Next came the final test for him, when as he was already tied to the stake and his fiery fate so imminent he was presented with (perhaps better, 'tempted' with?) a final offer of pardon in return for his recantation, ready prepared in writing on an official document. This was probably presented by one of the official witnesses from the Council and representatives of the authority under which this barbaric ceremony was taking place – being on this occasion Sir Robert Rochester and Sir Richard Southwell.

Rogers, as you would expect from him by now, summarily dismisses the pardon, still not prepared to recant of the beliefs on which he has built his life and saw as the foundation for his salvation.

The noise from the crowd grew in fear and apprehension and expectation, with people crying out to God to grant him the strength to persevere and bear the coming pain. Rogers was not permitted to speak long, but he was given the opportunity at least to say a few words.

He raised his hands to quiet the crowd.

And as their noise subsided he spoke out in firm voice.

"Brothers and sisters, hear these my final words! I tell you, follow the faith I have taught you and always stay true to it! I have defended it all my life, I have suffered for it through cruel imprisonment and mistreatment; and now …" he paused and the crowd stilled further, "… now I gladly sacrifice my life, for the temporary troubles of this fire serve only to cleanse me ready for an eternal comfort with my Saviour!"

A great and seemingly victorious roar rose up from the crowd in support and encouragement.

He spoke no more.

And then the order was given.

And the fire was lit.

Quite remarkably, the bravery of this man had only just begun to be witnessed. As the flames grew up around his legs and waist and up toward his chest, he did not cry out in fear or pain or for mercy. Rather, he calmly washed his hands in the fire - 'as if it were cold water' as the historian J C Ryle put it - perhaps in a final act of cleansing, as if ridding himself of the last vestiges of his earthly sin.

Having completed this extraordinary and symbolic act, he raised his hands heavenward as if to welcome heaven.

And his hands remained aloft.

Until at last he had no breath.

And as his hands descended, his soul ascended to be with his Lord.

Some said that at that moment the life passed from him, they saw a dule of doves fly overhead, which they took to be a sign from the heavens that the Holy Spirit was present to accompany the soul of John Rogers heavenward. A lovely thought.

The crowd became becalmed and even as prayers rang out for the soul of this colossus of a man, began to thin. The 'beast' that John Rogers had encountered at the boiling of the

Bishop of Rochester's cook on this very same spot, some twenty four years prior, was tamed.

Some lingered longer and waited until evening, when the embers of the ferocious fire had finally burned out. They then picked through the remaining rubble and took for themselves some remnants of the bones of John Rogers and wrapped them in paper to hold and revere sacredly.

Rogers himself would surely have railed against such superstition.

***

No record exists of what became of those pitiful remains of his human form.

Although in 1849 excavation work was carried out on the road outside St Bartholomew's Church in Smithfield, London, which was reputed to be the exact spot of the burning of the Marian Martyrs. Sure enough, as the workmen dug down three feet into the road, they found some rough stones and ashes.

In the middle of those ashes were a few remnants of human remains, showing signs of having endured a diabolical heat providing a chilling clue as to the demise those poor folk met in the fires of Smithfield.

Might some of those bones have belonged to Rogers?

Perhaps.

What is certain, though, is that plenty remains on record as to the impact of his strength of spirit and conduct at this, his final and greatest test.

Firstly, the example he set in his final hour was honoured and revered and repeated by far too many further martyrs in Queen Mary's reign. Two hundred and eighty seven in fact, including one archbishop, four bishops, twenty other clergymen, fifty five women and, even more appallingly, four children (according to historian J C Ryle). In fact the fires never stopped burning whilst Queen Mary was alive, with someone being executed virtually every week of her reign and five martyrs burned in Canterbury only a week before her death. As Ryle points out, these were not political rebels against the Queen's authority nor criminals such as thieves, murderers or drunkards. No, to the contrary, they were 'some of the holiest, purest and best Christians in England and several of them the most learned men of their day'.

Hooper, with whom Rogers expected to burn, was next to face the fire just five days after Rogers. To his apparent delight, Hooper was sent back to his diocese and died, bravely, within view of his own cathedral in Gloucester.

Third to face the fire was a man called Rowland Taylor, Rector of Hadleigh in Suffolk; and he was followed by the first martyr in Wales under Queen Mary, Robert Ferrar, Bishop of St David's, burned at Carmarthen on 30th March 1555.

Fifth then, was Rogers' colleague and friend, John Bradford – of whom we have heard from Rogers and of St Paul's Cross fame – another Prebend of St Paul's and Chaplain to Bishop Ridley. He was the next after Hooper to be burned at Smithfield on June 1st at the age of only 35, twenty years Rogers' junior.

It was Bradford who provided a powerful testimony as to the impact Rogers' brave behaviour had on the remainder of the leading Reformers at the time. Writing to Cranmer, Latimer and Ridley just four days after Rogers' death, he rejoiced that their "dear brother (Rogers) ... had broken the ice valiantly". As the historian Chester states, 'He (Rogers) had set them an example worthy of imitation, and, whither he had led the way, they could now more confidently follow'.

Ridley in turn wrote to Austin Bernher the very next day, 10th February 1555, with an even more direct reference to the impact Rogers' fortitude facing the fire had had on him, declaring, "I bless God with all my heart, in His manifold merciful gifts given unto our dear brethren in Christ, especially to our brother Rogers, whom it pleased Him to set forth first, no doubt but of his gracious goodness and fatherly favour towards him ... I trust to God it shall please Him, of his goodness, to strengthen me to make up the Trinity out of St Paul's Church (meaning himself, Rogers and Bradford), to suffer for Christ."

Ridley (Bishop of London, before Bonner replaced him under Queen Mary) went on to write to Bradford himself, "I thank our Lord God and Heavenly Father by Christ that, since I heard of our dear brother Rogers' departing, and stout confession of Christ and His truth even unto the death, my heart - blessed be God! - so rejoiced of it, that, since that time, I never felt any lumpish heaviness in my heart, as I grant I have felt sometimes before."

Ridley's wish was soon to be realised, as he was able to make his stand and sacrifice his life for his faith as the sixth martyr, along with Hugh Latimer, ex Bishop of Worcester on

16th October 1555. They were burned, back to back, in Oxford, outside Balliol College (the college, incidentally, that I attended, as I mentioned in the Preface). Ridley's prayer whilst tied to the stake demonstrated how he was true to his intent to maintain his strong faith until the very end; he prayed aloud, "Heavenly Father, I give you most hearty thanks that You have called me to a profession of You even unto death. I beseech You, Lord God, have mercy on this realm of England, and deliver the same from all her enemies."

Tied to the same stake, Latimer – over eighty years of age by this time – was able to comfort and encourage his younger brother in Christ. He declared, "Be of good comfort, Master Ridley, and play the man; we shall this day, by God's Grace, light such a candle in England as I trust shall never be put out!" Aged as he was, Latimer passed quickly after the flames were lit, but Ridley had to endure a long and painful death, as a result of the ineptitude and mismanagement of the fire by the attendants. Nonetheless, he was brave and faithful to the bitter end.

But as Ryle pointed out, it was Rogers who first 'broke the ice and crossed the river, as a Martyr in Mary's reign' and 'in one respect, had done more for the cause of Protestantism than any of his fellow sufferers'. He was referring, of course, to Rogers' role in completing and having published and had authorised the Thomas Matthew Bible.

So if his faith and fortitude in that last terrifying act had great impact and legacy, so too did the great work of his life, that Thomas Matthew Bible. This first authorised Bible in the English language in England was to have ramifications that resonated and reverberated down the ages – and still does.

Having access to Scripture in the native tongue was something that could never be removed once the people of England had experienced and tasted it. And in so doing, they became equipped to challenge some of the established practices and more aggregious doctrines of Papist Catholicism at the time. Indeed, the Roman Catholic church itself would soon sanction a Bible in English, although this took some time to come to fruition.

The core translations from Tyndale in Rogers' Thomas Matthew Bible were in turn incorporated into the Great Bible that Coverdale was commissioned to produce two years after Rogers' version in 1539, together with Coverdale's own translated passages. The direct criticism and critique Rogers included in the Thomas Matthew Bible against aspects of Papist Catholic doctrine counted against his version continuing in wide circulation during the later period of Henry's reign, when the king returned to a more conservative version of faith (perhaps where his heart always lay).

Queen Mary's attempt to obliterate and burn away all vestiges of Protestant Reform in England proved short lived as she herself died aged only forty two in 1558. Tragically what she had hoped was the blessing of a child in her womb – perhaps a son and heir to her throne, with King Philip of Spain, to maintain her familial line and faith – turned out to be uterine or ovarian cancer, which compounded with a virulent influenza (not unlike the Sweating Sickness we heard John Rogers describe) was to claim her life prematurely.

The throne then reverted, of course, to her younger sister Elizabeth, daughter of King Henry and his second wife Ann Boleyn, who had likely been instrumental in influencing her husband to look sympathetically on Protestant Reform in general and an English translation of the Bible in particular.

Protestantism returned to England.

The burning came to an end (temporarily at least) in 1559 when the Act 'De Heretico Comburendo', which had originally been enacted in 1401 under King Henry IV, was revoked. This had decreed burning at the stake for heretics in reaction to the Bible translation by John Wycliffe (some two hundred years before John Rogers) and the proliferation of new thought and criticism of the Catholic Church at the time; it was this Act that Queen Mary had re-enacted to capture and punish the sixteenth century Protestant Reformers, including Rogers, who was the first victim just days after it was re-adopted.

When Queen Elizabeth in turn died without issue, after a long and dramatic reign, it was her relative the Protestant King of Scotland, James – also related to King Henry VII – who succeeded her. He too, therefore, sustained Protestantism in England.

When in due course the King James Bible was published in 1611, it was around eighty percent based on the original Tyndale and Coverdale translations, as published in the Thomas Matthew Bible. And this King James Bible played a most remarkable role in spreading Scripture not just in England and the United Kingdom, but all around the world as first the British Empire spread awareness of and adherence to Christianity around the world and then the influence of the United States of America was felt practically and culturally globally.

Perhaps extraordinarily, as recently as 2014 – over four hundred and fifty years after Rogers' death at Smithfield – it is reported that fifty five percent of Americans who read the Bible still use the King James version (with its roots firmly based in the Thomas Matthew Bible and the original Tyndale and Coverdale translations captured there).

And so even today the impact of Rogers' faith and fortitude in life – perhaps even more than his famous and dramatic courage and steadfastness in death – is felt and seen in the lives of countless Christians around the world.

Even though many, indeed most, do not even know it.

***

Until now and the discovery of this record of his own life by John Rogers, it has been his manuscript of his Examinations that has most illuminated our understanding of the man. How perspicacious of Rogers to have not only written two separate manuscripts – one covering a virtually verbatim record of his trials and the other, shared here after such a long time undiscovered, covering the full vista of his life – but then to have stowed them in separate locations to increase the chances of each being hidden from his enemies and found by his supporters.

The manuscripts of his Examinations also almost went undiscovered at the time. The contemporary historian John Foxe records how Adriana and Daniel, their eldest son, had visited Rogers' cell soon after the execution (perhaps even that same day?). History does not recall the specific reason for the visit. Were they collecting the pitiful collection of his possessions after a year's imprisonment? Did they know of the manuscripts somehow and go looking to retrieve them? Or – as I consider the most likely – did Adriana simply feel the need to occupy the same space as her recently departed husband, to take in the melancholy view and breathe the putrid air where he had spent his last cold and lonely months, awaiting his fate and separated from both her and their beloved family?

Whatever the reason for their visit, Foxe records that it was only as they were leaving – having found nothing of particular note – that Daniel saw something tucked away in a dark corner of the cell: The manuscript recording the Examinations, witnessing his cruel treatment and thwarted attempts to explain himself and prove his faith through his beloved Scriptures.

So it was that they were able to retrieve that first hand record and – presumably at some risk to themselves – smuggle the papers out of Newgate and keep them securely until they could be safely shared amongst supporters for their own encouragement and warning. Foxe eventually takes possession of them and includes the detailed write up of his experiences in his Actes and Monuments, later to become known as his Book of Martyrs; this itself a mainstay of respectable, Christian libraries across the land for generations to come – including my dad's.

Whilst that ensured Rogers' description of his last days became immortalised for generations, his other manuscript – begun a year earlier and covering all aspects of his life, as we have seen – remained hidden from view in the cold and dark of the Newgate prison wall, where he had left the final sheets just prior to his final fiery end.

And so periods of his life equally remained in the dark, with speculation and postulation only filling the gaps.

Until now.

**

So what new light does this manuscript shed on this man?

For the most part, his telling of his own story only serves to re-enforce what was already known about him; his honesty, integrity and bravery as much in life as in death, his aptitude and dedication in producing the first authorised English Bible and the depth of his love of God and preparedness to sacrifice all before it.

But other fascinating flashes of insight enlighten our understanding and freshly illuminate his character. The re-telling of his courage in facing the fire, when only a child, to rescue his little sister – and his choice to recall that when faced with the fearsome circumstances of his imprisonment and potential trial for heresy, leading to a new fiery trial, is telling. Was he reassuring himself in the telling of it that this was an element he had faced down before? Did he read some supernatural prophecy into it and take comfort from that? And was the dramatic image of him knee deep in the pond, passing out buckets of water intended as a metaphor for his future role in teaching the ways of the Lord; passing on the Living Waters from Him as his vocation?

Perhaps.

And yet we also see admirable honesty and vulnerability in the telling of his slow journey to knowing God fully. How fascinating that although he was surrounded with the foremost thinkers and pioneers of Reform at both Oxford and, especially, Cambridge, he admits his reticence and that he did not commit his life to the cause and encounter God powerfully until at Antwerp. The grisly report of his witnessing the Bishop of Rochester's cook's execution is surely testimony to the sealing of his cautious and conservative nature during this time, prior to his conversion, driven quite simply by fear. He tells it, surely, to explain how this hideous scene served to seal his natural inclination toward a perhaps fearful respect and reverence to authority at the time. It is hard for us to imagine today the visceral impact such a public and dramatic show of the state's strength and ultimate power over the individual would have had.

He can hardly be blamed for taking the conservative, wider path at this point in his young life.

There is no doubt that he saw God's hand in what happened next, with his spirit disturbed and uneasy, leading to his leaving the familiarity of these shores and taking up the adventure in Antwerp, that bristling centre of trade and cauldron of Reformist thought and advocacy.

One of the most powerful aspects of the manuscript is the extent to which it provides testimony of the impact of key influencers on Rogers' life at critical junctures. There in Antwerp is William Tyndale, a giant of his generation and so critical in bringing to life the English translation of the Bible, at the greatest personal cost. We learn here, what we might only have guessed at, that it was Tyndale's example as well as Rogers' own deep interactions with Scripture, that brought about his revelation and evangelical conversion.

Similarly, we see his trust in his friend and landlord for a period in Antwerp, Richard Hawkins, providing him with the counsel that will change his life in other ways. Rogers is clear that it was Hawkins who, late one sleepless night, persuaded him to follow his heart and ask for Adriana's hand in marriage.

So it was he embarked upon his lifelong partnership with his much beloved wife, Adriana, whom we see in these manuscripts as not only the love of his life, but also his friend, companion and wise counsellor throughout his days. How touching and fitting that his last written words should be tender ones to her. The children she brought him were clearly a joy and delight to him and provided a fulfilment in his life for which he had great gratitude. How evident is his pride when they are naturalised Englishmen and women by Act of Parliament – and how ironic and cruel that this was not recognised, indeed was used against Rogers in his trial. Rogers witnesses himself to the fact that missing them, their growing up and the rights of passage they would pass through at different life stages was surely the greatest sacrifice he had to make for his cause.

But still it did not deter him

For even greater was his love of God and hope in an eternal future with Him.

Melanchthon also features as a further great influence in his life. His was the counsel that it seems led Rogers away from academia and into pastoral ministry. How many lives were touched – in Germany and in England – because of this change in pathway? We cannot know; but we can know that Rogers' trust in his friend prevailed until the end. Surely he was the 'dear friend PM' to which Rogers refers in his parting message to Adriana. We do not know for sure whether Adriana used her own initiative to reach out to Melanchthon or even return to Wittenberg after her husband's death; although there is good reason to think that perhaps she did, for we certainly see Daniel, the eldest son, studying there and indeed building a subsequent career on his good relations with Germany as an envoy for Queen Elizabeth.

We are left only to imagine whether Adriana made that long and arduous journey alone with her eleven children, from baby Hester to Daniel as a young man aged seventeen. What an emotional reunion that would have been for Philip Melanchthon and his wife and family, with the sizeable absence of Melanchthon's friend, the Rogers patriarch.

We also get a valuable glimpse in these manuscripts into something more of Rogers' character. We see the cerebral and orderly approach to addressing issues we might have imagined, given what we already knew of his orderly approach to the Thomas Matthew Bible layout, associated descriptive tables and commentary. So too we see the list of ten criteria he and Adriana drew up to be met to facilitate and trigger their return to England. How ironic and sad that the only one that was not met – the parish and diocesan oversight and supervision to ensure all Papist practices were wiped out – was to come back to haunt him when those Roman Catholic clergy were raised to the Council by Queen Mary.

Perhaps Mary would have sought them out and restored them in any event.

We saw this same analytical mind in something as emotional as his advice to his children, from the discussion with Robert Smith that he records in the manuscript. Ironically Smith did indeed translate his own thoughts and the additions of Rogers into a poem, which was then wrongly and inexplicably attributed by Foxe to Rogers himslef. The poem was included in the New England Primer and as such became a part of the curriculum in schools in America for generations to come. This perhaps did more than anything else to immortalise Rogers and his martyrdom, with truth and fiction blurred for centuries as a result.

Perhaps Rogers would have seen the funny side to that.

We see from the manuscripts that this erudite, earnest man also had a great sense of humour. His retort that 'man does not live on bread alone' when he heard from Poyntz and Tyndale about their method of smuggling Bibles into England in sacks of flour shows his quick wit as well as good humour. His enjoyment of his sons escapades in dressing up the already dead cat in Papist garb is another example, despite the obvious disapproval of his wife. Even at the last, his immediate response on being woken by the jailer's wife and being told his time had come – 'If it be so, I need not tie my points' – he maintained that innate sense of humour which in turn demonstrated both a deep humility and confidence in being ultimately secure in the hands of his Lord.

So what should we make of this man, over 450 years after his fiery martyrdom?

It will be hard for most to understand the depth of his conviction that led him to hold firm into and through that most bitter of torments. Even harder for most to conceive that the prime accusation, on which he stood firm and was convicted related simply to the nature of the sacrament of Holy Communion. For not only Rogers, but for all the Protestant Martyrs that followed, this was the litmus test which the Roman Catholic leadership in England applied – and if the recalcitrant failed to repent on this, condemnation as a heretic and the fiery consequences followed. Not only Rogers, but Hooper, Bradford, Ridley, Latimer, Philpot, Cranmer and many others were condemned of this specific 'heresy' which the Papist Catholics could not tolerate, but which the Protestant Reformers could not deny.

For Rogers the related charge was that he rejected the Roman Catholic Church as the antithesis of what he saw as the True Church of Christ, as such using inflammatory language that might make us flinch today, labelling it the Church of the Antichrist.

How did it come to these ultimate accusations that Rogers felt he could not deny, on pain of horrific death?

He and the other Martyrs clearly associated this doctrine and related judgement of the Papist Catholic Church as critical to a true understanding and relationship with God. Christians today in England may grasp something of the importance he might place on that, determining as it would their view on the life after death of each individual. For Rogers and the other

Marian Martyrs, nothing could stand in the way of the revelation they felt they had from the Lord that these Papist Catholic practices, and what they saw as associated superstitions, were deadly stumbling blocks to people receiving the mercy and Grace of their loving God.

We have become accustomed today to a degree of religious tolerance in England that was undreamed of in Rogers' time – when tolerance of sin and heretical doctrines was deemed worse for the individual, and any contacts they may contaminate, than earthly death itself.

The issue of the nature of Holy Communion in particular, on which today we may be quite happy to allow differences of opinion, acted as the ultimate lightning rod for all other differences in doctrine at the time. The Victorian historian J C Ryle identified this and summarised it as follows:

"The doctrine in question was the real presence of the body and blood of Christ in the consecrated elements of bread and wine in the Lord's Supper. Did they, or did they not, believe that the body and blood of Christ were really, that is, corporally, literally, locally, and materially, present under the forms of bread and wine after the words of consecration were pronounced? Did they or did they not believe that the real body of Christ, which was born of the Virgin Mary, was present on the so-called altar, as soon as the mystical words had passed the lips of the priest? Did they or did they not? That was the simple question. If they did not believe and admit it — they were burned!"

Cranmer summarised the difference in view thus, "They (the Papists) say that Christ is corporally under or in the form of bread and wine. We say that Christ is not there, neither corporally nor spiritually; but in those who worthily eat and drink the bread and wine He is spiritually, and corporally in Heaven."

And so he was burned.

Ryle – himself an evangelical Protestant minister - goes on to unpack further for us the theological reasons why the issue was deemed so serious and fundamental by the Martyrs. It is worth us dwelling on these for a moment, to truly ground our understanding of John Rogers and the beliefs on which he felt compelled to stand and for which he was prepared to sacrifice his life.

Ryle explained the key reasons why the Protestant Martyrs would not and could never agree to the Papist Catholic doctrine of Mass, with its insistence that the blood and body of Christ was corporally truly present in the sacrament. Accepting that, he explained, implies Christ's sacrifice needs to be repeated, so it was not in itself a finished and completed work. Furthermore, he claimed it gives priests an authority they do not deserve by suggesting they can offer the sacrifice of God, 'robbing the High Priest (Jesus) of His glory'. This in turn would puts sinful men - the priests - into the position of mediator between God and man, contrary to Scripture, as they saw it. Added to that, they considered that the Mass made the bread and wine into idols, giving them an honour and veneration they were never meant to receive which is 'to be abhorred by faithful Christians'. And finally, it overthrows the 'true doctrine of Christ's human nature', by suggesting Jesus' body can be in more places than one at the same time.

So whilst to us this might seem an esoteric, academic point of theology - even to many Christians today - to them it was fundamental to their faith, to their understanding of Scripture and as such to their belief in what is required for a living relationship with God, not just here on this earth, but for eternity hereafter.

Certainly, something to which they could not acquiesce, could not allow as it would undermine what they saw as the true message of the mercy and Grace of the Good News

Indeed, something for which they were prepared to die.

How desperately sad and ironic that this persecution of innocent, faithful and well-meaning men should have been inflicted on them in the name of the very same God that they acknowledged, revered and worshipped with their whole selves. A God whose message was one of love, forgiveness, mercy and Grace. Who called on His people simply to love Him and to love one another.

How much that God must have wept over the pain and sadness inflicted in His Name.

Do we have beliefs or causes or cares or loves for which we would be prepared to stand and to die? To face even the most horrific of deaths? Would we be able to find sufficient faith and fortitude to stand such a test?

I hope and pray that you and I shall not be so tested.

Sadly though, around the world, some 340 million Christians still do indeed suffer persecution and discrimination, according to the charity Open Doors. They also cite that a staggering 4,761 Christians were murdered for their faith last year: Truly, modern day Martyrs.

May they rest in peace with God in heaven and may He console their families here on earth.

Perhaps today the very word 'martyr' has become tainted for some, associated as it might often be with terms 'extremist', 'fundamentalist' and various types of abhorrent violence caused by the 'martyr' to others.

But the connotations of the word here, as applied to John Rogers and many of his fellow Marian Martyrs, are very different indeed.

Surely the character traits that come to mind having read the story of John Rogers, told in his own voice, include noble, loving, kind, holy, faithful, spirited, steadfast, loyal, courageous, brave, earnest, good, learned, erudite, patient, peaceful, joyous. That these attributes should sustain even to his death – indeed even through his death, in the unforgiving and torturous heat of the fire – is the greatest possible testimony to the greatness of the man and to his complete and absolute trust in his loving and sustaining Lord.

As a man, John Rogers had weaknesses too, of course. Perhaps he procrastinated early on in life in making some big decisions; perhaps fear and anxiety drove his decisions in early life and certainly it seemed he wrestled with the boundaries passing on mercy and Grace, the case of poor Joan Bocher comes troublingly to mind. Indeed, his language used against the Roman Catholic Church can appear to us to be inflammatory, even allowing for the situation in which he found himself, speaking truth to power. Doubtless other smaller faults and sins were ever present, but went unreported in the telling of his own story, as it would should any of us tell our own story.

He was, after all, just a man.

And yet I understand more fully now why my dad had such a fascination, respect and awe for this man of God and took such pride that he could be, should be a blood ancestor of ours.

Ultimately, though, there is perhaps a greater testimony still that we could witness to John Rogers the Martyr.

I have absolute certainty that if John Rogers were able to have the last word in this, the story of his life, at the last he would wish to deflect the attention and focus entirely away from himself and his own character.

Rather he would sincerely and deeply hope that his whole, colourful life and his brave, even glorious death would point to someone else; one who Himself suffered cruelly and unfairly and died utterly innocent.

Who died not by fire, but nailed to a tree – in an act of sacrifice made earth shatteringly more extraordinary by dint of the fact of who He was: Able to reconcile a fallen mankind with a perfect, all-loving Creator God.

The one in whom John Rogers had a complete and utter faith.

And the one from whom John Rogers found the source of his most astounding fortitude.

The Son of God.

Jesus.

***

Epilogue - Confession

DO NOT READ UNTIL YOU HAVE COMPLETED THE BOOK

The most remarkable parts of this story are in fact true, but it is time to admit that elements are from my imagination.

John Rogers most certainly was the first Protestant Martyr under Queen Mary and was indeed responsible for pulling together the first authorised Bible in English in 1537 – the foundation for The Great Bible and the King James Bible which were to have such great impact not only in England, but around the world as the British Empire grew in the coming centuries.

And he really did leave a secret manuscript that he hid in his cell in Newgate Prison which transcribed verbatim his examinations under Gardiner, Bonner et al. This was indeed discovered by his wife Adriana and eldest son Daniel when they visited his cell after his death to pick up his belongings (or simply to linger where he had spent his last days, we do not know for sure). Specifically, it was only as they were leaving that Daniel noticed something in a dark corner of the room that the manuscript was saved and with it Rogers' recounting of the Examinations. John Foxe relayed them in his Book of Martyrs (formally known as The Actes and

Monuments) first published in 1563, just eight years after Rogers' martyrdom, in Elizabeth I's reign just five years after Mary's death. He exercised some editorial rights over the copy, for reasons lost in the mists of time and that can now only be guessed at.

Joseph Lemuel Chester, an American who wrote the definitive history and biography of John Rogers in 1861 went to the trouble of printing both Rogers' exact manuscript of his Examinations and that of Foxe's version. He did this, it seems, to discredit Foxe and question his motives, having a low regard for Foxe's rigour when it came to historical impartiality and accuracy.

I was indeed inspired by an 1860s version of this Book of Martyrs from an early age as it was to be found on my dad's voluminous book shelves, alongside Chester's biography of John Rogers. I am proud to have them both now on my own bookshelves. And this later John Rogers, my dad, did indeed have a fascination with the Martyr and enjoyed seeking to fill in gaps in his understanding of the man with near and distant family members and anyone else with an interest, as well as seeking to confirm our genealogical links to him.

The dedication in this book to my dad, with the inscription "Ich bin der Gott deiner Väter" – translating as "I am the God of your fathers" – is a reference to a Preface that my father wrote to a book on John Rogers that he never got to write himself. That handwritten Preface, that I discovered in a lever arch file containing various clippings, correspondence and musings on the Martyr only after his death, explained the context and deep meaning of this phrase.

My father was representing the Methodist Church in Great Britain on a trip to the then communist German Democratic Republic (East Germany). He had been given a rare and old German translation of the Bible to take to the church in that country – a risky venture, as the import of Bibles into the country was illegal at the time. Naturally nervous about the task ahead – especially with some last minute difficulties over securing a visa (perhaps related to his time in the British Intelligence Corps some decades prior) – he recalls how he grew prayerful whilst sat in the Sheraton Hotel at Frankfurt Airport, ahead of travelling to East Germany.

And it was at this point he recounts being drawn to Acts 7 (and wondering for a while why) and then hearing the voice of the Lord – "I say spoke;" he writes, "He shouted it, boomed it at me!" – verse 32, in German, "Ich bin der Gott deiner Väter". He goes on, "He is that same God whom generations of Rogers had known and trusted and worshipped in spirit; He wasn't about to let me down now. In a little way, I was for a while to be His ambassador… Come to think of it, Rogers family history ran deep into Eastern Germany, with Dr John in Wittenberg, his wife Adriana, and eight children born over there (sic), over four hundred years ago. And so you see, my children, how the seed of this book dropped – deafeningly!"

So this might explain why, my dad having passed away three years ago without completing the story, I really do hope that he will look down with fondness, love and fascination at what I have done with it; to help bring it back to life and to the attention of more people. I know he would have agreed that the story deserves to be more widely known.

But there was no second manuscript covering the rest of Rogers' life.

It was not discovered in the remains of Newgate prison by me or anyone else - that was my subterfuge to enable John Rogers' story to be told in full. Although such a wall does exist bordering Amen Corner, belonging to St Paul's Cathedral behind the Old Bailey, the only remaining part of the infamous prison.

Let me take the other key elements of the story sequentially, to disentangle truth from fiction.

John Rogers was indeed born in Deritend, likely between 1500 and 1505, to John Rogers the lorimer (maker of bits, spurs, and metal mountings for bridles and saddles) and his mother was Margery nee Wyatt. John Rogers' father was indeed Thomas, although the discussions over the guild and costs for candles for his remembrance is a fabrication to help us into the culture of the time.

There was no fire in the Rogers household when he was young where I imagined him bravely rescuing his sister and first fearlessly encountering that element that was to define our memory of him - fire.

Nor was there an archery competition, although it is true that Henry VIII mandated the teaching of archery around that time, in order to build a more warlike and war ready nation to seek to satisfy his warlike ambitions and delusions of European hegemony.

We don't know where John Rogers was schooled, although my speculation is quite feasible as records suggest that one of the priests in the parish church at Deritend did indeed teach the children.

He did indeed go to Pembroke Hall at Cambridge and was a contemporary of the other men that would go on to be leading lights in the Reformation – Thomas Cranmer, Nicholas Ridley, William Tyndale, Hugh Latimer, Robert Barnes, Thomas Bilney and others (either as students or dons at the time). He is recorded amongst those that frequented the White Horse Tavern, known as 'Little Germany' as it was used by those interested in the Reform under Luther and Melanchthon taking place in that country, although no specific record exists of the discussions there, as I have imagined.

He would have been in Cambridge at the time of the Christmas Eve preaching of Robert Barnes, considered by many to be the starting gun for the Protestant Reformation in England – so it is quite possible, even likely (the church being so close to his college) that he was in attendance there.

It is also a matter of record that he went on to Oxford, as part of the initial intake of the best and brightest students in the land for the new Wolsey College and he did indeed proceed from there to become a priest (in what was the Catholic Church in England at the time, of course), being granted the parish of Holy Trinity the Less in Knightrider Street, London. Sadly this church is no longer there, having been destroyed along with so much else of London in the Great Fire in 1666.

Henry VIII did indeed bring in a new punishment for the crime of poisoning as a result of the incident with the cook and the Bishop of Rochester and the poor fellow was indeed executed by boiling at Smithfield. That Rogers was there and witnessed this and that that tipped his thinking further toward compliance to authority and away from rebellion by taking a living in a church in London is my convenient imagining – both as a pivotal moment in his life and indeed as an insight into his psyche at the time.

However, Rogers did indeed give up that position to be appointed chaplain to the Merchant Adventurers in Antwerp in 1534, where William Tyndale was already employed. Tyndale did indeed live in the home of Thomas Poyntz, where he embarked on completing the full Bible in English – putting his host at considerable personal risk, not to mention the risk he faced himself.

We do not know where John Rogers resided in Antwerp; the portrayal of him living in Poyntz's household with Tyndale is my imagining. As was his removal to the home of Richard Hawkins (a fictional character); although it is certainly true that when Tyndale was arrested his lodgings were searched and no record of his works were found. John Rogers is assumed to have been instrumental in moving and hiding them as is evidenced by his working on their completion, in secret, after Tyndale's arrest and execution.

Tyndale was indeed betrayed by Henry Phillips at the door of Thomas Poyntz's house whilst Poyntz was away at a fayre in Bergen op Zoom (yes, really!). He was executed by both strangulation and burning in Brussels, although the detail and manner of execution is of my imagining – and there is no record of Rogers being present. But his famous last words were indeed "Lord, open the King of England's eyes" – with the Lord apparently responding to that request, sufficiently at least to see the Thomas Matthew Bible authorised by Henry just a few years later, once Rogers had completed the compilation and had it published.

Poyntz himself was also arrested, but managed to escape captivity and flee back to England. His business was ruined by the scandal, as was his marriage as his wife refused to join him in penury back in England.

It was my conjecture that Rogers experienced a powerful encounter with Jesus whilst working with Tyndale in Antwerp and was thereby 'born again' as an evangelical Protestant. Although he does appear to have undergone a hardening of his commitment and grew in his faith – which perhaps is unsurprising given the closeness with which he was working with God's Word whilst producing the English Bible, with and then after Tyndale.

Details of John Rogers' publishers Richard Grafton and Edward Whitchurch are true, although the specific exchanges between them are imagined, as is the reason given for the Bible being named the Thomas Matthew Bible (although again, quite feasible).

The Thomas Matthew Bible was indeed the first one to be authorised in English by Henry VIII through communication by Grafton to Cranmer, in turn to Cromwell and then to the King himself. With Ann Boleyn's prior influence in the background, as well, of course, as the overarching political climate and state of affairs. It is true also that Rogers has not received the recognition that he deserves for his role in bringing this first authorised English Bible to England – even today if you search 'Bible translations into English' in Google and look at the Wikipedia entry, you will find no reference to Rogers, but only to Coverdale's unauthorised 1535 edition and then his authorised 1539 version, two years later than Rogers' Thomas Matthew Bible. It is at least gratifying that Rogers does have his own Wikipedia page with an accurate summary of his recorded life.

Rogers really was married to Adriana, daughter of the printer Jacob van Metern, around this time in Antwerp, although the detail of how they met and his decision process to break so firmly from his priestly celibacy is my conjecture. They did indeed go on to have eleven children, although the exact timing of their births is speculative. It is true that Rogers cited the number of children he brought from Meldorf as eight, suggesting that the last three were born in England and he also cited the number he believed he had in his last days at Newgate as ten. So it is true that he only met his last child, Hester, tragically, as a baby as he walked to Smithfield on that final, fateful day.

Rogers did indeed move to Wittenberg, cradle of the Protestant Reformation, in 1540 and was indeed well acquainted and firm friends with Melanchthon. It is very likely he met Martin Luther whilst there, although there is no specific record of this.

It is also true that he went on from there in 1543 to Meldorf as the pastor for the Lutheran church there and as Superintendent of the Lutheran Church for the region of Dietmarsh in North West Germany; although thre is no record that Melanchthon had any part in that decision. It is even true that his predecessor had been lynched by the people of Meldorf, although the specific portrayal of that and of the individuals involved is imagined.

Back in London at the time, the plight of poor Anne Askew is true, with the Lord Chancellor Thomas Wriothesley and Privy Councillor Sir Richard Rich taking on the torture themselves, to disastrous effect. She was indeed carried to her burning at Smithfield in a chair, unable to walk on her broken limbs, but her spirit still not broken despite everything she had endured. There was indeed a speedy end to her and the three men burned with her as a result of gunpowder given to one of the martyrs, which became a not uncommon practice in order to reduce their suffering.

We know Rogers returned to London by 1548 and produced the commentary on Melanchthon's 'Weighing and Considering the Interim', relating to the infamous Augsburg Interim published in that year. Although the idea that he first went ahead of Adriana and the children to test out the safety of the country now that Edward had become king is speculative as is his residing with his old friend Edward Whitchurch. As is also the list of 'criteria' for the Rogers family to return to England, although there can be little doubt that they would have supported and upheld those listed.

The idea that he was first chaplain to the Ridley household for two years prior to being given a parish is mine, conveniently filling in as it does a two year gap in the true historical record – although it is true that he was close to Ridley and this is therefore not inconceivable.

He was indeed then granted the parishes of St Margaret Moyses and St Sepulchre's in 1550 and lived in the rectory at the latter. He was then appointed prebendal stall of St Pancras at St Paul's in 1551 and as such he did indeed have official lodgings there, in addition to the rectory at St Sepulchre's, very nearby. He was then appointed Divinity Lecturer in St Paul's, probably a little after receiving the prebend.

Whilst in London there is indeed record that he was consulted on the plight of poor Joan Bocher and John Foxe intimates that it was in fact he personally who implored Rogers to intervene. Foxe records Rogers' unwillingness to do so and his (to us, perplexing and disturbing) affirmation that she should be burned at the stake for her heresy. Foxe also records his own reaction that Rogers may come to rue such an outcome for heresy – "perchance you may yet find that you, yourself, shall have your hands full of this gentle fire" - although that might have been some retrospective re-writing of the actual exchange by him. However, Rogers' defence of his stance is my supposition and extrapolation rather than recorded fact.

Rogers resigned his living at St Margaret Moyses just a year after being granted it, presumably finding the roles at St Sepulchre's and St Paul's, as well as his new living at Chigwell, Essex, as much as he could handle. And the following year his wife and children were indeed naturalised by Act of Parliament, which one imagines would have been a joy to him and given him a sense of safeguarding his family, unaware of the turbulence to follow.

The Sweating Sickness was real and prevalent in London around the time Rogers was at St Sepulchre's and St Paul's. The horrible and fearsome symptoms were broadly as I have described, although the specific incident described is imagined, with William Tomson a fictional character intended to represent all of the poor souls who suffered from this strange and terrifying disease.

Also true was Rogers' stance on his priestly attire – following the example of Hooper - and his compromise only to wear a rounded hat. One can surmise that these controversies took on increased significance due to the uncharted territory that the Reformers were navigating as they sought to peel back the (to them) unhelpful, manmade trappings of the Roman Catholic Church of the time to recapture what they saw as the true spirit of the New Testament and the early church.

It is a matter of recorded fact that very soon after Queen Mary's accession as a result of the death of her younger brother, the King Edward, before she had even arrived in London, Rogers preached at St Paul's Cross on 16th July 1553. This followed Nicholas Ridley preaching at the same place the week prior, just days after Mary had been pronounced Queen and whilst Lady Jane Grey was still in contention to take the crown and keep the Protestant Reformation alive in England. Ridley was critical of Mary's attachment to Roman Catholicism in contrast to the young Lady Jane Grey's Protestant credentials and thereby greatly antagonised the Catholic faction. This was therefore a dangerous assignment for Rogers, but it was reported that he preached a sermon that avoided contention or conflict.

He was indeed instructed to preach again just three weeks later, which is unusual given the number of potential preachers from St Paul's which meant that there was normally a longer gap between a preacher taking a sermon. Was it intended as a trap and part of the conspiracy to move against the Reformers? We do not know. But we do know that rather than take the path of discretion as he had three weeks previously, he vehemently and vigorously attacked what he saw as the shortcomings of the Roman Catholic Church. Although as he claimed in his defence under examination, he was again careful not to criticise Queen Mary in any way. Even so, he must have known that there would be dire consequences. He was in fact summoned before the Privy Council on the same day at the Tower of London, but so vindicated himself in defending his position that he was released – for the time being.

Further the following month he was indeed present when Gilbert Bourne preached at St Paul's Cross and the congregation there rioted. Missiles were indeed thrown, including a dagger which hit the Reformer and colleague of Rogers at St Paul's, John Bradford. Together with Bradford, he did indeed help quell the crowd and escort Bourne to safety. Whether or not the riot was deliberately incited is not known, but it certainly served as a pivotal moment in turning the tide on reigning in the Reformers.

Soon after these events, Mary sanctioned two Proclamations that restricted the actions and freedom of speech of the Protestants to speak out against the Queen or Council and effectively stripped them of their freedom to preach. On 16th August 1553, even before these Proclamations were made public, Rogers was summoned again before the Council to answer for the same purported 'crime' of his preaching at St Paul's Cross. Despite having already been summoned for that event with no consequences, this time he was placed under effective house arrest – in part for his supposed role in instigating riot there when Bourne preached. The vindication for this was – bizarrely – given that Rogers and Bradford had so easily quelled the crowd, they must have been their ring leaders and have planned the insurrection.

He was confined to his home and allowed interaction only with his household, but resisted the temptation to flee to the safety of the continent as he surely could have done (and perhaps as his persecutors had expected) and as so many of his contemporaries had done.

During this time, there was indeed a case of a cat being dressed in Roman Catholic vestments in London and left in the street as an act of protest. But it was my invention that the Rogers boys were the ones to do this, as is therefore Adriana's wrath and Rogers' secret pride.

Rogers remained under this kind of house arrest until he was finally moved to Newgate prison on 27th January 1554, apparently on the insistence of Bonner, Bishop of London who eventually persuaded Gardiner, the Lord Chancellor, that he should be removed to prison (and away from Bonner's own living quarters at St Paul's). The detail of his arrest are from my imagination.

That he also encountered sympathetic congregation members from St Sepulchre's as gaolers in Newgate prison is my conjecture, although the proximity of the church would make that quite feasible. He was to remain there for just over a year.

Lady Jane Grey was indeed executed at the tender age of sixteen following the Privy Council switching their allegiance to Mary. She did indeed recite Psalm 51 at her execution, although the exploration of that Psalm I gave to Rogers in prison is a fiction, albeit given credence as he did indeed recite that same Psalm Miserere as he headed toward his own end.

He and his Reformer colleagues did indeed sacrifice one of their two meals a day to be given to those even less fortunate convicts in the even less pleasant parts of the prison – which was indeed a remarkable act of Christian charity from them.

The Declaration of the Preachers in Prison was indeed a real document and the response of those Reformers invited to a theological 'debate' in Cambridge after their colleagues Cranmer, Latimer and Ridley had been ridiculed and poorly treated at a similar event in Oxford. The reasons for declining the live debate and their eight Articles of Faith are a true reflection of those they committed to writing as well as a valuable insight into the theological issues on which they were making their stand.

The depiction of Rogers meeting with Robert Smith, Martyr and poet, is my fiction, born of the fact that there was indeed a poem - two poems in fact, which were blended together to make a longer one - written by Smith to his children ahead of his own martyrdom. Foxe incorrectly attributed this to Rogers, for reasons unexplained and rather strange, such that generations of Americans studied this poem and assumed it to be written by Rogers. It formed part of the curriculum for many years, being included in The New England Primer, first published in New England in the United States of America around 1690. The content that I have included in their imagined exchange aligns with that of the poem and one can imagine Rogers being well aligned to the counsel. My fabricated listing of the ten specific points of advice from Rogers, based on Scriptures, are indeed referenced in the poem, albeit indirectly – I have made the link back to the Scriptures, but I have no doubt the Scriptures inspired the sentiment and words themselves for Smith, Rogers' fellow Martyr. (See Appendix for this poem).

Rogers did indeed meet John Day when the latter was imprisoned in 1554. It was Day who went on to print Foxe's Book of Martyrs / Actes and Monuments, to great acclaim and huge popularity – which in turn had a great impact on the English people in popularising the bravery and faith of the Marian Martyrs in particular, including Rogers as the very first. Foxe recorded the conversation Day had had with Rogers, regarding the latter's proposed supervision of the clergy that he felt would help secure the path of Reform in England and prevent the back-sliding that he had witnessed all too closely.

The description of the Examinations are intended to be as accurate a synopsis as I could manage of the true events and transcript – much of the verbal exchanges being relayed verbatim - as secretly captured by Rogers himself and passed on by Foxe. The key aspects of the report Rogers gives of his Examinations tally with the official record of the events, which give that content the greatest degree of historical credibility (see Appendix).

The heartfelt – and heart wrenching – prayer cited after his first Examination was included in that write up of events that Rogers himself recorded. Written, as with the rest of his Examination records, in the English of the time and with some short hand, I have simply translated as best I can into modern English – but without changing or redacting anything in this instance.

Rogers was indeed incarcerated in the Clink in Southwark the night after his second Examination and before the final Examination the following day. And he was indeed returned there, with Hooper, after his condemnation – and smuggled through the Bishop of Winchester's house and onto the dark streets of London, an advance party having already gone out before them to extinguish the street lights so as to be able to move them covertly back to Newgate. This plan was indeed foiled by the faithful supporters of Rogers and Hooper, who lit their way with candles held aloft amidst the clamour of much shouting of encouragement and blessings. Although unexpected, the show of support and protest remained peaceful – something which Rogers and Hooper would surely have appreciated.

The final words from Rogers to Adriana are my own invention, although I hope capture some essence of truth about what he might have said to her, had he been able. We do not know whether the family withdrew back to Wittenberg after Rogers' execution, although it is recorded that Daniel was to be found there studying some years later, so it is not inconceivable that Adriana should have escaped back there to a safer environment, surrounded by old friends. She and the children are recorded back in England, however, with Adriana being buried in the cemetery of St Bartholomew the Great in Smithfield, just yards from where her husband met his end.

My retelling of Rogers' final day is intended to be as accurate as I could make it based on the historical record, including the fact that the jailer's wife found it hard to wake him, so fast was he asleep; his quip regarding there being no need to tie his points; his exchanges with Bonner and Sheriff Woodroffe, including famously his comment that 'That which I have preached I will seal with my blood'; the extraordinary scenes on the way to Smithfield including seeing Adriana and his children; his final words and his final acts of courage, washing his hands in the fire and holding his arms aloft until his strength failed him. All true.

All of which is why I stand by my contention, that which was my conjecture is nowhere near as remarkable in this story as that which is true. Indeed, my imaginings serve only to bring to light and life the extraordinary truth about this man of God.

John Rogers the Martyr was indeed the most remarkable of men, who held these two outstanding character traits in equal, astonishing measure:-

Faith and fortitude.

***

END

Appendix 1

John Rogers' Official Sentence

Translated from original Latin by Joseph L. Chester 1861

In the name of God, Amen. We, Stephen, by the permission of God Bishop of Winchester, lawfully and rightly proceeding with all godly favour, by authority and virtue of our office, against thee, John Rogers, priest, alias called Matthew, before us personally here present, being accused and detected, and notoriously slandered of heresy; having heard, seen and understood, and with all diligent deliberation weighed, discussed, and considered the merits of the cause: all things being observed which by us, in this behalf, in order of law, ought to be observed, sitting in our judgement seat, the name of Christ being first called upon, and having God only before our eyes:

Because by the acts enacted, propounded, and exhibited in this matter, and by thine own confession judicially made before us, we do find that thou hast taught, holden and affirmed, and obstinately defended divers errors, heresies, and damnable opinions, contrary to the doctrine and determination of the holy Church, as namely these:

That the catholic Church of Rome is the Church of Antichrist: Item, that in the Sacrament of the Altar there is not, nor substantially really, the natural body and blood of Christ:

The which foresaid heresies and damnable opinions, being contrary to the law of God, and determination of the universal and apostolic Church, thou hast arrogantly, stubbornly, and wittingly maintained, held and affirmed, and also defended before us, as well in this judgement as also otherwise; and with the like obstinacy, stubbornness, malice, and blindness of heart, both wittingly and willingly hast affirmed that thou wilt believe, maintain and hold, affirm and declare the same:

We, therefore, Stephen Winchester, Bishop Ordinary and Diocesan aforesaid, by the consent and assent, as well of our reverend brethren the Lord Bishops here present and assistant, as also by the counsel and judgement of divers worshipful lawyers and professors of divinity with whom we have communicated in this behalf, do declare and pronounce thee, the said John Rogers, otherwise called Matthew, through thy demerits, transgressions, obstinacies and wilfulness (which thou manifold ways hast incurred by thine own wicked and stubborn obstinacy), to have been and to be guilty of the detestable, horrible, and wicked offences of heretical pravity and execrable doctrine: and that thou hast before us sundry times spoken, maintained, and wittingly and stubbornly defended the said cursed and execrable doctrine, in thy sundry confessions, assertions, and recognitions here judicially before us oftentimes repeated: and yet still dost maintain, affirm and believe the same:

And that thou hast been and art lawfully and ordinarily convicted in this behalf: We, therefore (I say), albeit (following the example of Christ, which would not the death of a sinner, but rather that he should convert and live) we have gone oftentimes to correct thee, and, by all lawful means that we could, and all wholesome admonitions that we did know, to reduce thee again unto the true faith and unity of the universal catholic Church; notwithstanding we have found thee obstinate and stiff-necked, willingly continuing in the damnable opinions and heresies, and refusing to return again unto the true faith and unity of the holy mother Church, and, as the child of the wickedness and darkness, so to have hardened thy heart that thou wilt not understand the voice of thy shepherd, be allured with his fatherly affection, doth seek after thee, nor wilt be allured with his fatherly and godly admonitions:-

We, therefore, Stephen, the Bishop aforesaid, not willing that thou which art wicked shouldst now become more wicked and infect the Lord's flock

with thine heresy (which we are greatly afraid of),
with sorrow of mind and bitterness of heart, do
judge thee and definitively condemn thee, the
said John Rogers, otherwise called Matthew, thy
demerits and defaults being aggravated through
thy damnable obstinacy, as guilty of most
detestable heresies, and as an obstinate
impenitent sinner refusing penitently to return
to the lap and unity of the holy mother Church:
and that thou hast been and art by law
excommunicate: and do pronounce and declare
thee to be an excommunicate person:

Also we pronounce and declare thee, being a
heretic, to be cast out from the Church, and left
unto the judgement of the secular power, and
now presently do leave thee as an obstinate
heretic, and a person wrapped in the sentence of
the great curse, to be degraded worthily for thy
demerits (requiring them, notwithstanding, in
the bowels of our Lord Jesus Christ, that this
execution and punishment, worthily to be done
upon thee, may so be moderated that the
rigour thereof be not too extreme, nor yet the
gentleness too much mitigated, but that it
may be to the salvation of thy soul, to the
extirpation, terror, and conversion of the heretic,
and to the unity of the catholic faith), by this
our sentence definitive, which we here lay upon
and against thee, and do with sorrow of heart
promulgate in this form aforesaid.

***

Appendix 2

Poem wrongly attributed to John Rogers – actually written by fellow Martyr Robert Smith

New England Primer 1687

MR. JOHN ROGERS, minister of the gospel in London, was the first martyr in Queen MARY's reign, and was burnt at Smithfield, February 14, 1554. His wife with nine small children (sic), and one at her breast following him to the stake; with which sorrowful sight he was not in the least daunted, but with wonderful patience died courageously for the gospel of JESUS CHRIST.

Some few days before his death, he wrote the following Advice to his Children.

GIVE ear, my children, to my word,
    Whom God hath dearly bought;
Lay up his laws within your heart,
    And print them in your thought.

I leave you here a little book,
    For you to look upon,

That you may see your father's face,
    When he is dead and gone,—

Who, for the hope of heavenly things,
    While he did here remain,
Gave over all his golden years
    To prison and to pain;—

Where I, among my iron bands,
    Enclosed in the dark,
Not many days before my death,
    Composed for you this work.

And for example to your youth,
    To whom I wish all good,
I send you here God's perfect truth,
    And seal it with my blood;—

To on, my heirs of earthly things,
    Whom I do leave behind,
That you may read and understand,
    And keep it in your mind;—

That as you have been heirs of that
    Which once will wear away,
You also may possess that part
    Which never will decay.

Keep always God before your eyes,
    With all your whole intent,
Commit no sin in any wise,
    But keep his commandments.

Abhor that arrant whore of Rome,
    And all her blasphemies,
And drink not of her cursed cup;
    Obey not her decrees.

Give honour to your mother dear;
    Remember well her pain;
And recompense her, in her age,
    With the like love again.

Be always ready for her help,
    And let her not decay;
Remember well your father all,
    Who should have been your stay.

Give of your portion to the poor,
    As riches do arise;
Arid from the needy, naked soul,
    Turn not away your eyes.

For he who doth not hear the cry
    Of those who stand in need,
Will cry himself; and not be heard,
    When he does hope to speed.

If God hath given you increase,
    And blessed well your store,
Remember you are put in trust,
    And should relieve the poor.

Beware of foul and filthy lusts;
    Let such things have no place,

Keep clean your vessels in the Lord,
 That he may you embrace.

You are the temples of the Lord,
 For you are dearly bought,
And they who do defile the same
 Will surely come to nought.

Be never proud, by any means,
 Build not your house too high;
But always have before your eyes
 That you were born to die.

Defraud not him who hired is,
 Your labour to sustain;
But pay him still, without delay,
 His wages for his pain.

And as you would that other men
 Towards you should proceed,
Do you the same to them again,
 When they do stand in need.

Impart your portion to the poor
 In money and in meat;
And send the feeble, fainting son,
 Of that which you do eat.

Ask counsel always of the wise
 Give ear unto the end,
And ne'er refuse the sweet rebuke
 Of him who is your friend.

Be always thankful to the Lord,
  With prayer and with praise,
Begging of him to bless your work,
  And to direct your ways.

Seek first, I say, the living God,
  And always him adore,
And then be sure that he will bless
  Your basket and your store.

And I beseech Almighty God,
  To replenish you with Grace,
That I may meet you in the heavens,
  And see you face to face.

And though the fire my body burn,
  Contrary to my kind,
That I cannot enjoy your love,
  According to my mind,—

Yet I do hope that when the heavens
  Shall vanish like a scroll,
I shall see you in perfect shape
  In body and in soul.

And that I may enjoy your love,
  And you enjoy the land,
I do beseech the living Lord
  To hold you in his hand.

Though here my body be adjudged
  In flaming fire to fry,

My soul, I trust, will straight ascend
    To dwell with God on high.

What though this carcass smart awhile?
    What though this life decay?
My soul, I hope, will be with God,
    And live with him for aye.

I know I am a sinner born,
    From the original,
And that I do deserve to die,
    By my forefather's fall.

But by our Saviour's precious blood,
    Which on the cross was spilt,
Who freely offered up his life,
    To save our souls from guilt,—

I hope redemption I shall have,
    And all who in him trust,
When I shall see him face to face,
    And live among the just.

Why, then, should I fear death's grim look,
    Since Christ for me did die?
For king and Cesar, rich and poor,
    The force of death must try.

When I am chained to the stake,
    And fagots gird me round,
Then pray the Lord my soul in heaven
    May be with glory crowned.

Come, welcome, death, the end of fears,
    I am prepared to die;
These earthly flames will send my soul
    Up to the Lord on high.

Farewell, my children, to the world,
    Where you must yet remain;
The Lord of hosts is your defence
    Till we do meet again.

Farewell, my true, my loving wife,
    My children, and my friends;
I hope in heaven to see you all,
    When all things have their ends.

If you go on to serve the Lord,
    As you have now begun,
You shall walk safely all your days,
    Until your life, be done.

God grant you so to end your days,
    As he shall think it best,
That I may meet you in the heavens,
    Where I do hope to rest.

***

More to explore

Visit http://johnrogersmartyr.com to explore further
the history and ongoing impact of the life
and death of John Rogers the Martyr.

CPSIA information can be obtained
at www.ICGtesting.com
Printed in the USA
LVHW101527120522
718522LV00002B/12

9 781839 759963